STRONTIUM DOG

DAY OF THE DOGS

Mutated by nuclear fallout, the Strontium Dogs are second-class citizens, only trusted with the worst jobs: hunting down criminals and claiming bounties in the most hostile parts of the galaxy. Among these misfit bounty hunters, Johnny Alpha is the best of the best and no one can hide from his psychic "stare".

When tearful tycoon Asdoel Zo enlists the help of Johnny and his fellow Strontium Dogs to track down the man who killed his family, it looks like easy credits in the bank. However, Asdoel Zo has something far more sinister in mind. Zo is a big-game hunter, and he wants to hunt the most dangerous prey there is: Strontium Dogs!

Ultra-violent, spaghetti western-style action mixed with dark humour and SF thrills, *Day of the Dogs* is frontier gunslinging and edge-of-your-seat action!

STRONTIUM DOG

DAY OF
THE DOGS

ANDREW CARTMEL

BLACK FLAME

For Peter O'Donnell, master storyteller.

A Black Flame Publication
www.blackflame.com

First published in 2005 by BL Publishing, Games Workshop Ltd.,
Willow Road, Nottingham NG7 2WS, UK.

Distributed in the US by Simon & Schuster, 1230 Avenue of the
Americas, New York, NY 10020, USA.

10 9 8 7 6 5 4 3 2 1

Cover illustration by Karl Richardson.

ISBN 13: 978 1 84416 218 5
ISBN 10: 1 84416 218 4

A CIP record for this book is available from the British Library.

Printed in the UK by Bookmarque, Surrey, UK.

CHAPTER ONE
RANCHERO ZO

As the man trudged across the desert the last light of evening glared down on him. The sun was low in the sky, a glaring ball of burning hydrogen a hundred million kilometres away. It cast sharp, ink-black shadows on the glaring expanse of desert sand: the shadow of a cactus and, standing slouched beside it, the shadow of the man, who had paused as if he could walk no further.

The man wore scuffed cowboy boots that had seen many years of hard wear. Spurs jangled musically on the boots as the man stirred his feet restlessly, scuffing them in the sand. A small green and yellow lizard appeared from the ground, stared with great concentration at the boots that had disturbed its slumber, then blinked in disgust and darted angrily away.

"Hello," said the man. He ran a finger inside his collar and brought it out again, slick with sweat. "Hot, isn't it?" He was a florid, amiable-looking fellow with thin, liver-coloured lips and a raptorial jut of freckled pink nose. Set close to this nose were piercing, stony grey eyes that bespoke cold depths of intelligence that seemed at odds with a man stranded in the middle of a desert, blazing sun-harrowed leagues from the nearest sip of cool water or the sweet solace of shade.

Despite his considerable paunch, the man was tall and powerfully built, his broad shoulders curved with age and the twin burdens they bore. On his right shoulder he carried a saddle, a magnificent broad black curve of leather set with Mexican silver.

The man sighed. "Heavy burden," he said. "And I've carried it a long way. How far? Couldn't rightly say. But I've been lugging this load ever since my fool horse lay down and died on me." He turned his head and squinted back into the endless distance behind him. "It was back that way. In an alkali gulch. I was counting on that horse to get me through this long, flat, baking chunk of hell that calls itself a desert. But now it looks like I'm going to have to walk out under my own steam."

The man dropped the saddle at his feet. It thudded to the ground, dust and sand rising around it. The dust settled on the leather and silver, and the gleaming, oiled length of the Sharps that was sheathed in the saddle. On the man's other shoulder was what looked at first glance like a rifle. He swung down the object and cradled it in his hands. It gleamed in the fading rays of late sunlight. He caressed the strings that were stretched across it. The thing was a banjo.

"My name is Charlie Yuletide," said the man, clearing his throat and spitting. His voice was low and croaky, clotted with dust. As before, he seemed to be addressing someone, but there was no one to be seen in the vast baking plain of the desert. Even the lizard had disappeared. There was just the man called Charlie Yuletide, the tall cactus standing beside him, and the saddle and rifle at his feet.

Charlie Yuletide glanced up at the blazing sun as he strummed a plaintive chord on his banjo. Long purple shadows were gathering in the distant canyons as the sun moved past its zenith. From far off in the distance came the unearthly, echoing howl of what might have been a coyote. The desert afternoon had begun its swift slide towards twilight.

"I'm Charlie Yuletide," the man repeated, but this time instead of speaking the words he sang them, in a quavering, plangent voice that suggested hillbillies, malnutrition, heartbroken cowpokes and unduly protracted sing-alongs beside guttering campfires. The lonesome howl of the coyote joined in, just a harmonic or two away. "That's my name," sang the man, "and this here's my story...

"I've come here to sing of daring deeds. And men with needs. Needs like the unholy hunger for gold. That leaves many a man lying so cold. Out in the desert, out like a light. Lying so lonesome in the desolate night."

Charlie Yuletide strummed his banjo and lifted his yodelling, plaintive voice into the darkening desert. In the distance the coyote howled again, as if in pain.

"I'll sing of the hunters and the hunted and killers of men. And of lost souls loved and hated and loved yet again. Killers who'll shoot down a fellow and leave him to feed the hogs. The killers who are converging on the Day of the Dogs.

"I'm singing of Johnny Alpha and the man at his side. As up to the ranch of the rich man did they ride..."

Johnny and Middenface McNulty stared out the window of the bus. The bus was a stubby, box-shaped vehicle which glided over the ground, using a silent hover mechanism that enabled them to flit, ghost-like, along the corridor of trees. Green and silver light flashed through the window of the bus, conjuring eerie reflections in the pale eyes of Johnny Alpha.

"The man must be cracked," said Middenface, a note of petulance creeping into in his voice.

"Maybe," said Johnny. "Most rich people are, one way or another. Their money makes them crazy."

"And he's got more money than most. So that makes him more crazy than most." Middenface studied his reflection in the window, the ugly ridged profile of his mutant head flickering incongruously over a velvety green backdrop of exquisite trees and lush shrubs. Nature at its finest juxtaposed with nature at its most aberrant.

A garland of fat, star-shaped, white and purple flowers fluttered past, curving around the mossy bole of a vast tree. Those flowers had blossomed in this place just as Middenface McNulty had blossomed in the radioactive rubble of Shytehill, the mutant ghetto where he'd led his brief but eventful childhood. He'd come a long way. Now here he was on a small private planet called SG977, travelling in a bus through paradise. Or at least a garden fashioned to look like paradise.

The garden stretched away from Middenface and Johnny for endless hectares in every direction. It was a lush tropical forest, a tame and neatly trimmed jungle. The bus was gliding through it along a narrow track that cut through the lush growth, a track paved with a smooth grey plastic surface that ran all the way from the space port to the mansion of Asdoel Zo, forming a direct if winding road.

Middenface supposed that all the roads on this planet led to the same place. After all, Asdoel Zo owned the planet.

"Why do you suppose he never made this track straight?" said Middenface.

"It's designed for enjoying the scenery, not for getting anywhere in a hurry." Johnny kept staring out the window.

"I'd be enjoying the scenery more if we were on the way back to the space port," said Middenface. "Why does he want to see us in person, anyway? He could have arranged this all with a call."

"Wants to look at the men he's hiring for the job," said Johnny. He turned to Middenface, the cold silver light of his strange eyes burning in the shadows of the bus. "Wants to look us in the eye."

The bus deposited them at the bottom of a slope that led up to Asdoel Zo's titanic mansion, or at least the first instalment of that mansion. The green expanse of gardens ended abruptly, the jungle theme terminating as a new look took over. The narrow track debouched into a grey plastic-surfaced circle where the bus floated to a halt, its entire front wall hissing open. Johnny and Middenface stepped out onto the circle. Several other buses were parked near their vehicle, all empty, all floating silently over their shadows. The sun was high overhead and Middenface felt the warmth of its one point two Sol-type radiation on the back of his neck, comforting on the old scars there.

Beyond the circle where the buses floated, a desert theme took over. The slope rising up to the house was terraced into banks of sand and pebble with ornamental cactuses planted on them. Each bank ended in a low wall of rough-hewn tree stumps that rose up to form the lip of the next bank above. The terraced banks rose like steps on a giant staircase up towards the house at the top. The house was a low, wide structure formed panels from mirror-like glass, gleaming steel and red wood.

Through the centre of the terraced slope a winding footpath of crushed, chocolate-coloured shell led up to the house. "What, no welcoming party?" said Middenface.

"Doesn't look like it," said Johnny. They started up the slope, their boots crunching on the shells. Middenface reflected that billions of tiny sea creatures, who'd once lived in the ocean of some distant planet, had given their lives to make this attractive footpath for the rich man who lived high on the hill above them.

"I've not met the man and I don't like him already," said Middenface.

"What got your goat?" said Johnny.

"What do you mean?"

Johnny Alpha smiled. "You've been spoiling for a fight ever since we arrived."

"Well, it bothered me. Didn't it bother you? The way they treated us back at the space port."

"They told you, the man has allergies."

"That's no reason for him to make us wear this ridiculous garb." Middenface lifted his arms to emphasise the ridiculous, and humiliating, cut of the white paper garment he'd been made to wear. It was a narrow bathrobe affair with a white belt at the front that Middenface had knotted tight in fury.

"It's undignified," he said. "I look like some wee geisha girlie or a patient in a hospital or something." He inspected his footwear with disgust. Like Johnny, he was naked under the paper robe, bare legs jutting out, bare feet shod in disposable blue and white plastic sandals. Together they trudged up the chocolate brown pathway on their sandals, crushing the shells underfoot.

Middenface paused to watch the busy gardening team on the terrace above. They seemed to know what they were doing and they were an uncommonly good-looking lot, all girls and all skimpily dressed in abbreviated olive green shorts and tank tops, with pert military-style green caps on their heads and sturdy combat boots on their little feet. They were busy planting a bed of ornamental cacti, ranging in size from huge monstrosities to tiny specimens that wouldn't have come up to Johnny's knee. The cacti came in various shapes and in a dramatic variety of colours, ranging from green to bruised purple and dusty pink.

One of the girls suddenly looked over at Middenface, then looked away again. She said something in a low voice and the others all giggled. Middenface turned bright red.

He turned away and hurried off up the path, moving hastily, his sandals slapping on the crushed shells. Johnny was moving ahead of him at a leisurely pace.

"It's us they're bloody laughing at, you know," said Middenface as he caught up with his friend. "And it's no wonder, the way we look in these bloody stupid outfits." Johnny just grunted. The men continued their ascent in silence, making their laborious way up towards the distant, gleaming house, paper robes rustling in the fresh breeze that blew from the moist green depths of jungle garden behind them.

They could see the details of the front of the house, tall windows gleaming behind a wide wooden-floored balcony, which was open at the front, facing the terraced slope. "I don't care how bloody rich and powerful he is," said Middenface, wiping sweat from his brow. "He's got no call to treat us like this. He could have sent a gravity pad for us, or let us use an elevator. There must be an elevator around the place. But not for the tradesmen, oh no. We're not good enough for the grav pad or the elevator. Instead we can just slog our guts out, walking up and down this bloody hill."

"Only up it so far," said Johnny.

"Well, it's going to be back down it any minute now," snarled Middenface.

"Don't go into meltdown," murmured Johnny. They had now reached the top of the shell footpath and they were confronted with a short flight of broad wooden steps. They started climbing the steps together. The steps creaked underfoot. From the direction of the house came an answering screech. It sounded to Johnny like some kind of tropical bird.

"It's Mr Zo who's going to go into meltdown when he hears just what I've got to say to him," said Middenface. "You just can't treat people like this. I don't care if he is a multi-billionaire or trillionaire or whatever he is. Who does he think he is? Insisting we take off our shoes at the space port like that, ordering us to strip and shower."

"They're concerned about off-world contamination," said Johnny in a reasonable voice.

They stepped onto the balcony. It was a cool, wide and pleasantly shadowy structure that spanned the entire width of the front of the house, a long wall of floor-to-ceiling windows reflecting blue sky and slants of sunlight and distant cloud. Their sandals slapped loudly on the wooden floor.

"And giving us these ridiculous wee things to wear." The paper robe rustled around Middenface's lanky frame as he stirred his shoulders pugnaciously, like a fighter warming up. "And that *thing* they did to us with the *vacuum cleaner*," he said. "I swear it ripped half my pubes out."

"Welcome, gentlemen," said a deep, lazy voice.

"I heard your remark, Mr McNulty," said Asdoel Zo.

"Remark?" said Middenface cravenly. "You must be mistaken, Mr Zo, sir. I didn't make no remark. I didn't say anything at all."

Asdoel Zo smiled. He was a sun-tanned man of medium height, wearing a blue and white Hawaiian shirt and black silk shorts. His bare legs and his stubby muscular arms were covered with thick coppery hair. His feet were bare. He had a shaved head and bushy red eyebrows, and a red moustache that looked like a third eyebrow that had escaped down his face and taken refuge under his nose. When he smiled you could see his teeth, which were bright and white and even, and Middenface noticed the tiny twin gleams of small diamonds, one set in each upper canine. The man had diamonds in his teeth, and Middenface was willing to wager that they weren't synthetics, either. He was awe struck. Imagine having the money to do that. And to keep all those wee girls on tap... He looked up from the shining dental gems to the man's eyes. They were alert and intelligent, the greyish-green colour of wet pebbles, and they seemed to be sizing Middenface up with amusement and possibly a little contempt. Middenface immediately dropped his gaze.

"You see, my friend," said Asdoel Zo, putting a furry arm over Middenface's shoulder, "I suffer from a range of allergies."

"Oh, now, isn't that a shame," said Middenface, hastening to inject concern into his voice.

"And the best efforts of the most highly paid homeopaths in the local galaxy have failed to budge these allergies."

"That's dreadful, dreadful," said Middenface. Asdoel Zo was leading him across the balcony. Johnny followed, silent, a step behind them.

"In particular," said Zo, "I'm allergic to dust. So I make a point of trying to achieve and maintain a dust-free environment."

"Well, of course, naturally, very sensible," said Middenface.

"Which is why I keep this place scrupulously well hoovered," said Zo, releasing Middenface's shoulder to gesture at a small vacuum cleaner robot that buzzed past them at shoulder level. The vacuum cleaner was about the size of a large bird. It darted through a gap between the tall windows and disappeared into the shadows of the house. "It is also why I insist on every visitor to my planet receiving a shower, followed by a good thorough vacuum cleaning when they first land."

"Quite right too," said Middenface.

"And those vacuum cleaners my people use are very powerful."

"Oh yes, they certainly are that," agreed Middenface enthusiastically.

"And my people wield them with enthusiasm. Sometimes too much enthusiasm. Which is why you suffered a certain... unfortunate loss of hair on your private parts."

"Never mind, Mr Zo. Never mind," said Middenface. "I've got plenty more where that came from. But if you don't mind, there isn't any need to give me another hoovering. I'm not the dusty type. No dust on me."

Asdoel Zo chuckled, though his grey-green eyes were cold. "Do you know what dust is, Mr McNulty?"

"Human skin cells," said Johnny Alpha. Middenface glanced at him, surprised at this sudden interruption. "That's what dust mostly is. At least, in places where you have a lot of humans."

"Exactly correct, Mr Alpha," said Asdoel Zo. He patted Middenface on the back again. "So you see, Mr McNulty, you are dusty. All human beings are. You're emanating a constant plume of dust as you shed your skin cells, like invisible smoke rising from your body."

"Ugh," said Middenface, shuddering. Then a sudden musical note rang out, echoing through the spacious shadowy balcony.

"Excuse me," said Zo, digging in the capacious pocket of his shorts and producing a phone. The phone was a golden rectangle, as thin as a sheet of paper, hinged in the middle. Zo opened it along the hinge and pressed it to his ear. He glanced at Johnny and Middenface. "Forgive me, gentlemen, I've got to take this." He turned and strolled to the far end of the balcony, out of earshot, and began talking into the phone.

Middenface looked at Johnny. "He's a nice chap, isn't he? All those billions in his bank account haven't affected him at all. Just a nice, down to earth guy, don't you think, Johnny?"

By way of reply Johnny sarcastically murmured "You must be mistaken, Mr Zo. I didn't say *anything*."

"What?" said Middenface. Then he realised that Johnny was imitating him. "What do you mean by that?"

"I thought you were going to give him a piece of your mind."

"I reconsidered."

"Reconsidered? I thought it was called grovelling," said Johnny Alpha with a grin.

"Now, now, Johnny. There's no harm in being nice, and Mr Zo is an important man. It does well to stay on the right side of him."

Asdoel Zo came back across the balcony, padding along the wooden floor on his bare feet. His call was evidently concluded and the phone back in his pocket. Instead he was holding a Cuban cigar. Blue smoke spooled from the glowing end, spreading a fruity scent across the balcony.

"Sorry about that, gentlemen. Now come along inside and we can have a proper discussion." Johnny and Middenface followed Asdoel Zo as he crossed the balcony towards the windowed front of his house, the odour of powerful marijuana drifting back to them from his cigar. "That's the biggest wee blunt I've ever seen," whispered Middenface.

The windows in front of them were overlapping panels of glass that automatically slid under each other, like a deck of cards, allowing access at any point. Now the windows sensed the approach of the three men and slid open. They stepped through out of the cool shadows of the balcony into the quiet splendour of the house. Immediately inside the entrance three more girls in gardening uniform, all blondes, were busy working on a large indoor planting, a raised bed of ferns and brightly coloured orchids with a

gently pulsing fountain set in a ring of stones in the centre.

It seemed to Middenface's somewhat overheated eye
that this trio of gardeners were wearing even less than the
girls installing the cactus outside. Johnny wasn't looking at
the women. Instead his alert gaze had shifted instantly to
something moving in the corner of the room. On two tall
perches fashioned from slender metal pipes, stood a pair of
birds. Parrots with gorgeous scarlet and emerald green
plumage. The birds stirred on their perches, inspecting
their master and his visitors.

The parrots were the only living animals in the room.
The rest were emphatically dead. The large space was
devoted to hunting trophies. Dozens of stuffed and
mounted heads of beasts hung on the high walls, with
small hovering vacuum cleaners, like the one they'd seen
outside dodging amongst them. One of the machines flew
too close to one of the parrots on its perch. The bird flew
at Middenface, a blur of dazzling tropical plumage.

"It's all right, gents," said Asdoel Zo, sucking on his
cigar. "He won't go far. He's a well trained pet." He exhaled
a perfect smoke ring and turned to the trio of girls working
on the planter. "Safira, would you mind getting a drink for
my guests."

"No, Mr Zo," said the girl, flashing a brilliant white
smile. She wiped a hand across her forehead and hastened
off into the depths of the large house.

"Actually," said Zo, "Phoebe, Jan, we could probably do
with some snacks as well. Nothing too major, we'll be having a meal later. Just some hors d'oeuvres to accompany
the drinks."

"Yes, Mr Zo," said the other two girls promptly, downing
their trowels and hurrying off. Middenface realised that
these women were all-purpose servants not just gardeners.
He started speculating fretfully on just how all-purpose.

Asdoel Zo's phone rang again and he sighed. "Once again, my apologies, gentlemen." He took the phone out of his pocket and moved away, puffing on his cigar as he spoke into the instrument. Middenface moved close to Johnny and murmured "Did you see those birds?"

"The parrots?" said Johnny dryly.

"No, not the bloody parrots. His gardeners-cum-jacks of all trades. Jills of all trades in this case. And a very nice bunch of jills they are. They're all knock-outs."

"Keep your mind on your job and out of your pants," said Johnny. "Or out of *their* pants."

"But Johnny. Just think about it. He can do anything he likes with them."

"I reckon he can. The rich generally get to do whatever they like."

"And they're crackers. Little beauties, all of them. And not simulated. Flesh and blood, not robotic. And I bet they're not even genetically modified." Middenface's voice was growing shrill and attenuated with envy. At that moment their host returned from the far end of the room where he'd been conversing in hushed tones. He snapped his phone shut and beckoned to them. "Come on in to my study, gentlemen."

They walked through the doorway in the far wall, under a vast spreading set of antlers mounted on a mahogany plaque, into a small room decorated in a masculine style with a stone fireplace. There were several more hunting trophies on the wall, including three buffalo heads – a black one, a brown one and a startling white furred albino head with fearsome holographic eyes that seemed to follow the viewer around the room. There was an antique wooden desk of the roll-top variety and a red leather sofa with two matching chairs. Over the fireplace, which was stacked with wood ready for a fire, but was thankfully not in use on this warm summer's day, were several antique rifles. Middenface was familiar with the weapons from numerous movies he'd seen as a boy, but he couldn't have named them. Johnny probably could.

Middenface looked away from the rifles and stared up at the albino buffalo head. Its mad, pink eyes stared at him in a murderous rage. Middenface could swear he could still see the gleam of ferocious life flaring in their depths. "Ugly bugger," he said.

Asdoel Zo chuckled. "Aren't those eyes something? I'm particularly proud of the way the taxidermist managed to make them look so lifelike. It's all hologram trickery of course."

"Oh, of course," said Middenface. "They never had me fooled."

"You should have seen what they were like in real life, bearing down on you at the business end of several tons of enraged mammal, charging full speed straight at you, hell bent on your destruction."

"You shot him yourself?" said Johnny.

"That I did. With a vintage Winchester 79."

"Sounds a little lightweight for taking down an animal of that size," said Johnny.

Zo glanced at Johnny in what might have been annoyance. "Of course I performed the coup de grace with a Sharps," he said.

"That would do it," allowed Johnny.

Asdoel Zo sank down on the leather sofa and gestured for his guests to sit in the adjacent armchairs. Middenface took his seat with trepidation, afraid that he might damage a valuable piece of antique furniture. But the chair was sturdy enough, although the leather seat generated an embarrassing farting noise as he sat down on it. Middenface crossed his legs, then uncrossed them again, tugging at the hem of his paper robe, afraid of exposing his wedding tackle to their prospective employer. "I don't suppose we can get rid of these ridiculous outfits, Mr Zo? And change into something a little more..."

"Dignified and befitting a man?" said Asdoel Zo with a smile.

"Yes, sir, Mr Zo, please," said Middenface.

"Well I'll certainly see what we can do. There are a number of outfits available, all well hoovered and dust free. I picked up a selection on McLoughlin's World, where I went on the safari that yielded our friend up there." He nodded at the albino buffalo head. "McLoughlin's is a class act all the way. The clothes are perfect period pieces."

"Period pieces?"

"Yes. Just wait until you get into character."

"Into character?" said Middenface.

"Yes. It's quite a thrill. I'm sure we've got something that will fit you, and Mr Alpha too. Like I say, I snapped up a selection on McLoughlin's World. They were beautifully made and quite the bargain. I'll get the girls to look them out in just a minute." Zo was grinning with enthusiasm.

"We didn't come here to play dress up," said Johnny Alpha. Asdoel Zo fell silent, his grin fading. Middenface wished Johnny hadn't spoken up like that. He shot his partner an annoyed glance. Couldn't he just for once be a little more tactful? Asdoel Zo stared at Johnny Alpha, his stony grey-green eyes locking coldly onto the mutant's eerie glowing gaze. The room fell silent and Middenface felt the contest of two powerful wills struggling for dominance. He cleared his throat. "Now Johnny, we're guests in Mr Zo's house. If he wants us to put on some wee costumes, there's no reason why we shouldn't..."

"No," said Asdoel Zo, lifting a hand in the air and waving it as though to disperse smoke, although his cigar had already gone out. "No, Mr Alpha is right. You're not here to indulge my enthusiasm for one of the more colourful periods of Earth's ancient history. Ancient history has nothing to do with it." He glanced at the dead cigar in his hand, then threw it savagely into the fireplace. He rose from the sofa and stalked across the room towards the roll-top desk. Middenface wondered for a moment if he should get up too, but Johnny remained seated so he did too.

Asdoel Zo stood with his hands on the desk. His face had assumed a faraway look. All trace of the genial host was gone. "Let's get down to business." There was a tormented, strangled, note in his voice, as if it pained him to speak. "I've asked you gentlemen here to do what you do best, to track down a vicious criminal and bring him back – dead or alive." Zo's voice subsided to a cracked whisper. "Preferably dead." He turned and looked at the two Strontium Dogs. "And you'll be rewarded if you succeed, gentlemen, very generously rewarded. I doubt anybody has ever provided you with the kind of pay-day Asdoel Zo can provide."

Middenface felt a warm glow at the mention of money. But Johnny broke the spell by speaking up. "What's this fellow done that makes you think he deserves killing?"

"What has he done?" said Asdoel Zo. He stared at Johnny blankly, as if the question was in a language that he didn't understand. He was silent for so long that Middenface began to squirm uncomfortably in his chair, which caused the leather seat to make the embarrassing farting noise again. Middenface hastily cleared his throat to cover the sound. "What Johnny means–"

Asdoel Zo interrupted him in an icy voice. "I'll show you what the bastard's done," he said. He grabbed the handles on the roll-top desk and wrenched its lid open with a clatter. Inside the antique desk was an incongruous, high-tech computer console with glowing buttons. Asdoel Zo pressed one of the buttons and there was a deep, melodious tone, like a brass gong being struck somewhere deep in the house.

Zo slammed the desk shut and turned back to Johnny and Middenface. "I'd like you to meet my family," he said. A section of the wood-panelled wall beside the fireplace slid open to reveal a doorway and through the doorway stepped a woman and two teenage children, both girls. They were dressed in formal black clothing, which contrasted tastefully with their healthy golden skin and the beautiful features the rich always seemed to possess, either through the efforts of genetic manipulation or cosmetic surgery. The girls had the same coppery hair as Asdoel Zo. The woman's hair was strikingly black and white striped. The beautiful trio came into the room and stood beside Zo at the desk.

"This is my wife Kathleen and my children Jodi and Lorna," said Zo in an odd, husky voice.

"Pleased to meet you," said Middenface. He was politely rising from his chair when he noticed Johnny urgently gesturing for him to stay put. Middenface sank back down, puzzled by Johnny's behaviour, but careful not to make the embarrassing noise.

Asdoel Zo was staring at his wife and children with a strange intensity. They in turn gazed back at him with what looked like a blend of mild affection and polite interest. The silence in the room grew and grew, until Middenface felt himself beginning to sweat. It was just a man standing looking at his family, but somehow there was a terrible tension in the room.

Finally, the newcomers broke the silence. "I love you, dear," said Kathleen, the wife. "I love you too, Daddy," chimed the older daughter. "You're my best friend, Dad," said the younger daughter.

It was a perfect vignette of domestic contentment. Then suddenly Kathleen, a tall, beautiful woman with jade eyes and that zebra-striped hair, seemed to tremble. It was as if she had been seized by a vicious attack of fever. Her whole body shook, her skin seeming to crawl across her body. Then, to Middenface's astonishment, she flickered. Asdoel Zo let out an enormous sob and lunged at her.

He went right through his wife, then right through his two children, like a man charging through mist. They were holograms, Middenface belatedly realised. The wife and kids were just projected images. Asdoel Zo stood gasping on the far side of them, then blundered back through the wraiths to the desk and the computer controls inside it. He touched another button and the woman and the two children disappeared.

He slammed the desk shut with trembling hands. Then the man began to sob. Middenface glanced over at Johnny in embarrassment.

Two of the gardening girls hurried in with trays of food, which they set aside as they rushed to embrace the sobbing man. The third girl stepped through the door with a tray of drinks and immediately sized up the situation. She too discarded her tray and threw herself into the group hug. Asdoel Zo suffered the attention of the women for a few moments, then waved them aside. He turned to Johnny and Middenface, his eyes red with weeping, his voice moist and unsteady.

"I want you to find the man who killed my family. I want you to find him and make the bastard pay."

CHAPTER TWO
TARGET TARKETTLE

Night had settled over the desolate landscape. The only sound was the sighing of the wind and, deep in the distant canyons, the uncanny intermittent cries of the coyotes.

Light flickered in the flames of a small campfire. In the glow of the campfire, the man called Charlie Yuletide lay wrapped in a threadbare blanket, using his saddle for a pillow, with his pistol lying close at his side, ready for instant use.

Charlie Yuletide shifted restlessly under his blankets, then sat bolt upright, like a man who had seen a ghost. He reached under his blanket and drew something out.

It wasn't a gun. It was his banjo. Charlie Yuletide strummed its resonant strings with his trembling hand. A melodious chord rose in the desert night. Then Charlie Yuletide began to sing.

"Welcome back to our story, my friends. A story already begun in blood, that promises more blood when it ends. A story of Johnny Alpha and his loyal saddle mate and the mission they accepted that would determine their fate. When a man who had buried the ones he loved in the ground showed them the face of the killer who had yet to be found..."

There was a prolonged rumbling sound as the stone fireplace sank away into the wooden floor of the study, revealing behind it a large vid screen set in the wall. The screen took on a creamy glow, then flickered to polychromatic life, revealing in grotesque close up the pitted pink face of a man, every pore, freckle, mole and whisker pitilessly displayed.

It was a ratlike face, with a sharp nose, receding chin and disquietingly full and sensual red lips. Oily wings of silver hair were scraped back over the man's delicate ears. The rotating three-dimensional image on the screen revealed that his left ear was pierced with a large ring of crudely worked gold. The man wore a battered black felt hat, and a frayed white shirt with a pearl pin across the collar and a narrow black tie.

"This is Preacher Tarkettle," said Asdoel Zo. The billionaire had dried his eyes and recovered his composure somewhat, much to Middenface's relief. He had also sent the solicitous trio of girls back out of the room, unfortunately sending the trays of food and drink with them. Middenface was beginning to feel a trifle hungry and more than a trifle thirsty. It had been a long morning, but he didn't feel he could raise these issues. After all, the poor man was talking about the fiend who'd murdered his family.

"We first met him on McLoughlin's World," said Asdoel Zo in a toneless voice. "He said he had come there to enjoy an authentic old west adventure, just like myself and my family. He was quite a character, very popular at the hotel. Everyone liked him. Everyone wanted to sit on the same table as him."

"So he must be pretty well-heeled, this Tarkettle," said Johnny. "To be able to afford an exclusive holiday like that."

"On the contrary," said Asdoel Zo, "it seems he pawned everything he owned for the ticket there. Spent every penny he could borrow and mortgaged everything except his soul."

"Why?"

"Because it was his self-appointed mission in life. He wanted to get close to us, close to me and my family. We didn't know it at the time, of course. He cunningly concealed his true motive under a wild enthusiasm for the old west experience on McLoughlin's world. He was genuinely having the time of his life, investigating the haunted saloon in the old ghost town, or blasting away while riding shotgun in a stagecoach under Indian attack, or when riding with us through the long grass of the prairie on a buffalo hunt. He was enjoying himself all right, but he was also keeping an eye on us every minute. We never suspected a thing. We just thought he was the sort of harmless eccentric who is obsessed with this period in Earth's history."

"The same period which you're so fond of," said Johnny.

Asdoel Zo's voice was dangerously calm, all trace of the emotionally bereaved husband and father utterly gone. "I hope you're not comparing me with this psychotic murdering scum."

"Just making an observation," said Johnny calmly.

"In my case, fascination with the old west is a lifestyle choice. For Tarkettle it's a compulsive fixation. One of the two which rule his life."

"And the other one?"

"Is me," said Asdoel Zo. "He's obsessed with me."

"But you didn't realise this when you met him on McLoughlin's World?"

Asdoel Zo sighed and subsided back onto the leather sofa. "No. I only wish to God I had. Maybe everything would have turned out differently." He punched himself with great violence on his bare thigh just below the cuff of his black shorts. The brutal impact of the blow left a white mark at the centre of a flaring patch of red flesh.

Middenface winced. "You can't blame yourself, Mr Zo," he said gently.

"Oh yes I can," said Zo savagely. "Not that it does a damned bit of good." He looked at Johnny imploringly. "When we first met him he seemed perfectly harmless."

"Even though you say he was obsessed with you."

"When you're as rich as I am, Mr Alpha, you become accustomed to unwanted attention from the little people. People who want to idolise you. People who want to be like you. Or *be* you. I thought Tarkettle was just another one of that breed."

"When did you learn different?"

"Not until it was too late. Much too late." Asdoel Zo took a deep breath. "I was attending a charity event on Beesom 12 with my family when my security people got word about an alleged threat on my life. It was a very specific threat. I was supposed to be the sole target and the assassination attempt was supposed to take place when I was on the shuttle, returning to my star yacht in orbit above B12. So naturally, I insisted that Kathleen and the kids should stay on the planet."

"Naturally," agreed Johnny.

"We sent the shuttle back up with a robot crew and a squad of trained mercenaries on board. I followed it up into low orbit in a second craft, my personal ketch, with my bodyguards, to watch what happened." Zo fell silent.

"What happened?" said Middenface.

"Nothing," said Asdoel Zo. "The shuttle docked with my star yacht without incident. No sign of any trouble at all. My ketch also docked. I was on board the star yacht, safe and sound. Then we got word from the planet's surface..."

"Tarkettle had gone after your family instead."

Asdoel Zo looked at Johnny bleakly. "Precisely," he said. "We don't know if he got wind of the trap we set on the shuttle and switched targets, or whether it had been his fiendish plan all along to convince us that the threat was against me, and then to go after my family." Zo's voice was suddenly hoarse with old pain. "But whatever the precise details of his plan were, it worked. We put all the security effort on me and the shuttle, and only left a skeleton staff protecting Kathleen and Jodi and Lorna." He sighed. "And Tarkettle wiped them all out."

The room was silent for a moment. Then Johnny said, "Why?"

Asdoel Zo looked at him bleakly. "Why?"

"What was Tarkettle's motive?"

"Motive?" Zo's voice trembled. "Does it matter? He killed everyone I loved in my life. What the hell does his motive matter?"

"It matters if it helps us find him."

Zo sighed again. "You're right," he said. He paused and sat staring into space for a moment. "You see this?" He raised his hands in a gesture that took in the room, the house, the whole planet. "I built all this with money I earned from my business. And my business is advertising."

"You make adverts?" said Middenface. It made absolute sense to him. Asdoel Zo's lifestyle was the kind of existence that Middenface had always enviously imagined highly paid media people enjoyed. Norms, that is. No mutant would ever be allowed to enjoy a glamorous career like that. Wealth and luxury were reserved for the norms.

"I don't make ads. I own the companies that make them. If you've ever bought anything, I guarantee that one of my companies was involved in the business of selling it to you at some point. The gentle art of hidden persuasion. Gentlemen, that's the cornerstone of my fortune."

Johnny nodded. "And this is why Tarkettle had a grudge against you?"

Zo also nodded. "He had a hatred of advertising that amounted to a mania. It seems he felt his free will was in jeopardy, that his thoughts were under assault from outside influences, trying to take over his mind and control his behaviour."

"He had a point though, didn't he?" said Johnny.

Middenface stared in astonishment at his friend. The room had gone icily silent again. How could Johnny say something like that? "What do you mean, Johnny? You don't mean that this bloodthirsty lunatic had some kind of a point when he attacked the poor man's wife and kids?"

Asdoel Zo held up his hand for silence. He was a man accustomed to having his orders obeyed and despite his laid-back appearance he possessed an enormous quiet authority. Middenface immediately shut up. Asdoel Zo peered at Johnny as if he was having trouble making out his features. "Are you referring to subliminals?"

Johnny shrugged. "Isn't that the whole point of subliminal advertising? To get into the mind of consumers and affect their thinking?"

Asdoel Zo took his phone out of his pocket and for a moment Middenface thought he was going to make a call, arranging for him and Johnny to be thrown out on their arses, and then presumably replaced by a pair of more compliant and less rude bounty hunters. He saw all the wonderful money Zo had promised, fluttering away.

But instead Zo used the phone as a remote control, pointing it at the screen on the wall with Tarkettle's face on it.

"I understand what you're saying about subliminals, Mr Alpha. And you may think you have a point. Or that Preacher Tarkettle had a point. But look at this man." The image kept on zooming in until Tarkettle's bloodshot eyes, blue as the sky and equally empty, filled the screen.

"The notion that you're having your thoughts controlled by others is a classic symptom of psychotic schizophrenia," said Asdoel Zo. "That is to say, madness. Look at these eyes. Are they not the eyes of a madman?

"Tarkettle was obsessed with the notion that he was no longer the sovereign ruler of his mind. He hated advertising and he hated the technology that had made it possible. In fact he was a Luddite."

"A what?" said Middenface, imagining some exotic sexual perversion. He could see just such vicious strangeness lurking in the limitlessly cold blue eyes that filled the screen.

"He means someone who hates machines," said Johnny Alpha. "Someone who hates them and smashes them every chance he gets."

"You mean like the Picket Line Robot Assassins?" said Middenface.

"Exactly like that. Except the PLRA is an organisation and Tarkettle was a lone fanatic who carried the concept well beyond the thresholds of madness. He intended to topple the entire empire of technology that made subliminal advertising possible and he saw me as the man at the head of the empire." He shrugged in self deprecation. "I suppose he saw himself as the man who was going to assassinate the emperor."

"But he ended up getting the emperor's family instead."

"Precisely, Mr Alpha."

"And you want us to find him and bring him back?"

"Dead or alive," said Asdoel Zo.

"Okay," said Johnny. He leaned forward and shook hands with Asdoel Zo. Middenface released a sigh of relief. He felt like he'd been holding his breath for an hour. At last the deal was secured. Johnny wasn't going to lose them this dream job after all. Middenface leaned forward to take his turn shaking hands with their new employer. Zo grasped his mutant flesh without hesitation, squeezing Middenface's hand firmly and warmly.

Johnny stood up. "Come on, Middenface."

Asdoel Zo glanced at him in surprise. "Are you going somewhere?" Middenface was equally surprised, but the disappointment he began to feel was a familiar sensation. Johnny was all business. The idea of hanging around in the billionaire's mansion with all the beautiful girls bringing them food and drink just wouldn't feature in Johnny's mind. Johnny Alpha was a Strontium Dog, eager to be unleashed on his prey.

"The sooner we get started, the sooner we can track down this Tarkettle." Johnny smiled a thin smile. "And collect our pay."

Asdoel Zo stood up. "Very practical and very commendable. Obviously I want you to get started as soon as possible. But first there's something we must do." He lifted the phone and pointed at the wall. The image of Preacher Tarkettle's face vanished. The screen was swallowed by the wooden wall and a deep low grinding noise began somewhere below them. The fireplace rose back out of the floor again, the planks in the floor neatly moving aside to make way for it. This time there was a roaring fire flaring in the hearth. The flames cast golden light and shadows in a weaving pattern across Asdoel Zo's face. He smiled at Johnny and Middenface. "There's someone I want you to meet."

Asdoel Zo led them back out through the trophy room where the parrots squawked and the flying vacuum cleaners buzzed. They passed back through the shuffling panels of the tall glass windows out onto the balcony. The cool perfumed wind from the jungle blew over them as they emerged from the house. The balcony was cool and spacious, and for some reason Middenface was glad to be back out. The rich man's house was a kind of temple of luxury and all the time he'd been in there, Middenface had been feeling uncomfortable, as though he was in the church of some strange religion – the religion of money – and might do something that was sacreligious or offensive. It was good to be back outside. He stretched and took a deep breath of fresh air, standing legs spread, arms akimbo and mouth wide open when he saw the woman.

She was small with a preposterously narrow waist and, Middenface couldn't help noticing, firm, round breasts. She was wearing blue jeans that might have been painted on her shapely legs and bottom, and a red and white checked shirt that was open to reveal a golden shadow of cleavage. Her face was oval with a full mouth, and button nose. The eyes were extraordinary: her left one pale blue and her right, deep brown. Middenface had once seen a picture of a wolf with eyes like that, and the woman had something of the same quality of a beautiful feral creature about her. She had severely cropped black hair with a silver streak running through it which would have been unflattering on anyone else, but on her it just served to emphasise the purity of her face.

Middenface tried to extricate himself from his embarrassing stretch. "Er, hello," he said, casually lowering his arms to his side.

"This is Hari Mata Karma," said Asdoel Zo.

"Just call me HMK," said the woman.

"Pleased to make your acquaintance," said Johnny.

"HMK will be accompanying you on your mission," said Asdoel Zo. Johnny flashed the man a look of irritation and Middenface felt his heart sink. Just when the deal looked like it had been sealed, Johnny Alpha was going to pick a fight with their employer. Middenface could see this job swirling down the sewer after all.

"What do you mean, accompany us?"

"I'm an independent operator working under special licence," said the woman.

"You mean without a licence."

HMK smiled at him. "Don't be so distrusting, Mr Alpha. If you look into my background I'm sure you'll find all my paperwork in order." The way she said it, it seemed almost to be a sexual proposition, as if by paperwork she meant something else entirely. Middenface glanced at Johnny. Was he imagining things?

"And besides," said HMK, "I have some special talents that you might find very interesting."

Middenface decided he wasn't imagining things. The woman was being deliberately provocative, coming on to Johnny in a big way. And now she was glancing over at Asdoel Zo, as if to estimate what effect her behaviour was having on him. But the billionaire simply stood there, cool and relaxed as he took out another cigar and ignited it by touching it on his phone. He puffed away watching HMK and Johnny Alpha.

"What do you think, Johnny?" said the woman. Middenface stared at his friend, waiting for a response. Surely even Johnny wasn't entirely immune from this woman's smouldering charms?

"I think you're going to be trouble," said Johnny Alpha, and suddenly everybody on the balcony laughed. Asdoel Zo released a big lungful of cannabis smoke that shimmered in the air like a writhing blue veil. Middenface got a whiff of it and felt his head swim. Johnny waved his hand in the air, brushing the smoke away. "I don't like this, Mr Zo," he said.

"I'm sorry to hear that, Mr Alpha."

"I don't like working with people I don't know."

Asdoel Zo held his cigar out in front of him, frowning as he watch the smoke rising from the tip of it. "I'd hate to lose your services, Mr Alpha." He glanced at Middenface. "Mr McNulty..."

"Johnny, can't we just..."

"Stay out of this, Middenface. If we take someone on board with us they might turn out to be a dead weight. And that might get us killed." Johnny turned his glowing eyes to HMK. "No offence, ma'am."

Hari Mata Karma smiled. "None taken."

Asdoel Zo took another drag on his cigar. "Mr Alpha, you don't seem to quite grasp the scope of this operation. This is no ordinary manhunt, and Tarkettle is no ordinary adversary. It's not going to be a two man job."

"You don't think so?" said Johnny coolly.

"No. In fact I think it's more like a seven man job."

"Seven!"

"I'm footing the bill for this operation, Mr Alpha, and I intend to see that it's done right, with no scrimping or false economy."

"I've had experience working with large teams before," said Johnny, "and I don't like it. It's an unwieldy size for a hunting party and people get killed." Middenface knew what Johnny was thinking of. Their ill-fated mission on the strange world of Epsilon 5 with its lethal time distortion effect. Middenface shuddered to remember it.

"I'm convinced it's a seven man – or man and woman – job," Zo glanced at HMK. "And I'm perfectly willing to let you vet the other members of your team. You can decide if they're good enough for you to take on. You have absolute right of veto." Zo paused and put his hand lightly on the woman's shoulder, "Except in the case of Hari Mata Karma. I insist that she goes along with you. She is what you might call a deal breaker."

"Okay," said Johnny. "Maybe breaking this deal is exactly what we ought to do."

"Oh, no," said Middenface. "Just when we were home and dry. Come on, Johnny..."

"Stay out of this, partner," said Johnny Alpha. "I'm not taking anybody on my team if I think they're wrong. That includes this little lady."

"Little lady," said HMK. "I love it. You're so chivalrous, Mr Alpha. Now I absolutely insist on joining you in the hunt for this Tarkettle bastard."

"Hari Mata Karma is part of the deal," said Asdoel Zo firmly, with a note of amusement in his voice, "or there is no deal." Johnny directed his searching, glowing gaze as Asdoel Zo. The contest of wills between the two men was palpable. "In that case," said Johnny, "I guess me and Middenface are just going to have to say thanks but no..."

"Wait a minute, Mr Alpha," said HMK. The woman smiled a brilliant, provocative smile. "Why don't you test drive me?" Middenface shook his head in wonder. Was the woman utterly incapable of uttering anything that wasn't couched in sexual innuendo?

"Test drive you?" said Johnny.

"Put me in a situation and see how I behave. Test me. Then decide for yourself if I'm the breed of Strontium Dog you want in your pack."

"You'll let me choose the situation?" said Johnny.

"Naturally." The small woman smiled. "You're the boss."

She glanced over at Asdoel Zo, who shrugged good-naturedly and took his cigar out of his mouth. "I suppose a test run won't do any harm," he said. "But take it from me. I know this woman's reputation. I had my people research her carefully. She'll be a real asset to your team."

"I'll be the judge of that," said Johnny Alpha. "Now who else do you want on this team?" Asdoel Zo took a slip of paper from his pocket and held it out.

"I've got a list."

Middenface read the list over Johnny's shoulder. It consisted of half a dozen of the top Strontium Dogs operating in the local sector. He watched as Johnny nodded, a tiny nod indicating the most grudging of acceptance, but acceptance nonetheless. Middenface heaved one final sigh of relief.

The first name on the list was Slim Drago.

Slim was famed for his ruthless manhunting skills and his junk food orgies, Slim being vastly obese. The word from the Dog House was that Slim was between missions and was, as usual, spending his hard earned bounty money on huge quantities of low quality food.

But Slim was not to be found at any of his usual haunts. After three days of hunting through the cheapest and greasiest of junk food meccas on seven planets, HMK unexpectedly came up with a lead. "He's in orbit around Elgar 4."

"How the hell do you know that?" demanded Johnny. Hari Mata Karma just smiled and said, "I have my sources."

So the fourth day of their search found them in a small fleet, star clipper loaned to them by Asdoel Zo. They flew up past the vast arch of a pink and white streaked giant of a planet that looked like marble, approaching a medium sized space station of the old fashioned double wheel configuration. It was the notorious Burger Heaven Drive-In.

"People come here from all over the galaxy," said Middenface.

"You can see why," said HMK. The double wheels of the space station had been covered by a bright shell in the shape of a gargantuan hamburger, orbiting gracefully in the beautifully eerie light of the pink and white planet below. "It's such an object of beauty," she said. There was a scattering of space vehicles docked all around the giant burger. "No doubt full of hungry burger fans," said HMK as Johnny skilfully and expertly put their ship into the docking pattern. The view of the space station vanished from their screen to be replaced by a dancing banana singing a high-pitched song, the gist of which was that Johnny Alpha, Middenface and HMK should not dare to leave Burger Heaven without sampling the "taste bud-bogglingly delicious banana burger, banana shake and banana fries".

"Good God," said Middenface. "I've heard of a banana burger and banana fries before, but a banana milkshake? People consume the strangest muck."

Johnny was cursing as his fingers skimmed smoothly across the control panel, making adjustments to the screen. "What are you doing?" said HMK.

"Trying to get this damned ad off our forward viewing screen," said Johnny.

"You can use one of the small screens," suggested HMK.

"But why should I have to?" said Johnny. He kept struggling with the controls, but the singing banana still dominated their screen. "I don't understand why that screen doesn't have better anti-ad protection," said Middenface. "This ship belongs to a billionaire."

"A billionaire who made his money from advertising," said HMK.

"Got it!" said Johnny. The banana disappeared with a squeal and a flash, to be replaced by an image of the approaching space station, much closer now. They could see that there were layers of lettuce, tomato and onion tucked under the mammoth burger bun facade that clad the vast beef patty, which housed the main module of the space station. Suddenly a small vehicle popped up in front of them. It was a bronze-coloured, spherical vehicle. A robot-controlled satellite with twin white, slanting head-lights at the front, which were deliberately engineered for an anthropomorphic suggestion of eyes. Above the eyes was an oversized plastic replica of a white baseball cap with the words Burger Heaven emblazoned on it. The cap enhanced an otherwise strictly minimal resemblance of the spherical vehicle to a human head. Two large mechanical tentacles appeared from either side of the head, as though sprouting from its ears. The tentacles reached out towards their craft with dreamy slowness. "It's trying to grab us," said Middenface, reaching for the weapons systems on the control panel. Johnny reached out one fast, strong hand and seized Middenface's wrist, stopping him. HMK sat down beside Middenface, smiling at him.

"Not so fast, big man. It's only a parking drone."

"Combination parking drone and waiter," said a cheery voice over the intercom. "Allow me either to help you dock safely aboard Burger Heaven, or remain parked out here in the drive-through zone and allow me to fetch your order and bring it back to your vehicle!" The artificial cheerfulness of the voice reached a new peak of engaging sincerity. "Whichever choice you make, make sure you don't miss our special Banana Meal!" Johnny reached for the control panel and cut off the voice of the drone. He hit the transmit button. Now the thing could hear them, but they weren't forced to listen to its unctuous sales pitch. "We'll be coming aboard," said Johnny tersely.

The drone gestured cheerfully with its tentacles, beckoning them and flashing its lights to indicate that they should follow it towards the space station. Johnny looked at the others. "Check your weapons and make sure they're all set to stun."

HMK grinned at him. "What makes you think we'll be needing weapons, stun or otherwise?"

"Slim Drago can be kind of volatile if you approach him in the middle of a junk food binge," said Johnny. "Haven't you heard that about him?"

"I suppose I might have heard something," allowed HMK playfully. "I might have heard that he can be quite a handful."

"Handful is one way of putting it," said Johnny, strapping on his guns. "He has a mutation that doesn't allow him to metabolise certain foods properly. If he eats them it can make him berserk. And you don't want five hundred kilos of berserk Slim Drago coming at you."

"God help us if he's in the throes of a sugar rush," added Middenface. Johnny didn't reply. He was concentrating on coaxing their ship into the narrow space of the docking port. A reverberant clunking sound signalled that they had established themselves in the berth, followed by the buzzing and clicking of the umbilicals attaching themselves to provide the ship with power and communications lines. A rumbling clank and a green flash on their screen indicated that the docking berth had sealed and was pumped full of breathable atmosphere. Johnny pushed the airlock release and a cool flow of fresh air invaded the ship, displacing the stale, canned atmosphere they'd been breathing for the last twelve hours. Johnny leaned back in his seat.

"Before we go inside after Slim, there's a few things we need to familiarise ourselves with." He punched buttons on the control panel and the view of the docking bay on their screen vanished to be replaced by a photograph of a very fat, but very formidable-looking man with a rather silly fringe of tonsured blond hair. "This is Slim Drago," said Johnny, hunched over the control panel, frowning at the screen with concentration. "As we all know, Slim doesn't like to be interrupted while he's stuffing himself with junk food. But once he's had a chance to recover from the blowout, he'll be fine, a perfectly reasonable man. So the trick is to get him away from the trough without getting bitten, so to speak. Slim has even been known to pull a gun on a fellow Strontium Dog when he's at the height of a burger binge. So, I suggest we use some kind of anaesthetic gas, to render him semi-conscious, but docile. It will keep him out of action for a few minutes and give him a chance to recover from his feeding frenzy. By which time he should be in a more friendly and receptive frame of mind. In other words, we'll be able to talk to him and get some sense out of him. We've got several canisters of anaesthetic gas in the cargo bay in the rear of the ship."

"Johnny–" said Middenface.

"Just a minute, Middenface," said Johnny, still frowning with concentration at the screen. "Slim himself is just one of our problems. Here's the other one." The image on the screen changed. It showed a view of a dozen men in brightly coloured uniforms, all armed with what looked like giant ketchup bottles. Their uniforms had the Burger Heaven logo emblazoned on them. On close inspection, the oversized ketchup bottles revealed themselves to be some kind of weapon. "These are the Burger Heaven security guards. Just a small sample of them. There are something like a hundred and eighty employed full time in the space station, although only half of those will be on shift at any given time. That still leaves ninety fairly husky bouncer types around the place for us to deal with."

"Johnny–" said Middenface.

Johnny held up his hand. "Just a minute," he said. "Let me finish. The Burger Bouncers' job is to maintain order, not to go looking for trouble. Those ketchup bottles they're carrying are actually spray guns full of a crowd quelling compound, consisting of a psychedelic tranquilliser in foam form. It's topically active, which means if they spray it on you and it hits a patch of exposed skin on your body, you can count on being out of action for at least eight hours. The psychedelic foam sends a person of average size and weight into cloud cuckoo land in a state of euphoric helplessness. It renders troublemakers very easy to handle. The Burger Bouncers' job is to use it only if absolutely necessary. But absolutely necessary situations arise about once a week on this satellite, given the unstable nature of many junk food enthusiasts combined with the tendency of the human metabolism to run out of control when fed on a diet of the sort of garbage they sell here."

"Johnny–" repeated Middenface.

"I'm almost finished. Just hear me out. This is the important bit. The Burger Bouncers shouldn't intervene in our attempt to have a little chat with Slim Drago. It's none of their business. But unfortunately Slim has been known to bribe some of the bouncers to work for him as a kind of personal bodyguard. As I said before, he doesn't like to be bothered when he's stuffing his face and the Bouncers are a kind of insurance policy. We can pretty much guarantee that there's going to be trouble even if we so much as approach Slim. His personal Bouncers are going to jump us and try to spray us with their foam guns. Complicating this situation is the fact that we don't know which bouncers are working for Slim and which aren't, so we're just going to have to assume that all of them are our enemies for the purposes of this mission. This means that we should wear full body space suits with the visors down when we enter Burger Heaven. This ensures that no matter how much of that foam they spray on us, it's not going to knock us out. So long as no skin is exposed, we'll be safe. We should just be able to walk in their, grab Slim, and walk out again. Now, is all that clear?" As he finished speaking, Johnny turned to look at Middenface and Hari Mata Karma – but the woman was nowhere in sight.

"Where's HMK?" said Johnny.

"That's what I was trying to tell you," said Middenface in an accusing tone. "She slipped out the minute the ship's hatch opened. You didn't notice because you were staring at that bloody screen."

"Well, where's she gone?"

"I don't know," said Middenface.

"Why didn't you tell me?"

"Johnny, I *tried*," said Middenface.

Johnny Alpha scrambled out of his seat. "We'd better go and find her before she screws everything up for us." He hurried towards the rear of the ship.

"Johnny, wait!" said Middenface. This time his friend listened to him. He stopped and looked back. "What is it?" Middenface was bent over the control panel, staring at the screen.

"Look," he said.

MHK appeared on the screen, trotting back into the docking bay and moving quickly towards the ship. She was wearing a space suit with the visor down. The space suit had several patches of damp white foam clinging to it. On her utility belt were attached a number of bright yellow canisters. Trailing over her shoulder was a length of red and black mountain climbing rope.

"What are those canisters?" said Middenface, peering at the screen.

"Our anaesthetic gas. What's that on the end of the rope she's dragging?"

Johnny's question was answered by the viewing screen as HMK disappeared from sight, hauling the rope behind her and dragging her burden into view. It was Slim Drago, lurching unsteadily with the rope tied around his wrists. He was following HMK like a dog on a leash. "What the hell is she doing?" said Middenface.

Johnny didn't reply. He was already running to the back of the ship. Middenface followed. They reached the hatch just as HMK stumbled on board, dragging the huge, sleep-walking bulk of Slim behind her. As she entered the ship she hit the undocking control on the hull and the umbilical power and coms cords dropped off the ship with loud popping and sucking noises. HMK scrambled through the hatch, dodged past Johnny and Middenface and secured her rope to a bracket on the nearest bulkhead. She tugged her helmet off, revealing a face bright with sweat and excitement. "Don't touch me, boys. I've got that damned crowd control foam all over my space suit."

"Don't worry, I'm not going to touch you," said Middenface. Somehow it sounded stupid when he said it.

"What the hell do you think you're doing?" demanded Johnny.

"Bringing Slim Drago in for a chat," said HMK, tugging on the rope. The massive form of Slim came stumbling through the ship's hatch to join them. She smiled at Johnny. "Isn't that what you wanted?" Slim Drago was grinning stupidly at his new surroundings and the people all around him. He let out a loud, contented belch, then sat down on the floor and began to happily hum a snatch of song.

"You were supposed to go in there with Middenface and me," said Johnny.

"What difference does it make?" said HMK. She cracked open the chest plate on her space suit and slithered out of it, taking care to avoid the foam clinging to it. "We've got him now."

"She has a point, Johnny," said Middenface.

HMK strode to the control panel on the bulkhead and slapped it, causing the hatch to hum shut. "We'd better get out of here before those Burger Bouncers catch up with us."

"She has a point there, too, Johnny," said Middenface.

Six hours later Johnny, Middenface, HMK and Slim Drago were seated comfortably on the balcony outside Asdoel Zo's mansion, sipping beers in the evening sunlight while a bevy of Zo's beautiful gardening girls busied themselves cooking spare ribs on an infrared barbecue unit for the

Strontium Dogs. Asdoel Zo was busy somewhere in the depths of his mansion, mixing a bowl of spicy sauce to go with the ribs. The billionaire had insisted on a celebration; he'd been delighted that they'd managed to track down and enlist Slim Drago.

Slim, since he'd calmed down from his eating binge, was proving to be an amiable, polite and self-effacing man. He sat hunched beside Middenface, dwarfing the large wooden deck chair he sat in. He sipped at his bottle of beer and smiled shyly at Middenface.

"How are you feeling now, big fella?" said Middenface.

"Fine, thanks. Just a bit of a headache."

"That would be the anaesthetic gas I used on you," said HMK, seated opposite them. "Sorry about that."

"Heck, I don't blame you," said Slim. "Trying to talk to me when I'm eating is like taking a bone away from a starving wolf. Using that gas was the only safe way of getting me into a civilised conversation."

"That's what we figured," said Johnny, who was sitting beside HMK.

"But don't you mind us kidnapping you like that, Slim?" said Middenface.

The big man shrugged. "If you hadn't turned up I would have just stayed there at Burger Planet, eating, until I ran out of money. I'm like a compulsive gambler in a casino. I can't leave the table until I'm broke."

"So you're saying we did you a favour?" said HMK.

"That's right, miss. To tell the truth I'm kind of relieved to have my eating spree terminated. I know it's self destructive behaviour, but I just can't help it."

"Well then, here's to friendship," said Middenface, lifting his beer bottle. Slim smiled and did the same, and then Johnny and HMK joined in the toast. Four beer bottles clinked together, followed by four amiable gurgling sounds as the Strontium Dogs drank. Then they all sat back in a companionable, silence watching the sun sinking over Asdoel Zo's private jungle. As the shadows of night swallowed the balcony, the girls who were busy cooking could be glimpsed in the red glow of the barbecue, like labourers in front of an open furnace. Fragrant cooking smells wafted towards the bounty hunters.

HMK leaned over to Johnny. "So?" she said.

"So what?" said Johnny.

HMK shook her head. Her pearly teeth glowed in a smile in the darkness. "You know what I mean. How did I do?"

"Terribly. You disobeyed orders and acted on your own."

"I didn't disobey orders. I ducked out before you had a chance to give any."

"You acted independently instead of as part of the team."

"I figured that was the smartest move," said HMK. "One person could get in there and back out with Slim faster than three of us. And attract less attention along the way. That was my theory, anyhow." She smiled again and sipped her beer. "And it looks like I proved it."

"It's true, Johnny. She did."

"I don't like people taking charge," said Johnny Alpha. "Not when I'm in charge of this outfit."

"No question," said HMK. "You're the boss. And I promise not to make a move again without consulting you. But I wanted to prove myself back there at Burger Heaven. To show you what I'm made of."

"I guess you did that," said Johnny.

"So?" asked HMK.

"So what?" said Johnny.

HMK punched him playfully on the arm. "Don't keep a lady in suspense," she said. "Did I prove myself, or didn't I? Am I on the team, or not?"

Johnny shrugged grudgingly. "I guess you proved your-self. I guess you're on the team."

HMK howled with delight and poured beer on herself, on Middenface and on Slim Drago, who sat placidly and amiably, keeping an eye on the sizzling spare ribs on the barbecue. Asdoel Zo appeared on the balcony wearing a tall white chef's hat and carrying a large wooden bowl. "I hope all of you like your sauce spicy," he said.

While the others were busy eating, Johnny led Asdoel Zo down the steps from the balcony to the quiet and pri-vacy of the terrace garden for a talk. "What's on your mind, Mr Alpha?" said Zo, igniting another cannabis cigar.

"First I wanted to say thanks, for the food and beer."

"My pleasure."

"But I also want to make clear that this mission is not going to be one long happy barbecue."

Asdoel Zo puffed on his cigar and looked at Johnny. It was fully night on SG977 and one of the planet's three moons had come out from behind a wide bank of cloud. Its cold bone-coloured light shone on Johnny Alpha's unearthly eyes. Asdoel Zo sucked at his cigar until its tip glowed. He studied the glowing cigar tip instead of Johnny's disquieting eyes. "I'm aware of that," he said.

"You may be aware of that," said Johnny. "But I'm not sure the rest of my team are."

"They're all top professionals," said Asdoel Zo.

"They're top professionals all right. But if we want them playing at the top of their game we're going to have to keep them sharp. And you aren't helping by creating a party atmosphere like you did tonight."

"Party atmosphere? What are you, Mr Alpha? Some kind of neo-Puritan?"

"Call me anything you like," said Johnny.

"It's just some beers and a barbecue. A bit of fun."

"A bit of fun that could dull the reflexes, slow the reaction time and get somebody killed." Johnny turned and walked back up the stairs, leaving the billionaire smoking his cigar in his cactus garden. As Johnny crossed the balcony he paused at the corner where Slim, Middenface and HMK were sitting. "I want everyone to hit the sack soon."

"Hit the sack?" said HMK.

"And make sure you get plenty of rest," said Johnny. "I have the feeling tomorrow is going to be a tough day." He turned and walked into the house, heading for the guest wing where Asdoel Zo was providing rooms for the Strontium Dogs. HMK watched him go. "Mr Party Fun," she said.

Middenface sighed. "Johnny may not be a party animal, but he knows what he's talking about." Middenface rose from his chair to follow Johnny. "And if we all want to stay alive, we'd do well to listen to him."

CHAPTER THREE
LUNAR SHOOTOUT

Dawn painted the desert as a man sat prodding at the ashes of a campfire. The man was Charlie Yuletide. He had his blanket wrapped around his shoulders to protect him from the morning desert chill. He squatted awkwardly and poked at the grey ashes of his fire until he found a glowing fragment, and then he began to rebuild the fire, using blunt chips of kindling that he took from a paper sack in one of his saddlebags.

He stacked the kindling in a pyramid and blew on the red coal until the kindling caught and flames rose from the fire. Charlie Yuletide sighed and set a battered coffee pot in the centre of the flames. Then he picked up his banjo and began to sing.

"Johnny and friends went off in search of a siren. But before they knew it, guns was a-firin'."

Twelve hours later Johnny and his team were on a small moon called Disraeli 4.1.

The next name on their list was Stella Dysh. Johnny and the others knew Stella by reputation and all agreed that she would make a valuable addition to their elite group...

"Why don't we call it a posse?" said Middenface. Johnny frowned at his friend. "What are you talking about?"

"This team we're putting together. Why don't we call it a posse?"

"A what?"

"A posse," said Middenface. "You know, like in a western. The bad guy has to be hunted down, so they form a wee *posse* and go after him."

Johnny shook his head. "You've been hanging around Asdoel Zo too long. He's got you cowboy crazy."

"But it's exactly what we're doing. It's the perfect name."

"It's from the Latin *posse comitatus*," added Hari Mata Karma.

"She sure is one smart lady," said Slim Drago, gazing worshipfully up at HMK's space-suited form. Slim was in his own oversized vacuum suit, which gave him the appearance of some kind of giant teddy bear. Slim was proving a placid and amiable character when he was not on a junk food binge. In fact, Middenface had concluded that he was downright dull.

"I don't give a damn what we call it," said Johnny. "But we're not going to have a team or a posse, or anything else, unless we manage to get some more Strontium Dogs to join us. And Stella Dysh isn't exactly proving easy to contact. In fact, if Asdoel Zo wasn't so willing to throw his money around we wouldn't have come here looking for her. We would have crossed her off and moved on to the next name on our list."

"But we couldn't have that," giggled HMK. "Because then there wouldn't be seven of us, and seven is such a western number!"

"Why is that?" said Slim Drago in his adoring voice.

"Oh, it's just tradition," said HMK. She was hunched over the communications console in the crawler, which was situated in a small bubble cockpit in the roof of the vehicle. There wasn't room in the cockpit for two people; indeed there was hardly room for one full grown person, which is why HMK had volunteered to man the communications. Johnny stood under her in the main section of the vehicle, staring up at the diminutive woman in the bubble dome.

"Is she not answering?" said Johnny.

HMK shook her head. "Still no reply," she said. "Maybe she's just left her phone switched off."

"Maybe," Johnny said sceptically.

"Maybe she's just not at home," suggested Middenface.

"No," said Johnny. "If she'd left her base she would have notified the Dog House." Stella Dysh was notoriously scrupulous about such details. She liked money and never wanted to miss an opportunity for paid work. "She makes sure she's always available," said Johnny.

"Yes, that's what I've heard too," said HMK dryly.

"Keep trying," said Johnny.

"Yes boss," said HMK. Johnny moved forward to the front section of the vehicle where Middenface was sitting in the driver's seat in another transparent dome, this one vertically mounted on the face of the crawler and considerably larger than the communications cockpit. Large enough for two people – though not if one of them was Slim Drago. Slim had been assigned to a position in the rear of the crawler where it terminated in another dome, which housed the controls for the mechanical arms mounted on the sides of the vehicle.

The crawler was painted bright orange, for maximum visibility on the ashen dust of the moon. The orange cylinder had bubble cockpits at the front and rear, and another, for communications, mounted on the roof. The vehicle crawled along the lunar surface on three pairs of caterpillar treads that pivoted to accommodate even the most dramatic changes in the terrain. It made good speed and would bring them to the settlement where Stella Dysh lived in less than three hours' travel from the mining base where they landed. It was one of a small fleet of such vehicles designed for prospecting and ore gathering. The mine's manager, a woman with a set of ill-fitting steel teeth, had rented it out to Johnny and the others for an extortionate sum. But Asdoel Zo was footing the bill. It was the only way to get to Stella Dysh, who refused to respond to any attempt at communication.

"How far is it to the shite hole, anyway?" said Middenface.

"You're the one who's driving," said HMK.

"Well according to the map that steel-toothed bitch sold us, it was supposed be just ahead, at the foot of that bluff or tor or whatever the damned thing is called. Maybe old steel snappers lied to us... Ah, hang on. I'm doing her a disservice. That looks like it just up ahead."

The crawler was rounding the base of a huge outcrop of rock that threw a giant shadow on the white lunar terrain. Just as they emerged from the shadow they saw a cluster of buildings at the foot of the outcrop, gleaming in the pitiless glare of the sunshine pouring down from the black sky with no atmosphere to filter it. The buildings were seven or eight small domes and cylinders that could house fewer than a hundred people. It was a tiny community. As the crawler approached the buildings it passed a variety of ruined machinery, junked vehicles and other trash that had been dragged from the settlement and just dropped on the ground.

"They're some kind of lunar trailer trash," said HMK. "What kind of girl is this Stella Dysh anyway?"

"You said you knew her," said Johnny.

"Knew of her," HMK corrected him. "Like everyone else, I've heard about her special, ahem, talent and that she's not shy about using it. But I didn't expect to find her living in redneck squalor."

"Redneck? Aren't you being just a touch snobbish?" said Middenface.

HMK ignored the remark. "I mean just look out there," she said.

"I am," said Middenface. "I'm only steering the vehicle."

"Then while you're steering it, take a look at all those little gleaming objects strewn across the landscape. Do you see them, twinkling in the sunlight?"

"Yes, I see them," said Middenface. "What are they, deposits of valuable minerals?"

"Not quite. Beer cans."

"Good God," said Middenface.

"That's right. Thousands and thousands of beer cans, scattered here by the high class indigenous population. Like I said, redneck squalor. Or maybe I should say redneck heaven."

"What's that gleaming in the sun?" said Slim Drago, as if just waking up to the conversation.

"Beer cans. She told you," said Middenface. "For heaven's sake man, pay attention."

"No. Not those. That thing glinting over them. Looks like it's on the roof of one of those buildings."

Johnny threw himself into the cockpit, staring over Middenface's shoulder. "Shit," he said.

"What's the matter?" said Middenface.

"Everybody seal your suits!" said Johnny. "And grab your weapons. Hold on tight and brace yourself."

"Why?" said Middenface.

"Because," said Johnny, "that thing on the roof of the building is a–"

Middenface, hastening to obey Johnny's orders, already had his helmet sealed shut on his space suit and he was listening to Johnny, who was also now sealed into his helmet, on the intercom unit. The intercom buzzed as it came to life, obscuring Johnny's last two words. Middenface heard Slim Drago chuckle on the intercom. "That's funny, Johnny. I thought you said *rocket launcher*."

The side of the crawler exploded as a projectile tore through it, screaming and twisting and sending fat, white sparks tumbling through the interior of the vehicle and blasting out into the lunar vacuum.

The impact of the missile knocked the crawler onto its side, then onto its back. But orientation was irrelevant since the rush of escaping air created a suction strong enough to tear Middenface from his seat and throw him out onto the moon's surface. He hit the ground gently and bounced in slow motion, raising a confusing swirl of dust. As he spun, he got intermittent glimpses of the bright orange crawler lying on its side, tractor treads spinning and twisting in a futile attempt to get a grip, like a beetle on its back. There was an ugly gash in the cylindrical body of the vehicle and Middenface glimpsed another space-suited figure tumbling out into the void. It was a tiny figure, so Middenface knew it was HMK. As she hit the ground and skidded in a slowly rising plume of dust, another figure appeared in the hole in the side of the crawler. The figure was so large it had to squeeze its way out. Slim Drago's considerable bulk had saved him from being sucked out like Middenface, HMK and Johnny.

Johnny. Where was he? Middenface looked around for his friend, but he couldn't see anything, he was still spinning with the momentum of his fall and dust was still rising all around him, blotting everything out. Middenface stuck his arm out to break his fall and he hit the ground softly, his spin slowing. He put his other arm out, grabbing at the lunar dust with his clumsy space suit gloves and bringing himself to a halt. He knelt there for a moment, listening to the confusion of chatter from Slim Drago, squeals from HMK and a shocked voice cursing in the vilest possible terms that he gradually recognised as his own. There was no sound from Johnny.

Middenface rose unsteadily to his feet and then he saw Johnny, who was already up and running, back towards the wrecked crawler. "Take cover," shouted Johnny.

"Where?" demanded HMK in a voice that Middenface was pleased to note was more pissed off than frightened.

"Over here," said Johnny. "Behind the crawler. Keep it between you and the settlement as you move."

"Okay boss," said Slim obediently. He had been loping away from the crawler in great, distance-devouring, low-gravity lunar strides. Now he slowly brought himself to a halt and turned around to begin loping back in the other direction, towards the crawler. Middenface was already there, at Johnny's side, when first HMK and then the hulking Slim Drago joined them. He sidled up to Johnny and peered through the transparent curve of the abandoned cockpit. He took one quick look then ducked with comical haste. "It's a rocket launcher all right," said Slim.

"Yes, I think we'd gathered that," said HMK.

"Keep your head down," Johnny said sharply.

But he was too late. Slim had bobbed up for another look through the cockpit canopy that exploded all around him in a shower of glass fragments that looked like ice flakes. "Get down!" shouted Johnny. They all ducked low behind the crawler and the glass of the cockpit settled on them in a slow motion shower. It was being chewed away by some kind of projectile weapon. A machine gun, maybe. "And stay down," snarled Johnny.

"Yes, sir," said a chastened Slim Drago.

"Middenface, make sure these two don't get themselves killed in the next ten minutes."

"These two?" said HMK in a scandalised tone, "I hope you're not lumping me in with this careless oaf here."

"I am a careless oaf," said Slim over the helmet mikes in a tearful voice. "A careless, careless oaf."

"The next ten minutes?" said Middenface. "Where will you be, then, Johnny?"

"I'm going to drop back about a hundred metres, in a straight line, using the crawler for cover," said Johnny

Alpha. "Then I'm going to cut left for those rocks near the base of the butte. I'll use them for cover and make for the shadow of the butte. Once I'm in shadow I'm going to flank the settlement, or at least that one building housing the sniper."

"Or snipers," said HMK, stressing the plural.

"Or snipers," agreed Johnny. "Now keep your heads down."

"Wait Johnny," said Middenface desperately. "Take me with you."

"Somebody's got to stay and look after these two," said Johnny, slipping back from the vehicle and beginning his run for the rocks.

"That's ridiculous," howled Middenface.

"It is ridiculous," echoed HMK. "How do you expect to deal with those snipers on your own?"

"It's too late, save your breath," said Middenface. Johnny's figure was already dwindling in the distance, moving swiftly in the low lunar gravity. He ran gracefully, floating slightly above the ground, dust rising under his boots as he cut left towards the rocks at the base of the butte.

"He's a very stubborn man," said HMK.

"You're telling me," said Middenface.

"He's the boss," said Slim placidly.

Ten tense minutes ensued as they waited to hear from Johnny. Middenface managed to work out a crude system of mirrors, using glass fragments from the shattered cockpit, which allowed him to keep an eye on the rooftop sniper. Not that he could see much. There appeared to be a small group of figures with an assortment of weapons, including the projectile gun and the rocket launcher, which had so dramatically demonstrated its power earlier. But no detail was visible at this distance. The cheap space suits that Steel Teeth had rented them with the crawler had not come equipped with anything more sophisticated than UV filters. There was any amount of sophisticated image enhancement equipment inside the crawler, which would have brought the snipers into clear and detailed view, but it was impossible to get at any of it. When Middenface made a tentative attempt to re-enter the vehicle through the hole in its side he was met with a blast of bullets that tore new perforations in the crawler's orange skin and angled savagely into the moon's surface on the far side, sending up spouts of dust dangerously close to the crouching Strontium Dogs.

Thereafter, Middenface and the others stayed put. Middenface used his crude mirror system to keep an eye on the rooftop while Slim hummed, and HMK fumed and fretted. "What can he be doing?" she said.

"He's flanking them."

"I know that. But, having flanked them, what exactly does he then intend to do?"

"Whatever the situation demands, I imagine," said Middenface.

"What, like single-handedly gunning them all down in a blaze of glory, or a glorious blaze or something?"

"Yes, maybe something like that."

"I don't get it," said Slim Drago. "Why is Miss Stella Dysh firing at us anyway? She's supposed to be our friend, isn't she? Our fellow Strontium Dog?"

"We don't know that it's Stella Dysh who's shooting at us," snapped Middenface. He couldn't believe he'd ever thought that this big lout was intelligent.

"But that's where she lives," insisted Slim. "The place where they're shooting at us from."

"The place where they're shooting at us from," echoed HMK, laughing. "You really must remind me to buy you a grammar implant for your frontal lobe, Slim."

"That's a really kind offer, Miss Hari Mata Karma," said Slim adoringly. "Thank you."

"Look," said Middenface impatiently, "just because that settlement is where Stella Dysh lives, it doesn't necessarily follow that it's her shooting at us. There could be scores of other people living there."

"Scores?" said Slim in confusion.

"Dozens, then," said Middenface.

"Dozens?"

"A score is twenty, a dozen is twelve," explained HMK.

"Oh, so there could be lots of other people there besides Stella Dysh who are shooting at us," said Slim.

"Precisely," said Middenface.

"So what you're saying is that there's lots of people there."

"Right."

"And there could be lots of snipers."

"Right."

Slim Drago painfully puzzled it out. "So... what you're saying is that... Miss Dysh... she's just *one* of the snipers."

"No!" said Middenface in exasperation. "That's not what I'm saying at all. We don't know that Stella Dysh is shooting at us. In fact, the people who *are* shooting at us may have taken her prisoner."

"Oh," said Slim. "I see. So Miss Dysh is being held hostage and we have to go in to rescue her."

"Yes. No. Maybe. Look, I have no precise idea of what is going on, and I won't know until Johnny gets back, so everybody just stop jumping to conclusions until he does get back, and reports."

"All right, Mr Middenface," said Slim Drago, and he resumed his tuneless humming. Middenface turned down the volume for Slim's feed on his helmet and the humming faded. But then another voice rang in his ear. "I still don't see what Johnny thinks he's doing," said HMK in her familiar lilting sarcastic tone. "What is he going to achieve on his own? You don't seriously believe that he'll be able to take on all these snipers and gun them all down?"

"Oh yes," said Middenface. "Or take them all prisoner."

"Take them prisoner?" HMK chuckled. "Oh yes. Get the drop on an entire nest of snipers and take them prisoner. That's *very* likely to happen. And once having taken them all prisoner, what will he do with them? Rehabilitate them?"

"No, march them back here to the crawler where we're waiting," said Middenface. And he stood up and moved around the front of the vehicle, past the shattered cockpit. "Come back Mr Middenface!" brayed Slim Drago anxiously. "They'll shoot you."

"Get down, you fool!" HMK cried simultaneously.

Middenface was touched by the note of concern in their voices, but he was no fool. He had only stepped out of cover because of what he had seen, through his arrangement of mirrors. "Don't fret yourselves," he said to Slim and Hari Mata Karma. "In fact, why don't you step out here and join me?"

Slowly and hesitantly HMK and Slim emerged from the cover of the wrecked crawler. They came and stood beside Middenface on a low outcrop of rock near the mangled middle caterpillar tread on the vehicle's elevated offside. They stood on the outcrop and stared towards the settlement. From there they could see a small group of figures in space suits approaching, raising a trail of dust in their wake. The white lunar dust gleamed in the sunlight, giving a ghostly aspect to the marching figures.

As they grew closer, it became clear that all of the marchers were humanoid. Most of them, however, were unusually small. Only about a metre tall. Johnny, who marched behind the individuals with his gun slung at his side, towered over them.

"Look!" cried Slim, his voice reduced to a distant bellow in Middenface's helmet. "It's Mr Alpha and he's got a whole bunch of little snipers with him."

"He took them all prisoner," murmured Hari Mata Karma in wonder.

"That's what I said," said Middenface proudly. "That's my boy."

They sealed the huge gash in the side of the crawler using an emergency repair kit that came with the vehicle. It provided spray canisters of plastic sealant that formed a membrane to seal holes. The various small bullet holes were dealt with easily enough, but the manufacturers hadn't planned on dealing with a hole the size of the one torn by the rocket in the crawler's hull.

In the end, they managed to create several small membranes and join them together, finally filling the hole with a patchwork of sealant. They dealt with the shattered front cockpit by the simple expedient of sealing off the airlock that led through to the driving compartment. Then they activated the reserve oxygen tanks in the crawler to give the newly sealed vehicle a breathable atmosphere so they could take their helmets off.

"We've got a healthy reserve of air," said Johnny Alpha, "but I don't want anyone wasting it by doing any vigorous physical activity."

"Not much chance of that," said Hari Mata Karma. "We've barely got room to budge, with all of us crushed in here like this."

"That's exactly what I mean," said Johnny patiently. "There's so many of us in this confined space we're going to be using up our oxygen reserves damned quick if we're not careful."

There were eight people jammed into the wreck of the small vehicle: Johnny and his team, and the four dwarfish figures still sealed in their space suits. The miniature humanoids stood around looking sheepish under the gaze of their captors – or at least, as sheepish as it was possible to look with one's face concealed behind the blacked-out visor of a polarised space helmet. "All right, take your helmets off," barked Johnny. "Let's get a proper look at you."

The dwarfish captives began to unclip their helmets, and Middenface saw that they weren't dwarfs at all. They were children. "Good heavens," said HMK, echoing his astonishment. "They can't be more than eight or nine years old."

"Ten this week," said a pugnacious, freckled blonde girl. She had a dirty face and long golden hair gathered back into an elaborate braid that curled around the broad inner collar of her space suit like a friendly slumbering serpent. Her brother said, "Me too." He too had his hair twined in a long braid that coiled around his neck. But unlike his sister, the rest of his hair was shaved. The pair were obviously twins. Middenface noticed that they both had pointed ears.

"This is Greta and Grün," said Johnny, by way of introduction.

"They've got funny names!" chortled Slim Drago.

"They're of German derivation," explained Hari Mata Karma. "Grün means green."

"Really?" said Johnny. "I had a chance to get acquainted with Greta and her green brother on our walk back to this vehicle, after getting the drop on them in their sniper nest on that rooftop."

"You never would have 'got the drop on us', as you put it, if it hadn't been for your stinky cheating," said the little girl called Greta, who was clearly the ringleader of the group.

"Cheating?"

"Yes. Coming at us out of the shadows like that."

"What did you expect me to do, stand out in the open sunlight and let you shoot at me?"

"That's what an honourable man would have done," sniffed Greta.

Johnny ignored her. He indicated the other two children, a boy with Oriental features and a heavy-set black girl. Like the twins, they had smudges of oil and dirt on their faces. "This is Hung Tay and Albertine. They don't say much."

"Hung Tay can't say much," said Grün helpfully. "He's mute."

"It's a mutation," said his sister.

"He's a mute mutant," said Grün, and they both giggled.

"Mutants?" said HMK in a startled voice. "That's right," said Johnny. "They're muties like the rest of us."

"What's that smell?" said Slim Drago, pinching his nose and frowning with distaste. He waved his free hand through the stale air. With eight bodies respiring in the small space it hadn't taken long for the air to become warm, damp and less than fresh smelling. "It's the ripe odour of unwashed children," said HMK.

"You try showering when you have to roll stolen canisters of water fifty kilometres," snarled Greta.

"Don't anyone get excited or raise their voices," said Johnny, coolly. "It will just use the oxygen up quicker and make it a lot less pleasant in here for all of us. Now, kids, let's have a little talk."

"Excuse me, Mr Alpha, sir," said Slim. "Why do we have to talk to them in here? Why can't we go back to their settlement and go into one of their houses? I imagine there would be a better air supply in there."

"I imagine you're right," said Johnny. "I just don't fancy going into any of those dwellings when we don't know how many of the little monsters are lurking in the settlement."

"Enough of us to crush you," said the little blonde girl.

"I see what you mean, Johnny," said Middenface. "An attitude like that and another rocket launcher could do a great deal of damage to our wee posse."

"He's determined to go with the posse word, isn't he?" said HMK. "I kind of like it myself."

"Are they all just bairns in the settlement?" said Middenface. "Or are there grown-ups too?"

"Judging by that pile of beer cans, some grown-ups too."

"Only Miss Dysh," said Albertine suddenly. She seemed to have trouble speaking and she licked her lips nervously between sentences. Middenface saw that her tongue was forked. Another mutation, one that would account for her speech impediment. "She's the one who drinks all the beer," said the girl in her odd, thick voice.

"Shut up, Albertine," snapped Greta. "Don't let these buffoons get a clear idea of our strength, or the disposition of our forces."

"Disposition of their forces," said HMK. "Listen to her, the little cutesy."

"It's kind of cute, isn't it?" said Slim Drago with a dopey grin. He reached out one big clumsy hand to pat Greta on the shoulder of her space suit. The little girl hissed and bared her teeth, Slim jerked his hand back as though menaced by a snake.

"Nice manners," said HMK. "Where did she learn to talk and behave like that?"

"Playing battle simulations on the games console," said Grün. He glanced at his sister. "It doesn't matter if they know that Miss Dysh is the only grown-up in Our Town. We kids can fight as good as any grown-ups." He scowled defiantly at the Strontium Dogs.

"You certainly managed to blow a hole in this crawler, little man," said Middenface, drumming his fingers against the taut plastic membrane sealing the wound in the ruptured hull.

"Don't try and butter me up," said Grün. His sister and the other kids giggled.

Johnny turned his piercing eyes on the children and they immediately fell silent. "Now we're going to ask our little friends some questions," he said.

"We won't answer them," said Greta. "We don't talk to kidnappers."

"That's fine, because we aren't kidnappers," said Johnny. Middenface thought that this wasn't strictly true, considering some of the rules they'd bent over the years to bring their quarries back to justice. But he elected to remain silent. "First question, how come there's a whole colony of you little kids living with just one grown-up?"

"Because Stella is our friend," said Grün. "And we aren't going to let you get away with what you did to her."

"We didn't do anything to her, kid," said Johnny. Hari Mata Karma came up close behind him and peered at the children. "As a matter of fact," she said, "We're eager to find Miss Dysh and talk to her ourselves. We thought she'd be staying in your little settlement. What do you call it... Our Town?"

"Not your town," said Greta. "Our Town."

"Fine," said HMK. "We'll discuss the ambiguity of pronouns later. But for now, why don't you accept the possibility that we're who we say we are?"

"You know, Greta," said Grün. "None of them look like the other one, the one who took Stella."

"No," said Greta. "You're right. The other one was more professional and better organised. He wouldn't have let us ambush him like this." She stared around at the wrecked vehicle with satisfaction.

"Hey, kid, watch it," said Middenface with stung pride.

HMK gestured for him to be quiet. She leaned towards Greta. "In that case, there's no reason for you not to answer Mr Alpha's question. What are a bunch of kids doing living together in the middle of nowhere, on some godforsaken third class moon? It's not some kind of absurd Peter Pan type setup, is it?"

"Where else did you expect us to go? We didn't have much choice after we escaped!"

"Escaped from where?" said Johnny.

"The Big Crater Mining Complex," said Albertine, as if repeating a lesson she had been forced to memorise. "We used to live there and it was a bad place. They were very bad to us and it wasn't a proper home. It was run by an evil monster witch. She had steel teeth."

"Yes, we know. We met her," said Middenface. "She certainly drives a hard bargain on vehicle rental."

"You kids used to live at the mine?" said HMK.

"What do you mean, they were bad to you?" said Johnny.

"They made us work the seams," said Greta. "They'd send us in with mineral extraction hoses. We had to crawl through the seams to the locations that their computers told them would be rich veins."

"Crawl through the seams?"

"Yes, where it was too small for the grown-up miners to go."

"Why not use wee robots?" said Middenface.

"Because it's cheaper to use mutant children," said Johnny. His face was flushed with anger. "If they break down, they're easier to replace."

"You poor things," said HMK. She knelt by the children and peered into their grubby faces. After a moment staring into the depths of her beautiful mismatched eyes, eyes that were brimming with emotion, the children's hostility began to soften. Their mouths began to tremble and tears started to gleam in their own eyes. Hari Mata Karma scooped them all into her arms in a clumsy embrace, made all the more clumsy by the space suits everyone was wearing. "You poor little things."

"Before everyone bursts into tears, I have a few more questions," said Johnny, dryly. But it was too late. The children dissolved into tears and HMK joined them. They were one sobbing, sodden, embracing mass. Johnny gave Middenface a disgusted look. Middenface, too, observed the weeping women and children with traditional male alarm. Slim Drago watched with a dopey, doting expression on his face. Finally the little blonde girl called Greta freed herself from HMK's embrace and stared defiantly up at Johnny Alpha. She wiped her face and her copiously running nose with the back of one space suit gauntlet and said, "You wanted to talk to us?"

"Yes," said Johnny impatiently. "Now from what you've been saying, Stella Dysh is gone. She's been gone for some time."

"Over fourteen cycles."

"That's about ten days," said HMK.

"He took her fourteen cycles ago."

"And what you're saying, little girl," said Middenface, "is that she's been spirited away by a mysterious assailant. You don't know who and you have no idea where he took her."

"No, stupid lump-headed man," said Greta. "We know exactly where he took her."

CHAPTER FOUR
UNDERSEA PRISON

In the middle of the desert, the wreck of a stagecoach lay on its side punctured by arrows. The stagecoach lay like a dead beast, bristling with the shafts that had killed it.

One pair of its wheels was trapped on the ground. The other pair of wheels hung high in the air. Charlie Yuletide stood beside the wreck. He reached up and snapped off one of the arrows. He examined it for a moment, then threw it aside, and began to strum his banjo and sing.

"Just like this stagecoach, Johnny was attacked by some varmints. But then they turned out to be kids under vacuum-proof garments..."

It turned out that the crawler wasn't as badly damaged as they'd initially believed. Once the holes in the side of the vehicle had been patched, the main problem was getting it upright again. But by judicious use of levers improvised from some lengths of pipe provided by the kids from Our Town, and with the help of Slim Drago's considerable brute strength, they were able to rock the vehicle back off its back and onto its caterpillar tracks, settling in gentle dusty bounces and shudders back onto the lunar surface.

One set of the crawler's tracks had been savaged beyond repair by the passage of the missile. But that still left five operational sets, and Johnny and the others had been able to drive the crawler back to the mine almost as fast as they'd left it. Once again, Middenface assumed driving duties, although within the shattered cockpit he'd been obliged to wear his spacesuit and keep the airlock sealed behind him, sitting out in a vacuum for the whole journey.

Once they got back to the Big Crater Mining Complex they parked the damaged crawler and separated. The four Strontium Dogs roamed the mine for almost an hour before meeting up again and going as a group to visit the manager they had done business with earlier. The woman was reclining in her personal quarters, on a circular green sofa in a room padded with matching silk in a moiré pattern. The room was dominated by a wide curved window that gave an impressive view of lunar mountain peaks. An elaborate mirrored drinks cabinet dominated one wall. Another was covered with antique oil paintings. Nothing at all in the room related to the business of mining.

The woman who lived in this room had a fat, combative face with yellowish eyes. Corkscrews of rust-coloured hair hung down over her forehead, and when she smiled her steel teeth glinted.

"So, you made it back in one piece."

"No, as a matter of fact we didn't."

"Huh?" The woman's yellow eyes clouded with puzzlement. They were such a weird colour that Middenface wondered if she was a mutant herself.

"Do you mean something went wrong?" said the woman whom Middenface now thought of as Iron Teeth.

"Yes," said Johnny.

"Like what?"

"Like your moon crawler getting a hole blown in its side by a rocket launcher."

"The hell you say! You're going to have to pay for the damage."

"You think so?" said Johnny. His voice was dangerously quiet.

"It was in our agreement when you rented it. It may not have been stated, but it was implied."

"Let me tell you what else was implied," said Johnny Alpha. "It was also implied that you should tell us about any hazards or dangers we were likely to encounter when we set out along that route you mapped out for us."

"Hazards and dangers like what?" said Iron Teeth.

"Like a colony of mutie kids with a rocket launcher."

"Those little bastards. You didn't let them kick your ass, did you?" Iron Teeth cackled. "A grown man like you? You ought to be ashamed."

Hari Mata Karma suddenly pushed past Johnny. "I'll tell you what we're ashamed of," she said. "We're ashamed of a bag of pus like you exploiting little kids and risking their lives in your mining operation."

"I deny any knowledge of any unethical practices that my junior managers might have implemented without my knowledge or consent," said Iron Teeth in what was obviously a much rehearsed statement.

HMK pulled out a gun and shoved the barrel of it between the woman's metal teeth with a clinking sound. "Deny all you want," she said in a hot, hissing whisper. "You're all finished in these parts."

"Figgish?" said the woman, trying to talk around the gun barrel.

"Finished is right," replied HMK. She pulled the gun out, causing it to rattle noisily off the woman's metal molars. HMK inspected the saliva moistened gun barrel with distaste and wiped it dry on the woman's tunic. "Tell her, Johnny."

Johnny held out a flat disc of plastic, about thirty centimetres in diameter and five centimetres thick. It had a curved upper surface and a flat base. On the base was a digital readout screen and some controls in a recessed panel. Iron Teeth's eyes widened when she saw it. She obviously recognised the object. "This is a detonation unit," said Johnny. "The kind you use here in your mine for blasting new seams."

"Where did you get it?"

"Those kids living out in that settlement had quite a collection of them."

"Those scavenging little rats!"

"Highly industrious rats," said HMK. She took the disc from Johnny and inspected it before offering it to Iron Teeth. "Over the years they've stolen enough of these explosives from your mine to blow the whole place into orbit." Iron Teeth refused to touch the deadly device.

"Which brings us to the point of this discussion," said Johnny.

"Oh no," said Iron Teeth. Her face went white.

"Oh yes," said HMK. "We've placed these charges all over your mining complex. We didn't miss a single shaft, machine or building. We've placed them at points of strategic weakness and concealed them so thoroughly that it would take you weeks to find them. And we've set the timers, and believe me, you don't have weeks. The entire crater is rigged and set to blow."

"Blow? No. When?" said the woman, who seemed to have been reduced to monosyllables.

Johnny Alpha smiled thinly and said, "One hour from now."

"Why are you doing this to me?" shrieked Iron Teeth.

"Because you're an evil old bag who's been sending wee kiddies to their doom," said Middenface.

"What do you want me to do?" begged Iron Teeth.

"Just one thing," said Johnny. "Get off this moon."

"Off it?"

"That's right. Clear out with your entire staff."

"But the mine–"

"Either you go now or you stay and get blown up with the mine when it goes," said Johnny.

"In exactly one hour," said HMK.

"Only fifty-seven minutes now," corrected Johnny.

"You can't do this to me!" squealed the woman.

"Listen, Iron Teeth," said Middenface. "You'd better get out of here before our demolition charges blow."

"My teeth are made of steel!" screamed the woman. But she lurched up from the sofa, ran into her bedroom and began hastily packing a suitcase.

Word got around the mining complex with impressive speed and within twenty minutes every living member of the mine's staff had crowded onto one of the large freight rockets with whatever belongings they had managed to pack. Johnny and the others watched their departure from the lounge of the manager's living quarters, sitting on the sofa with the twins Greta and Grün, who had been waiting in concealment in the crawler.

They watched through the window as the freight rocket took off, its ivory teardrop shape lifting on a silent column of blue flame rising over the distant mountains. "They made remarkably good time," said Middenface, inspecting a chronometer. "They've got off the moon with thirty-three minutes to spare before the place was set to blow up. That would certainly be a comfortable safety margin."

"It sure would," said Johnny. "If the place was actually rigged with explosives." HMK chuckled and handed Johnny the disc shaped explosive charge. "How many of these did we actually have?" she said.

"Just the one," said Johnny, turning the disc over in his hands. "And this one doesn't work. The explosive element was taken out years ago."

"Stella used it to blast a hole in the bedrock for a new latrine for Our Town," said Greta. "The old septic tank had blocked up back into the hydroponic farm and it was all a big mess."

"Don't feel obliged to go into any detail," said Midden-face.

"What do you think Iron Teeth is going to do when she learns we bluffed her into leaving?" said Middenface.

"She'll shit and go blind," said HMK. "If you'll pardon my French."

"It doesn't matter what she does," said Johnny. "By the laws of space salvage, this abandoned mining installation now belongs to whoever is first to take occupation of it." He looked at Greta and Grün. "That means you, kids."

"Well, we certainly won't do a worse job running it than that old metal mouthed monstrosity," said the little girl. She elbowed her brother. "Come on Grün, let's check the ore manifests and find out what the cash flow is for this place." The twins left the room through a hissing dilating door without a backward glance.

"They're going to run the place?" said Middenface.

"I don't see why not. They've been surviving against all odds ever since they could walk," said Johnny. "And they know this operation inside out from their days down the mines."

"But they're just naïve kids."

Johnny smiled his thin smile. "I have a funny feeling that those naïve kids are going to do just fine."

Middenface still wasn't convinced. "They may have a legal right to take over the mine by the laws of space salvage. But there are plenty of buggers out there who don't give two hoots about legal rights or laws. What if old Iron Teeth comes back with her friends and tries to take the place by force?"

Johnny's smile widened a fraction. "You saw what those kids managed to do with one old rocket launcher and a few assault rifles?"

"Sure," said Middenface. "They damned nearly wiped our arses for us. But–"

"But just imagine what they'll be able to do with an arsenal of state of the art weaponry," said Johnny.

Middenface grinned. "I dread to think. But where would the little perishers get hold of an arsenal of such state of the art weaponry?"

Johnny shrugged. "We may just be able to help them out with that." He looked at Hari Mata Karma. "Asdoel Zo can afford to pay for some excess fire power for a worthy cause, don't you think?"

HMK shrugged and inspected her finger nails. "Why ask me?" she said. Her voice was oddly icy.

"So, the little children are going to run the mine from now on?" said Slim Drago, who was always at pains to make sure he understood the current situation. "And we'll give them guns? And nobody will bother them?"

"That's about the size of it, big fella," said Middenface.

"We'll leave them so much ordnance it would take a full armada to shift them." Johnny stared out the window. "After all, this crater makes an excellent defensible position."

"Why Johnny," said HMK in a teasing voice. After her strange chilliness of a moment ago, she seemed to be back to her normal playful self. "You're just a big softie at heart. Why don't you settle down and raise a dynasty of rug rats? I think you'd make a great dad. I can just see you with a pipe and slippers. And of course up to your elbows in nappies."

"Ugh," said Middenface. "Nappies. Now there's a genuinely terrifying thought."

Johnny stood up. "Get your things together. We'd better be going. We've still got a posse to recruit."

"I still don't understand why we have to split up," said Hari Mata Karma in a petulant voice. Middenface sighed and braced himself. HMK was a lovely little woman all right, and a bundle of fun when she was in a good mood. But when anybody did anything to cross her she acquired the disposition of a pit viper. "Johnny's already explained once."

"I don't care. Let him explain again. In words of one syllable, so the stupid little woman is sure to understand." HMK almost spat the words out.

"Words of one syllable would be good," Slim Drago said hopefully. He stood slightly apart from Johnny, Middenface and HMK, as though he understood and accepted that he wasn't a full member of the team when it came to discussing matters of policy. Or maybe he simply wanted to stay out of the argument. Middenface couldn't blame him. It was supposed to be a friendly discussion, but whenever HMK thought she wasn't getting her way, things tended to turn vicious.

They were all sitting in the small dining area of the galley adjoining the *Louis L'Amour*, the sleek C-class star clipper which Asdoel Zo had provided for their use. The *Louis* was an ideal vehicle for flight or pursuit, though it wasn't armoured or equipped for any battle scenarios beyond a light skirmish. It was a large vessel, with the capacity to carry seventy passengers and crew, in addition to berthing a complement of three extremely fast and manoeuvrable ketches in its hold, each of which could be used as one- or two-man vessels. It also carried, by legal requirement, a sizeable life boat capable of safely carrying away the maximum number of people who were permitted to travel in its mother ship, albeit stacked in the cold paralysis of cryosleep. The *Louis L'Amour* was so well designed and so lavishly equipped with robots, servo-mechanisms and support software that it could be piloted by two humans or even, at a pinch, one.

They were twenty hours outward bound from the moon called Disraeli 4.1 where their search for Stella Dysh had reached an abrupt dead end. Johnny, however, had a pretty good idea where Stella could be found, thanks to the combative moppets Greta and Grün. The twins had told him that she had been taken prisoner by a fellow Strontium Dog – an unusual situation, but by no means unique. The Dogs had a code of conduct but, like any sentient beings, they found ways of bending the rules and accommodating their consciences to suit a given situation.

"You don't even know who this Strontium Dog is," growled Hari Mata Karma. "The one who kidnapped your precious Stella Dysh." She had a bowl of steaming mushroom and red pepper quinoa stew in front of her, served up by the galley's autochef. She had been picking at it with considerable dexterity but little enthusiasm, using a pair of chopsticks. Now she impatiently stabbed the chopsticks into the bowl with a savage gesture that made Middenface think that she'd rather be driving them into Johnny's windpipe. She was certainly a volatile wee woman. "I don't think you're in any sort of a position to chop your manpower in half and go on a kamikaze mission with your old chum just because you don't think I know my ass from my elbow."

"And me too," said Slim Drago. "I don't know my ass from my elbow either." He said it without any trace of anger towards Johnny. He was just reaffirming his loyalty to HMK. It was embarrassingly clear that the huge mutant was nursing a schoolboy crush of gargantuan proportions for the little woman.

Johnny took a deep breath. "Okay. Let me try to explain…" There was a note of growing impatience in his voice that Middenface recognised and understood. Johnny was a man of action. Negotiation and arbitration weren't his strong suits. Talk wasn't his strong suit. Violent combat was his strong suit. Nevertheless, he was taking pains to try and calm HMK down. Like Middenface, he had seen enough of her in action to begin to think of HMK as a valuable member of the team. It wasn't so much what she did; it was what she didn't do. Like panic, or lose her head. Even when they'd been under fire she'd maintained her own characteristic brand of pissed-off cool.

"I'll take your points one by one," said Johnny.

"Yes, that would be nice," said HMK with icy sarcasm. "Would you?"

"First of all, it's true that we don't know who the Strontium Dog is, the one who took Stella."

"Yes. That was one of the salient facts that your murderous, mop-headed cherubs failed to avail you of."

"Murderous cherubs," Slim Drago chortled ponderously. "You sure do talk pretty."

"Thank you, Slim," said HMK politely. But her steely blue and brown gaze didn't budge from Johnny's own extraordinary eyes.

"By the way, what's a cherub?" said Slim. "And what's salient? And what's avail?"

"Shut up, Slim," said HMK. "Just shut up, all right?"

"All right," said Slim cheerfully.

"It doesn't matter that we don't know who the bounty hunter was," said Johnny. "What matters is that we know where they took Stella Dysh." Johnny gestured towards the viewing screen mounted on the wall of the galley, in which the giant shape of an immense green and rust streaked planet hung. It looked to Middenface like a bowl of pea soup into which someone had stirred a few spoonfuls of chilli sauce. Middenface's mouth watered. He wished they could get this discussion over with so he could serve himself some food.

"That planet down there is the Queen Victoria Penal Colony," said Johnny.

"What, the entire planet?" said HMK caustically.

"Yes, pretty much," said Johnny. Middenface was pleased to see that the little spitfire didn't have him rattled at all. "Queen Victoria is an ocean planet. It's virtually all water except for some small island archipelagos at either pole, which are just barren rock. Underwater mountains pushing up into a toxic methane atmosphere."

"You make it sound divine," said HMK. "Have you considered a new career writing travel brochures?"

Johnny ignored her. "Like I say, the whole planet is basically ocean. And the penal colony is under water. Obviously the colony doesn't cover the whole ocean floor..."

"That would be a very big prison," said Slim Drago. "Whoops. Sorry. I'll shut up again."

"But the entire ocean floor is legally part of the prison's protectorate," said Johnny. "So anyone who sets foot on it is liable to be arrested and incarcerated."

"For a very long time," added Middenface.

"Without trial or sentencing?" demanded Hari Mata Karma.

Johnny smiled grimly. "On Queen Victoria they've done away with annoying details like due process. No one is imprisoned here because they've been tried or sentenced. They're here because somebody has paid to have them locked up."

"But that's terrible," said HMK. She appeared genuinely scandalised, even to the point of seeming to forget that she was supposed to be furious at Johnny. "How can they get away with that?"

"Because the people they lock up don't have money or influence. Or at least, not as much money or influence as their enemies who've paid to have them locked up."

"It's a total disgrace," said HMK. "And now you've told me about it, I'm all the more determined to join you in your prison break. I want to help you kick those Queen Victoria bastards in the balls."

"In the balls," chuckled Slim Drago. "Oops. Sorry."

"I appreciate the sentiment," said Johnny, "but–"

"But you still don't want me tagging along, because I'm a stupid little woman who couldn't possibly be of any use to you. Because of course I don't possess any useful talents or qualities."

At last Johnny's temper flared up. "Can't you get it through your thick head that this has nothing to do with you personally? You have plenty of talents and qualities. But none of them matter a damn."

"And why not?" said HMK coldly.

"Because this is a two-man operation."

"I see, you and Middenface against the entire staff of a heavily armed prison world. Yes, well I certainly find that a compelling and convincing argument."

"I don't care if you do or you don't," said Johnny. "The fact is that I've got a plan and the plan will work, but it only takes two of us to pull it off. And while we're busy breaking Stella Dysh out of prison, you and Slim can make yourselves useful doing something else for us."

"Oh really? Like what? Making cups of tea?"

"No," said Johnny. "Going after Bel/Ray."

"And who, dare I ask, is Bel/Ray?"

"The next name on the list of this posse we're recruiting."

HMK seemed fractionally mollified. "Well at least you're giving me and Slim something *fairly* important to do."

"Yeah, *fairly* important," said Slim.

"But why don't we all work together on the jail break," persisted HMK. "Then we can all work together on picking up Bel/Ray."

"Because, like you said, Queen Victoria is a heavily armed prison world." Johnny smiled. "And when we bust out one of their inmates there's going to be hell to pay. This whole sector is going to be too hot for us. So we need to make sure that Bel/Ray is recruited and ready to go by the time we've rescued Stella Dysh, so we can hightail it out of here."

There was a moment's silence, then HMK said, "I'm sure there's a flaw to your logic... But I can't see it immediately."

"That's a relief," said Johnny.

"Now, Johnny, are you sure you want to do this?" said Middenface as he strapped his friend into the gravity couch. Once Johnny was securely fastened, he began to cover his body with thick inflatable slabs of multi-ply soft plastic. The slabs were from the hold of the *Louis L'Amour* where they were used to pad cargo and protect it from damaging vibrations. Middenface was piling them on top of Johnny with much the same idea in mind.

"Don't you start," said Johnny Alpha. "That discussion with HMK nearly killed me."

Middenface chuckled for a moment, then was serious again. "Just make sure that this wee stratagem doesn't kill you, old friend," he said.

"Do you have a better plan?" said Johnny.

"No, but I've got an interesting variation on this one," said Middenface.

"What's that?"

"Let *me* pilot the crash ship and *you* wait in orbit until I send for you."

Now Johnny chuckled. "Nice try, Archibald. But I dreamed up this little endeavour so I get first shot at carrying it off."

Middenface sighed and shook his ugly, misshapen head. He adjusted the last of the soft plastic blocks and stepped away from the gravity couch. "This is a damned dangerous little scheme. And in aid of what? Springing this one wee lass Stella Dysh so she can join our team."

"Our posse," Johnny corrected him.

"Whatever we call it," said Middenface. "Do we really need her? Can't we just get someone else and leave her where she is?"

"Leave a fellow Stront locked up for the rest of her days in that hellhole, for a crime she never committed?"

"Ah yes, well, when you put it like that," said Middenface. "You're a stubborn man, you know that, Johnny Alpha. I don't suppose there's any point in trying to talk you out of blowing up the engine either."

Johnny shook his head. "It's got to look like a genuine accident. If the prison guards detect an explosion in low orbit with the distinctive signature of one of my engines blowing up, and then I fall down the gravity well in this crippled vehicle and splash down in the ocean near their colony it will all make for quite a convincing accident."

"Yes, well just mind it isn't *too* convincing," said Middenface.

He turned his back on his friend and made his way through the central axis of the ketch, floating in zero gravity. When he reached the airlock, he secured the helmet on his space suit, ducked inside the lock and set it to cycling. When the cycle was complete, he floated out of the ketch into space. Stars gleamed above him in an infinite ceiling. At his feet was the monstrous face of Queen Victoria, its curve filling his entire vision with its swirling green surface streaked rust red. Or blood red, thought Middenface.

He kicked away from Johnny's vehicle and let the momentum carry him back to his own ketch. The third ketch from the *Louis L'Amour* was now some billions of kilometres away, with HMK and Slim Drago piloting it in search of the next recruit for their team. Their posse. Middenface smiled for a moment, but the smile faded as soon as he thought of Johnny lying there in the control room of the ketch, strapped to the gravity couch like a man awaiting a lethal injection.

For a moment he wished that he and Johnny were the ones who'd gone in search of Ray/Bel, and that it was HMK and Slim Drago who were going to attempt the prison break.

But you couldn't send a woman and a simpleton on a mission like that. There was no way round it. This was the way things had to be. He took one last look at Johnny's ketch, a needle-nosed vehicle with black and yellow stripes that gave it something of the look of a giant wasp with its wings folded, floating in sharp relief against the bilious green clouds of Queen Victoria below. Then he turned to look at his own ketch, hanging above him, floating slowly closer, with the bulk of the *Louis L'Amour* suspended in space above it, filling the black infinite sky.

Middenface docked with his ketch, activated the airlock and made his way through to the control room. There he sat down on a gravity couch, just like the one Johnny was strapped to, watching the forward viewing screen. He suddenly remembered something and tapped the communications console. Johnny Alpha's voice came over the speakers. "What is it?"

"I was so busy sulking I forgot to say good luck."

"Thanks. You'll remember the signal to come and get me?"

"I'm hardly likely to forget it, am I?" said Middenface.

"Good. See you soon." Then, as Middenface watched, one of the wings of the wasp ignited in a ball of white flame as the engine exploded. Johnny's ketch tipped out

of orbit and began its long crippled sliding fall towards the
planet below.

Johnny's plan worked.

The staff at Queen Victoria saw the explosion in orbit
and their computers correctly identified it as the terminal
failure of a vehicle's engine. So when the vehicle itself was
detected, falling through the atmosphere, it was regarded
as a distressed traveller in need of rescue, rather than a
suspicious intruder to be captured, detained and ques-
tioned.

The crippled ketch fell through thousands of metres of
atmosphere, protected from the searing, white heat of re-
entry by its toughened, ceramic hull. Half a kilometre
above the surface of the ocean Johnny deployed a couple
of drag chutes to slow his descent, as though he'd been
struggling to release them all the way down and only
managed to at the last possible moment. The chutes
reduced the ketch's momentum enough to stop it breaking up as it hit the surging vast waves of the muddy ocean,
but the impact was still enough to knock Johnny unconscious, despite the gravity couch and all the padding
Middenface had used to fill the control room. Johnny
woke up out of a sick, giddy daze, forcing himself back to
consciousness. He checked a chronometer and gasped
with relief when he saw that he'd only been unconscious
for a couple of minutes. The ketch was floating safely on
the breast of the planet-spanning sea and any moment
now the undersea penal colony would send vehicles to
effect a rescue on the surface.

That wouldn't do at all.

Johnny hit the controls and cut free the drag chutes. On
the stern screens he saw their billowing, white shapes
with fringes of long cords attached to them. They floated
away on the water like giant jellyfish. He felt an absurd

pang at watching them go. It was like seeing old friends leave. After all, the chutes had saved his life.

The ketch was floating sturdily in the uneven tossing of the ocean swell. Despite its damage it was perfectly seaworthy. In addition to being an interstellar runner, the craft was designed for both atmospheric and aquatic use. It could dive and manoeuvre under water. But that wasn't what Johnny had in mind.

He took one last look at the parachutes floating away. Then he pressed the button that Middenface had secured to the arm of the gravity couch with gaffer tape. "It isn't pretty, but it's serviceable," he'd said. The serviceable button triggered an explosion deep in the belly of the ketch. Like the explosives that had blown the engine in orbit, it was one of the disc charges from the Big Crater Mine. Greta had provided them for the Strontium Dogs. Johnny had been amused that she charged him for them, instead of giving the explosives as a present. She'd given him a discount, though.

The charge in the belly of the ketch had blown a hole in the hull that allowed seawater inside the engine room. The engine room was sealed off from the control room where Johnny sat by two bulkheads that were airtight. Johnny prayed that they were also watertight. After a few moments he could feel the attitude of the small vehicle changing. It was no longer buoyant, but was on its way to becoming a dead weight. Finally, when a critical threshold had been passed, the nose of the ship went straight up, the tail fins straight down, and it sank like a stone.

CHAPTER FIVE
AQUA ESCAPE

In the desert night the square face of a fort shone. Charlie Yuletide stood in front of the mountain range, silhouetted against the fort, strumming his banjo and singing.

"Women like a man who wrestles with danger, who'll risk his neck to rescue a stranger. So all the girls were sighin' when Johnny Alpha stepped into the lion's den..."

"What astoundingly good luck you have, Mr Alpha," said Florien Lamarck, the chief warder and commander of the Queen Victoria Sub Aqua Penal Colony, wiping his haggard face with a linen napkin.

"You mean surviving my drop from low orbit?" said Johnny.

"No," said Lamarck. "Not that."

"You mean ending up on the seabed near enough to your colony that you could come and pick me up?"

"No," said Lamarck. "Not that either. I meant arriving on a Friday. Every other day of the week we have to eat fish in this godforsaken outpost. For obvious reasons. Living off the land and all that. Or, in this case, living off the ocean. But every Friday here at the Queen Victoria Penal Colony we allow ourselves the luxury of a little red meat."

"Thank all the deities above," added Luis Nova-Cruz.

Lamarck was a tall thin cadaverous man with thinning grey hair that exactly matched the colour of his watery eyes. He had large hands that manifested a perceptible tremor, which Johnny attributed to excessive consumption of alcohol or some other dangerous stimulant. Nova-Cruz on the other hand was short and fat with olive skin, gleaming brown eyes and an unruly head of thick, curly black hair. He was Lamarck's second in command. The two men and Johnny were sitting in a dining room of baronial splendour, equipped with a thick gleaming slab of polished wood for a table and elaborately carved chairs. A dazzling, white tablecloth didn't quite fit the table and therefore had been spread across it in a diamond shape. The table was covered with silver tureens and warming dishes, chunky silver cutlery and expensive china and heavy crystal decanters full of wine. Lamarck offered Johnny some wine from one of the decanters then refilled his own glass with trembling hands. Johnny noticed that he didn't offer any wine to Nova-Cruz. There was a definite undercurrent of hostility between the two men, although both of them had seemed delighted to meet Johnny.

Johnny had briefly lost consciousness again when his vehicle plunged to the bottom of the sea. The ketch was designed to withstand such pressures and had remained watertight inside the sealed bulkheads that contained Johnny's control cockpit. He had sunk safely to the ocean floor, still strapped in his gravity couch, unconscious. But the considerable strain of water pressure at that extreme depth had squeezed the ketch like a nut in a cracker and the little vessel had begun to make distinct groaning noises as its carbon steel skeleton flexed, as though in the grip of a great fist. It was these eerie groaning noises that summoned Johnny back to consciousness. He had awoken in time to see divers from the penal colony approaching him in their white scuba suits, moving like ghosts through the green water.

Johnny hurried to unstrap himself from the couch, grab a screwdriver and start puncturing all the plastic blocks of impact padding that had protected him. Then he deflated them, packed them into a small mass and concealed them in the hold. Anybody who saw them might put two and two together and realise that the accident had been deliberately staged. When they were safely stashed away, he strapped himself back into the couch just in time to play possum as the divers began to burn their way through the hull to rescue him.

He had then been sealed in a survival cocoon and towed back to the mini sub the divers had used. Still feigning unconsciousness, he was brought into the prison colony through the towering diamond shaped underwater airlock, given a cursory medical examination and a new set of clothing and then immediately invited to dinner with the two most senior officers in the colony, Lamarck and Nova-Cruz.

Watching these two men, it struck Johnny that stuck in this distant outpost, the two men were starved for company. For fresh blood.

The dining room they were sitting in was a long, low and had been decorated to look like a captain's cabin from the days of sailing ships. It even had fake portholes fastened onto the rough-hewn wooden walls. For the most part, though, the walls were decorated with stuffed fish of the most bizarre varieties Johnny had ever seen.

Nova-Cruz caught the direction of his gaze. "Ah, I see you are admiring the denizens of the deep that we have caught and used to decorate our humble abode."

"Humble abode?" snapped Lamarck. "I hope you're not referring to my private quarters in a slighting fashion."

"No, of course not, commander," said Nova-Cruz smoothly.

"No? It sounded to me as if you were."

"Forgive me if I'm mistaken, commander," said Nova-Cruz in a charming and urbane voice, "but didn't you just a moment earlier refer to the colony as a 'godforsaken outpost'?"

Lamarck simply ignored this comment and continued doggedly with his own tirade. "What precisely is so humble about this place?"

"It was just a form of words, commander."

"A very offensive one, if I may say so."

"You certainly may say so, commander. However, if you have anything else to say to me I suggest you do so now, because I find I must be going."

Lamarck's watery eyes hardened with rage. "What? You're leaving before I've served dinner? Before you've broken bread with our new guest?"

Nova-Cruz turned to Johnny and bowed. "For that I am sincerely sorry, Mr Alpha. I shall speak to you another time and perhaps you'll even do me the honour of dining with me."

"Sure," said Johnny.

"Dining with you?" demanded Lamarck. "But he's dining with you now, you ill-mannered cur. Or at least he would be, if you weren't so unfailingly ill-mannered."

Johnny could read anger in Nova-Cruz's dark eyes as he sat weathering this storm of abuse. But the small, fat man remained admirably composed. "I repeat, commander. My apologies. But I find I have quite lost my appetite and in any case I must now attend to my duties." He rose from the table, bowed to Johnny, snapped Lamarck a perfunctory salute, then strode out through the beaded curtain that separated the dining hall from the next room. Lamarck stared after him with undisguised hatred. Finally, the strands of the beaded curtain stopped swaying and he turned back to Johnny, making an obvious effort to compose himself.

"I'm sorry for my subordinate's appalling manners, Mr Alpha."

"No problem," said Johnny. It was clear to him in any case that Nova-Cruz had left the room because he couldn't stomach any more of his commanding officer. There was some kind of long-simmering resentment between the two men, but Johnny doubted he'd ever learn the cause of it. He had no intention of staying in this place long enough to find out.

"What were we discussing before that lamentable cur spoiled our meal with his disgraceful behaviour? Oh yes. The fish on the walls." Lamarck stared at the mounted specimens for a moment, in the manner of a man looking upon something overwhelmingly familiar and trying to force himself to see it through fresh eyes. "Yes they are an ugly lot. Verily, monsters of the deep. But fortunately we do not have to eat any of them, or their brethren. Not tonight. Tonight it is good fresh meat." Lamarck chuckled happily and lifted one of the silver lids that sat on the table. Underneath it was a coffin-shaped wooden chopping board with a large slab of undercooked meat on it. Bloody juice from the meat gathered in a deep groove that ran around the rim of the chopping board.

Johnny wondered where the hell you could get red meat like that from in a prison at the bottom of the sea. He decided he had no intention of finding out.

"You are indeed fortunate, Mr Alpha," continued Lamarck. He picked up a long and extremely sharp knife and studied the piece of meat, calculating the best angle of attack. Then he leaned forward and prodded the roast with one long pale index finger. "You know, I think this could do with a moment more resting before we carve it."

He set the knife down on the table with an audible clank and picked up a large silver ladle instead. "I believe I shall serve the soup first. That would be a civilised thing to do, wouldn't it?"

"Sure," said Johnny. Lamarck lifted the lid off a soup tureen and a puff of steam wafted out of it. He stirred the soup thoughtfully, making a slopping sound.

"Tell me, Mr Alpha, where were you travelling to when you had that dreadful and unfortunate accident with your engine? What was your destination?"

"Here," said Johnny.

"Here? You were travelling here? You mean to somewhere else in this planetary system?"

"No, to right here. To this prison, where I'm sitting with you now."

Lamarck chuckled. "What an extraordinary thing to say. Come, come, Mr Alpha. You're teasing me. Why would you want to come to this desolate place?"

"So I can arrange the escape of one of your inmates. You know, a good old fashioned jail break."

Lamarck laughed uproariously. "Better and better. You certainly are a card, Mr Alpha. I'm tremendously glad to have your company at my table. That foul dog Nova-Cruz doesn't know what he's missing. Tell me more about this 'jail break' of yours."

"Not much to tell really. I calculated the trajectory and sabotaged my own engine so I'd end up crashing on the ocean floor just about at the limits of reach for a rescue team from your penal colony."

Lamarck made no noise, but he was rocking back and forth with silent mirth. After a moment he managed to recover himself enough to knuckle tears of merriment from his eyes. "Ah, Mr Alpha, you are a tonic. But why crash at the limits of reach, as you put it when, with your obvious gift for precision crash-landing you could have set down just outside our gates?"

"Because I didn't think it was a good idea for me to be too close when the reactor on my ship goes critical and blows like a nuclear bomb."

Lamarck sighed and leaned back in his chair, idly stirring the soup with the silver ladle as he spoke. "Yes, I must say that's a good reason for parking your craft some distance away. But it's not, if you don't mind me saying so, quite as good as the rest of your story."

"No?" said Johnny.

"No, I fear. The rest of your story had a certain zany plausibility, or no, better call it authenticity, because while it possessed a certain dramatic purity it still remained utterly implausible. But this is a less successful, though still thoroughly amusing jape. I mean, why would you have a nuclear reactor going critical on your ship? A ketch of that designation doesn't even have a reactor on it."

"No, you're right," said Johnny. "That's why we had to take one off the starship and put it on board especially."

Lamarck slapped his legs and chortled again. "All right, all right, very good. That makes sense. But nevertheless, why should it go critical?"

"Because I set it to do just that."

"Just for the hell of it?" said Lamarck cheerfully.

"No, because a nuclear explosion will provide a useful diversion."

"For this 'jail break' of yours?"

"No, for my friend who'll be bringing his own ketch down here to pick us up. Me and the prisoner I'm going to free."

"I see. Yes. That does tie up most of the loose ends. Except for the most important ones of course."

"Like what?"

"Such as, how are you going to find the prisoner in this huge maze-like penal colony. And how are you going to set them free from their maximum security cell?"

"I wasn't exactly sure of my plan when I arrived. I decided I would improvise on the basis of any opportunities that presented themselves and, that being the case, I now think I'll get *you* to do it," said Johnny.

"Me?"

"Sure," said Johnny. "As chief warden you have access to the database of all your prisoners, and you'll also have the clearance for releasing the one I want."

"Mmm. Yes. True. But what about the other enormous loose end? *Why* am I going to do this for you? How are you going to threaten me? Because presumably some form of physical threat or intimidation would be essential. And you haven't provided one. Come, come, Mr Alpha, these little details are all-important. Where are you going to find a weapon to make me do your bidding? After all, you were thoroughly searched when we brought you into the colony, weren't you? Mr Alpha... What are you doing with that knife, Mr Alpha? Put it down. Put it down. Please put the knife down..."

The Strontium Dog called Stella Dysh had a cell in the isolation wing of the penal colony. Access to it was through a series of concrete tunnels with guard posts and gun emplacements at every junction. However, the designers of the colony had included a number of short cuts and concealed access passages, which allowed the warden to keep an eye on his staff. Travelling through these passages, with Lamarck leading the way, Johnny was able to make extremely good time. Lamarck's initial defiant resistance had crumbled as soon as Johnny looked him in the eyes.

Johnny's mutation had made his eyes like two tiny windows into some strange hell. When he turned his full gaze on someone, few men could resist the fierce weird flames that blazed there.

It was Johnny's eyes as much as the knife that made Lamarck his compliant hostage. Although it did help that it was a very large and very sharp carving knife. With it held to his throat, Lamarck had shown Johnny how to access the convict records on the computer and Johnny had then quickly determined the location of Stella Dysh.

When he'd told Lamarck that they were going to the isolation wing, the man had suddenly shown the first signs of resistance. But after another glimpse of the psychic inferno in Johnny's eyes he had set off with Johnny and was now leading him to the correct area of the sprawling colony.

Whenever Lamarck looked like he was going to weaken, or remember his sworn duty, Johnny clouted him with the soup ladle, which he'd also taken from the table. As a result, chief warden and commander Lamarck had acquired a number of lumps on his head, although nothing to rival Middenface's crenellated skull.

Johnny remembered his friend with a flash of affection. He hoped that Middenface was keeping an eye on his instruments for the tell-tale thermal plume of the nuclear explosion that was set to go off in – Johnny checked his watch – approximately twenty-seven minutes.

"Who are you looking for?" said Lamarck. "Who is it you want to take from my prison?"

"What difference does it make?" said Johnny. "Do you know every inmate by name?"

"Naturally not."

"Well, then," said Johnny. He paused by one of the metal doors that lined the narrow cement tunnels at regular intervals and checked the number on it against the cell number he'd memorised from the prison computer. "Why are we stopping here?" said Lamarck, nervously.

"Because we've reached our destination."

"But there are only six cells in this section of the tunnel."

"And the prisoner I'm looking for is in one of those cells," said Johnny. "Now let's go." He shoved Lamarck

through the metal door, but not before the man glanced
back at him with a strangely piteous, imploring look. The
door opened with a pneumatic sigh and puff of cement
dust, allowing them to step into a short section of tunnel,
oval in section like an egg standing on its base, painted an
unpleasant shade of institutional green with bright oval
lights recessed into the wall. The light shone on thick
glass doors spaced at regular intervals along the tunnel. In
the door nearest to them a tall, powerfully built white man
with tattoos all over his body, could be seen, crouched
naked, doing what looked like yoga exercises. He didn't
look up at them as they walked past.

"Can't he see us?"

"No," said Lamarck. "It's one way glass. Or a two way
mirror. Or whatever you call it." The man's voice had devel-
oped a nervous tremor. "Isn't he the one you're after?"

"Not by a long shot," said Johnny. "Keep walking." But
by now he was virtually having to drag Lamarck along
with him. The man had been fairly passive and tractable
up until this point, but it seemed that the nearer to Stella
Dysh's cell they got, the more unmanageable he became.
Maybe the full import of what he was doing was finally
hitting home, thought Johnny. After all, Lamarck was
betraying everything he stood for by helping a prisoner
escape, even under extreme duress.

"Is it him?" said Lamarck as they passed another prisoner in a cell, a hairy dwarf who was sleeping curled in a
foetal bundle on the concrete floor.

"No," said Johnny. Then they passed another cell, with
another male inmate. "Is it him?" gabbled Lamarck.
Johnny didn't bother to reply. Another cell, another man.

"Is it him?" bleated Lamarck, a desperate note of pleading in his voice.

Johnny ignored him. They passed a fifth cell, with a
fifth male convict inside, and when Johnny didn't pause

Lamarck let out a small animal cry of pure despair. "What's wrong?" said Johnny.

"Nothing," stuttered Lamarck. "Just my nerves. I'm only human you know. I don't know about you mutants, but we humans sometimes cry out when emotional stress becomes too much."

"No," said Johnny. "I meant, what's wrong with the cell door?"

The circular glass door of the cell was blacked out, the way the light sensitive lenses in sunglasses black out in bright light. "It's nothing. It's the opacity option on the door. You just press a button and it goes away."

"Then press the button," said Johnny. Lamarck reached up and obediently punched a stud on the wall. The darkness began to fade from the door, like black ink slowly thinning and dispersing in clear water. "Now open it," said Johnny. Lamarck pushed another button and there was a smooth sliding sound followed by a clunking noise and the door shivered and drifted open a whisker.

"After you," said Lamarck.

"Nice try," said Johnny, and pushed the man ahead of him into the cell. The slowly clearing door was still impossible to see through, so Johnny and Lamarck were just as surprised as the occupants of the cell when they stepped inside.

Stella Dysh was in the cell all right. She was a tall, skinny woman with lacklustre, and rather tangled, red hair that looked as if she had lost interest in combing it half way through. It hung down in lank strands over a thin face only brightened by a clumsy slash of lipstick that looked as if it had been applied by a child experimenting with make-up for the first time. Peeking through the straggly strands of hair, wide with surprise, Stella's eyes were a dull shade of blue, set in a face too angular for conventional prettiness, but not sufficiently angular to be distinctive or interesting.

Stella Dysh was simply very plain. The disposable green paper prison overall she was wearing did nothing to flatter a figure that was, in any case, less than alluring. Altogether, Stella was a woman you might forget within seconds of meeting her.

None of this bothered Johnny in the least. He wasn't expecting a vivacious beauty or a fascinating, distinctive ingenue. He knew that Stella's special talents lay elsewhere.

What did bother Johnny was that she wasn't alone in her cell.

"You cur!" said Lamarck, spittle flying with his words, when he saw his second in command, Luis Nova-Cruz, sitting with Stella Dysh on her narrow steel bunk.

Nova Cruz was wearing a red silk cravat with a pattern of white seahorses on it and a quilted jacket of iridescent oriental blue. He was sitting beside Stella and they were both bent over a narrow folding table that was spread with a generous selection of foodstuffs, including marinated octopus, curried shrimps, smoked salmon and a number of other seafood delicacies. There were also several bottles of chilled white wine on the table with white napkins tied around them. Half a dozen different wine glasses stood on the table, some of them already greasy with use, including two that had lurid smears of lipstick from Stella's mouth.

Nova-Cruz was frozen in the act of pouring wine from a champagne bottle into a fresh glass. The sparkling wine foamed up out of the glass and spilled on his sleeve, soaking it as he stared at Lamarck and Johnny in the doorway.

"Commander! Mr Alpha! What an unexpected pleasure. I was just interrogating one of our prisoners."

"Interrogating?" sputtered Lamarck. "Don't try and lie your way out of this one Nova-Cruz. It's clear that what you're actually doing is sexually harassing one of our prisoners."

Johnny shook his head. He didn't know whether to laugh or groan. One thing was clear to him, whatever was going on in the cell was not sexual harassment. In the far corner of the cell was a large graceful vase containing long delicate blossoms of yellow and purple that looked like attenuated orchids. Beside the vase were several dozen empty bottles of what looked like genuine vintage wine from Earth and brightly coloured twists of discarded wrappers from what had once been numerous bars of organic chocolate.

This wasn't the scene of some kind of harassment. It was a love nest, and a very sloppily kept one at that. In the other corner of room was a pile of expensive-looking female clothing, shimmery and silky in translucent colours, but obviously worn and dirty and waiting for the wash. His gaze moved on, to take in the primitive toilet and spartan wash basin built into the walls of the cell. The rim of the toilet bowl was hung with what Johnny at first thought was strings of beads, but he then realised were pearl necklaces. The taps on the sink were adorned with a number of delicate gold and silver chains and bracelets.

"You're pouring champagne on your sleeve, Luis," said Stella Dysh in a rather croaky and unpleasant voice.

"How clumsy of me," said Nova-Cruz. He set the bottle of wine down and wiped his sleeve with a white cloth napkin.

Lamarck was trembling with rage. It seemed he had quite forgotten that he was being held at knifepoint by Johnny and forced to assist in the escape of one of his prisoners. Indeed, his entire attention was focused on Nova-Cruz. "You're not getting away with this, you greasy little varlet. This is the end of your career in penal reform."

Nova-Cruz turned to Johnny and said, "I am sorry you had to witness this, Mr Alpha. It is a personal matter between myself and the commander, concerning the favours of this luscious, fascinating woman you see here at my side." Then Nova-Cruz noticed the knife Johnny was holding and fell silent. Evidently an apology was no longer necessary. He looked at Johnny with puzzlement in his warm brown eyes. "What is going on?" He rose to his feet, pushing the table gently to one side.

"Oh, she's a luscious, fascinating woman all right, but she is not yours," hissed Lamarck, standing toe to toe with Nova-Cruz and leaning into his face pugnaciously. "She belongs to someone else. She belongs to a much more worthy man. A man who is worthy of her charms!"

"That's very flattering of you, Florien," croaked Stella Dysh. "Did you bring me any presents this time? Surely you didn't forget."

Lamarck turned and stared at her. His voice changed, suddenly becoming frail and querulous and brittle. "Stella," he quavered. "How could you do this to me?"

"Do what? What are you talking about? As far as I can see, the only injured party here is me. Unless you've got a gift for me concealed about your person that I haven't been able to detect. Or perhaps this gent does."

She turned and looked at Johnny for the first time, giving him a bold, appraising glance. In the full glow of her attention Johnny realised that there was something about this woman. Something he couldn't identify or name. But in a peculiar, powerful way she was more than the sum of her unprepossessing parts. It wasn't her tangled hair or her colourless face, or her shapeless body under its shapeless garment. It was nothing he could identify or isolate, but she exerted some sort of profound allure to the male psyche. To *his* psyche. Johnny forced himself to look away from her.

Lamarck was now shouting at Stella. "Why should I bring you presents? You've already bled me dry."

"Bled you dry? What nonsense. You've still got most of your pension and several of your children's trust funds."

"You said you were mine, Stella! You said I filled your every waking thought. You said you couldn't even think of another man..."

"Oh, I said so many things, Florien." Stella turned to Nova-Cruz. "How about another splash of that fizz, Luis?"

"Vintage champagne for the princess," said Nova-Cruz cheerfully filling her glass. His gaze flickered to Johnny. "I don't suppose you'd care to join us, Mr Alpha? I could wash a glass for you."

"Don't bother," said Johnny.

"Are you sure? It's very good champagne. Anyway, to return to my earlier question, Mr Alpha, what is going on? Why are you holding that knife?"

"I've taken your commander hostage and I'm forcing him to help me free this prisoner," said Johnny. "Basically it's a jail break."

"A jail break?" said Nova-Cruz in astonishment. "Free the prisoner? You mean free Stella?" He suddenly rose to his feet in alarm, slopping champagne from his glass.

"Careful, you're splashing again," said Stella.

Nova-Cruz stared at Johnny, his brown eyes burning with indignation. "I cannot allow you to do that, Mr Alpha. Stella stays here. She is mine."

"She is not yours!" cried Lamarck. "She will never be yours." He looked at Stella. "Tell him."

"Actually," said Stella, "I've been meaning to have a little chat with you about this, Florien. I'm not saying that it wasn't wonderful while it lasted, but I have the feeling our time together has kind of reached a natural end, sort of thing."

"No, you're not, you're not, you're not," sputtered Lamarck. "You're not leaving me for this unctuous, epicene boulevardier."

"Now be nice, Florien. Luis is a very sweet and charming man. And let's face it, his family has cash reserves that make yours look positively pitiful."

"I have money," said Lamarck desperately. "I have money I haven't told you about. I can always get more money. Don't throw yourself into the arms of that primitive. Remember the times we had together, you and I, in this cell. The beautiful things I gave you. Why aren't you wearing the beautiful things I gave you?"

"Because Luis here likes me to dress up in full prisoner regalia. It gives him some kind of kinky thrill."

Nova-Cruz glanced at Johnny and shrugged without embarrassment. "I am a man, what can I say? A man has his urges. You understand, Mr Alpha?"

Johnny checked his watch. Twelve minutes until the detonation. Twelve minutes until Middenface would be arriving from low orbit in his ketch. "I understand that Stella Dysh is getting the hell out of this place," said Johnny, "I'm taking her now. That's what I understand."

"And what makes you think I want to go anywhere with you?" croaked Stella Dysh.

"Look Miss Dysh, I'm Johnny Alpha. I'm a Strontium Dog just like you."

"I know who you are. I recognised you. You've got quite a rep."

"Good. Here's the deal. We need your special talents. We're organising a manhunt and we want you to join our posse. You'll be extremely well paid for your services and we're throwing in this escape for you free of charge."

"But who says I want to escape?"

Johnny felt himself losing his temper. He glanced at his watch again. Only eleven minutes now. "We don't have time for games, Miss Dysh. Put something on your feet and let's go."

"We're not going anywhere," said Stella. Her voice was like two pieces of broken porcelain grinding together. "I've hardly begun to put the squeeze on these chumps. This is the cushiest gig I ever stumbled onto and I'm not about to leave it. Get lost, mister."

Johnny checked his watch. Less than ten minutes left now. He reached over and grabbed Stella Dysh, pulling her off her bunk and throwing her over his shoulder. As he did so, both Lamarck and Nova-Cruz reacted as though he'd thrown a switch. They threw themselves on Johnny in a concerted and violent attempt to retrieve the struggling Stella. Holding onto the squirming weight of the woman with one hand, Johnny had to fend the two of them off.

Nova-Cruz grabbed a wine bottle from the table and swung it at Johnny's head. Johnny knocked it aside with his forearm, receiving a glancing blow along the bone that tightened his teeth with agony. He was still holding the carving knife in his free hand. He reversed it and drove the blunt end of the handle down Nova-Cruz's head, striking the man's skull a resounding blow through his thick black curly hair. Nova-Cruz clutched his head with both hands, sat down on the cot again, turned very pale and fell back onto the pillow where he lay motionless, but breathing deeply.

Meanwhile Lamarck was attacking Johnny with his bare hands, trying to claw at Johnny's face with his fingernails like a hysterical woman. Johnny punched him on the point of the jaw and Lamarck collapsed like a sack of laundry, falling onto the cot on top of the stationary Nova-Cruz.

Johnny looked at the unconscious men for a moment, then turned and carried the struggling and spitting Stella Dysh towards the door of the cell. "At least let me take my jewellery," she snarled. Johnny ignored her, carrying her out of the cell. "What about my stock certificates?" she shrieked as he closed the door behind him, making sure it locked solidly. "What about my bearer bonds?" demanded Stella as he pressed the stud on the wall that he'd seen Lamarck use earlier.

The glass door of the cell darkened, hiding the men trapped inside. Johnny turned and walked down the corridor, carrying the furious woman on his shoulder, complaining all the way.

All went smoothly until they got to the maintenance tunnel for the main outer airlock. Even then it might have continued to go smoothly, if Stella Dysh hadn't spoiled everything.

Johnny should have been watching her more carefully, but he hadn't entirely adjusted to the idea that the woman he was rescuing wanted to stay in the prison and was the unwilling subject of an escape attempt.

There was a work crew in the access tunnel checking power conduits and communications hubs to make sure that they weren't being damaged by damp. Here near the main airlock they were in the outer skin of the prison colony and the vast cold mass of the ocean was only a few metres of concrete away. The chill expanse of the walls constantly wept condensation, which played havoc with even the best insulated electrical components, so a work crew had to be sent out and intervals to inspect them.

Johnny found the work crew easy enough to avoid, ducking into a side tunnel. Then Stella Dysh, who had for several minutes been behaving herself and apparently co-operating, had let out an ear-splitting screech. The work crew understandably dropped tools and rushed to investigate. By the time they got to the side tunnel Johnny was gone. Carrying Stella, with his hand firmly clasped over her mouth, Johnny bulled his way up an access ladder and struggled through a manhole, dragging Stella every centimetre of the way. He emerged into a corridor he recognised from his arrival. They were near the control room for the main airlock. He was almost at the rendezvous point. He checked his watch and saw that he'd arrived with three minutes to spare.

Unfortunately, at that moment two heavily armed prison guards walked around the corner. Johnny had momentarily loosened his hold on Stella to look at his watch and she opened her mouth wide and screamed like a banshee. "Help me!" she shrieked. "I'm being kidnapped!" The two guards froze in astonishment for a moment, then snapped into action. The guard nearest Johnny raced towards him, unholstering a sidearm as he ran. The other one took a communicator out of his pocket and urgently summoned backup.

"Put her down!" yelled the nearest guard. He had his gun out and was squinting as he took aim at Johnny. Johnny didn't give him time to draw a bead. He hefted, balanced, and threw the carving knife in one powerful, graceful motion. The knife tumbled through the air for an instant before hitting the guard in the throat with a horrible chopping sound. The man fell to the floor, clutching at the grotesque piece of metal lodged in his wind pipe. He made a terrible hissing attempt to breathe through the wound, one more sound for Johnny to file away in his gallery of personal nightmares. Then the man stopped breathing and just lay there twitching.

Johnny had already let go of Stella, and was stepping forward to scoop up the dying guard's gun. The other guard realised what was happening and began to scrabble for his own sidearm.

Johnny shot him down where he stood, then grabbed Stella again and dragged her towards the airlock control room. In the staging area under the control room, he found his own space suit hanging with an assortment of other diving gear. He stood over Stella Dysh while she found a scuba outfit of the correct size and put it on. She was somewhat subdued and less troublesome since Johnny had killed the guards. Maybe she realised she was responsible for the men's deaths.

Unfortunately, one guard had managed to send off a distress call before Johnny had got to him. That meant they could expect reinforcements to arrive looking for them any minute. But in a minute they were going to have something else to think about.

Johnny looked at his watch again. "Brace yourself," he said.

"Brace myself for what?" said Stella Dysh sourly.

And then the tidal wave hit.

The nuclear detonation Johnny had engineered served to create a diversion in two ways. It created an underwater tidal surge that sent millions of tons of water thundering through the depths in a chain reaction and arriving to collide against the walls of the undersea prison with the force of an earthquake's aftershock. Every vibration detector and alarm in the prison went off simultaneously.

The nuclear explosion had also tripped every radiation alarm.

The net result was pandemonium. The prison staff forgot all about Johnny and the escaping prisoner and wondered for a moment about their own survival. And that moment was all Johnny needed. He knew there was no question of escaping through the main air lock. It was far too well guarded. But there were bound to be subsidiary, smaller airlocks for maintenance and access routes. After a swift, tense search he found an ideal one.

"What the hell is this?" said Stella Dysh. Johnny had called her over to what looked like a narrow shelf sunk into the wall, surrounded by white tiles and an instruction plaque. But on closer inspection, the shelf turned out to disappear into a hole in the wall, a hole which extended into a tiled tube no more than a metre in diameter. The plaque on the wall beside it read *Mortuary Tube*.

"It's our route out of here."

"It's a hole in the goddamned wall."

"We're lucky to find it."

"It says 'Insert corpse head first'."

"Look," said Johnny impatiently, "the prison staff are off guard at the moment—"

"You mean the guards are off-guard?" said Stella Dysh.

"But they won't be for long. And when they arrive they're going to shoot instead of asking questions. Shoot you as well as me."

"All right, all right. I just don't like the sound of it. Who would? 'Insert corpse'."

"It's just another route out into the ocean. They use it for burials."

"No shit, Professor Hawking."

"It's our way out of here."

"Just so long as they don't use it for executions," said Stella Dysh, and she climbed into the hole in the wall, head first, followed by Johnny.

The mortuary tube carried them beyond the walls of the prison, sending them out into the cold vastness of the ocean in a plume of waste water. Johnny had grabbed one of the diving lamps and he switched it on, intending to make a signal that Middenface could see from a distance. But the instant he turned the light on, another light came on immediately in front of him, shining out of the dark ocean, straight into his eyes.

As Johnny blinked, momentarily dazzled by the beam of light, he moved his arm to shield his face. He used the arm holding the lamp and as he moved it, the beam of light immediately shifted off his face. Johnny squinted into the water in front of him. He lifted his light again and shone it in front of him. Another beam of light came shining back. Johnny moved his hand around experimentally and the beam of light moved with it.

It was a reflection of the diving lamp he was holding. A reflection from the front windscreen of the ketch that emerged, huge and silent, through the swaying curtain of cold ocean current. Johnny was shining his torch directly into the cockpit and now he could see Middenface sitting there, grinning.

Two minutes later they were safely on board, rubbing towels over their cold, soaked bodies as Middenface plotted a course back into orbit to rendezvous with the starship that hung overhead. Johnny led Stella Dysh into the control room.

"Good to see you, old pal," said Middenface, beaming at Johnny.

"Nice work with the rendezvous," said Alpha.

Stella Dysh was drying her hair. She lowered the towel from her face and peered at Middenface. "Who's this?" she said.

"McNulty is the name."

"I hope everyone on this posse isn't as ugly as he is."

"Well, *she* was certainly worth rescuing," said Middenface, hitting the button that sent them through the ocean, back up to the surface, and into space.

CHAPTER SIX
OLD BROILER IN THE BARBECUE

The moon was high over the desert and Charlie Yuletide stood with his banjo, plucking plangently and singing, "Johnny Alpha was hellishly brave. And when Johnny's guns finished firin', it turned out he'd escaped with the siren. Escape from the watery grave!"

Middenface observed the reaction of Asdoel Zo's gardeners to Stella Dysh. The girls' behaviour around the female mutant was interesting and instructive. They seemed to take an instant, visceral dislike to her. It appeared to be a gut reaction, an atavistic hatred of something alien and menacing. It was ridiculous, but there it was; the gorgeous gardeners found this drab stranger a threat. In this respect it seemed they were like all the women who encountered Stella.

The reaction of men was the polar opposite. They found themselves attracted to Stella without quite realising it, and without being able to consciously explain why.

Even Asdoel Zo wasn't immune to her siren's allure. He could be found wandering around with Stella at his side, the woman yawning openly and making no attempt to conceal her boredom as he showed her his enormous collection of western memorabilia and cowboy accoutrements. For her own part, Stella settled into life in the billionaire's mansion with what at first appeared to be resigned disgust, but gradually revealed itself to be guarded enthusiasm. She even stopped sulking about being freed from her undersea prison against her will, when Asdoel Zo promised to pay her an exorbitant fee for taking part in the posse's pursuit of Preacher Tarkettle.

"It wasn't just the money," said Stella, explaining her change of heart. "It was also, you know, the thrill of the hunt."

"Of course it was, darling," said Hari Mata Karma, who had hated Stella like poison from the moment they'd met. "We're all bounty hunters here. If there's anything we understand it's the thrill of the hunt. It's just a shame you couldn't have manifested it a bit sooner."

Stella raised her eyebrows. "I don't know what you mean."

"I mean, you seemed strangely reluctant to leave your watery prison and that sort of attitude made life more than a little tough on poor Johnny here, who'd gone to all that trouble for you. But then, men do seem to be willing to go to a lot of trouble for you."

"Yes, that they do," Stella said complacently.

"And it's so hard to imagine why."

But as HMK later confessed to Slim Drago, "It was a good insult but I was being disingenuous."

"Disingenuous?" said Slim Drago vaguely. The fat man was busy combing his hair with meticulous, frowning concentration.

"Pretending an innocence I don't really possess," explained HMK. "Because you see, I know exactly what makes her so irresistible to men."

"Irresistible," said Slim. The tip of his tongue was protruding from the corner of his mouth with dogged concentration as painstakingly, and painfully, he dragged his comb through his hair.

"Yes, it's a result of the same mutation that made her a Strontium Dog. You see, she's a female sharpshooter whose siren-like abilities enable her to lure her prey into range. And once they are there under her gun she will either fire a lethal round or an anaesthetic one."

HMK snorted with contempt. "So whether her prey is wanted dead or alive, she can deliver!" she announced, speaking in the tone of a vapid huckster from the Shopping Channel. Slim was still wrestling with his comb, trying to drag it through his unruly locks. HMK stared at him impatiently.

"You really are useless with that thing."

"I sure am. Useless."

"Here. Give it here." HMK took the comb from him and began to pass it through his hair with smooth, practised strokes. "There, is that better, you great lummox?"

"Yes thank you. Can you do the back as well, please? I tried, but I didn't do a very good job. I can't see the back of my head."

"You could use a series of mirrors, you buffoon, or a screen and cam arrangement. Never mind. Here. I'll do it for you." HMK wielded the comb with dextrous, finicky speed. "Why all this sudden interest in your appearance anyway?"

"Because I might see Stella Dysh," said Slim Drago. "I kinda like her." He blushed, his big ears glowing red. Then he yelped with sudden pain. "Ouch! You pulled out my hair with that comb."

"You'd better do it yourself then," snarled HMK, throwing the comb in his face and marching off.

Middenface witnessed the whole incident and was secretly amused. HMK might not have welcomed Slim's sloppy, foolish adoration but she certainly missed it now that it was gone. The big Strontium Dog had taken to following Stella Dysh around like a foolish little puppy and seemed to have forgotten that HMK existed.

That night Middenface and HMK had a drink on the balcony while Asdoel Zo cheerfully busied himself over the barbecue coals, and his bevy of beautiful gardeners discreetly, but firmly, made sure Stella came nowhere near him. HMK sipped her drink and glanced over at Stella, who was going down the balcony steps and out into the cactus garden to avoid having to talk to Slim.

HMK looked at Middenface and said, "Stella isn't a glamorous beauty like me, in fact she is downright dowdy, but she has another, more subtle and profoundly powerful appeal. She secretes pheromones, potent scent-attractors that draw males like dogs to a bitch in heat – as one might uncharitably put it. Indeed, some *women* are also vulnerable to Stella's unique charms – which might account for certain parties hostility towards the mutant siren."

Middenface looked across at Hari Mata Karma. In the gleaming sunset of SG977 her beautiful face looked flushed. There was a fine sheen of sweat on her brow. Middenface stared at her. Was she saying what he thought she was saying?

His thoughts were interrupted by a sudden burst of excited squealing and giggles from the girl gardeners. Middenface immediately spotted the source of their excitement. Johnny Alpha was ambling up from the shadowed terraced garden with his easy but powerful stride. Two silent figures followed him.

HMK leaned forward, peering over Middenface's shoulder. "Johnny's back."

"Looks like it."

"Who's that he's got with him?"

"Numbers six and seven on our list."

"You mean the final members of our posse?" said HMK. Her voice was suddenly alive with excitement. "Maybe we can finally get this manhunt started."

"Let's hope so," said Middenface. "It would be a shame to have to go on sitting around this billionaire's mansion being provided with unlimited food and drink, and attended by beautiful women."

"You have a dry sense of humour, Archibald. That's what I like about you."

Middenface was startled. "Who told you my name?" He thought only Johnny knew that particular dark secret. Hari Mata Karma dismissed the question with an impatient wave of her hand. "More importantly, what's the name of these two newcomers?" She peered down the hill towards Johnny and the strangers.

HMK and Slim had succeeded in the mission Johnny had given them while he was busy freeing Stella Dysh. They had been sent to another star system where they had located and made contact with the final members of the posse, and arranged the terms of their employment. Now these posse members had landed at the space port on Asdoel Zo's private planet and Johnny had gone to meet them.

"Their names? Ray/Bel."

"Ray/Bel? But that's only one name."

"True, though apparently they also answer to Bel/Ray."

"They? You mean they only have one name between them?"

"After all, they are mutants," said Middenface.

"No kidding. So what's their mutation?" She uttered this last phrase in a rising cadence of announcement, as though it was the title of a new game show. Middenface shrugged.

"I don't know a hell of a lot. Just that they're a Siamese twin, brother-sister combination. Except these twins have the ability to separate their joined bodies and move about autonomously."

"How convenient for them."

"Though they must fuse again at meal times or they will starve."

"Why?"

"Because they share a digestive system."

"*Eeee-yuk.*"

"They also share a psychic link, which apparently makes them a remarkable synchronised organism, ideal for stalking and catching prey."

"I can hardly wait to meet them," said HMK, peering down the hill. "I trust they won't be sharing their digestive system just yet."

Hari Mata Karma and Middenface had very little chance to form any impression of the twins. There was just a glimpse of white faces and long black hair as the two figures followed Johnny onto the balcony. Ray and Bel were both dressed all in black: black trenchcoats and, beneath these, black turtle neck sweaters, leggings and gleaming black boots. They were both carrying heavy bundles of luggage, which they refused to let anyone touch or help them with. They stayed close together, side by side like shy children at a party, but Middenface could see light between them. "They're not joined," he whispered to HMK. "Not at the moment, anyway."

"But how do they do it when they *do* join up?" she whispered back. "Do they have a special flap in the side of their trenchcoats that opens up or something? Once again I say, eeee-yuk. Maybe there's a special zippered aperture."

"I don't know, shall we ask them?"

Middenface and Hari Mata Karma approached Johnny and the newcomers. But after the briefest of introductions, the twins excused themselves and carried their luggage to their room, pleading fatigue after their long journey.

"You look tired, Johnny," said HMK, opening a bottle of beer for him. Johnny accepted it, enjoying the feel of the cold glass in his hand then the feel and flavour and cool, quenching moisture of the beer as he drank. Asdoel Zo came over and joined them.

"Oh no, what do you want?" quipped HMK. She had recently adopted a comic feigned insolence towards their billionaire employer, which he seemed to endure with detached amusement. "I just came to say thank you to Johnny," he said. "For collecting our guests."

"I guess the posse is complete now, Mr Zo," said Johnny. "And we can get started on our hunt for Tarkettle as soon as you're ready."

"Excellent. But let's not spoil a beautiful evening by talking about that murdering lunatic." Asdoel Zo took a deep breath, as though gaining control of his emotions. Then, after a moment, he said, "Let's just enjoy our final barbecue together."

"Sounds good to me," said Johnny, sipping his beer. "And smells good too."

"Oh, that's just the starters," said Asdoel Zo. "I cooked them on the infrared Hibachi up here on the balcony. The main course is going to be cooked down there in the cactus garden. I had the girls dig a barbecue pit and fill it with coals. I ignited it earlier today with my new laser prongs. It should be just about ready when we've finished the starters. Would you like some marinated prawns, Johnny?"

"No seafood, thanks," said Johnny. "I was at the bottom of the ocean myself, not too long ago."

Asdoel Zo, the gardening girls and the seven Strontium Dogs all gathered in the darkness, beside a clump of tall cactuses, in the flaring dry heat of the barbecue pit. The ruddy flames of the barbecue lit their faces with a festively hellish light. Big square grills were laid across the hot coals with choice cuts of meat and an assortment of exotic vegetables strewn on them, all gleaming with oil. "Welcome to the Ranchero Zo barbecue!" cried Asdoel Zo. "Plenty for everyone! Now, who'll be my first customer of the evening for some prime, tender beer-fed steak?"

"I wouldn't mind a piece, Mr Zo, sir," said Middenface.

"Creep," whispered HMK in his ear. Middenface didn't care. He just wanted to get his teeth into that delicious, delicate beef. He'd had some a few days ago and he was eager to repeat the experience. The meat wasn't cloned, genetically modified or grown in a tank. He'd never tasted anything like it.

"Here you go," said Asdoel Zo, lifting a huge, dripping piece of beef off the grill with a pair of long-handled tongs. The juices from the lump of meat splashed back onto the searing coals, hissing and vaporising with a delicious odour. One of the gardening girls handed Middenface a plate and he hastened forward to receive his steak from Zo, like an acolyte approaching the high priest for a benediction. Zo slapped the warm steak onto his plate with a moist, meaty sound, then moved on to the next person in line, Hari Mata Karma. "What would you like, little lady?"

"Gee, I don't know," said HMK. "Do you have anything for non-carnivores?"

"We certainly do. Just look at these here kebabs." Zo pointed at thin steel skewers, which lay across the grill with a colourful variety of oiled vegetables impaled on them.

"'These here'?" said HMK. "What's with the hayseed accent?"

"Just getting into the spirit of things," said Zo. He opened a slim box and peeled out a pair of tissue-thin gloves, which he slipped over his hands. Once he had the gloves on, Middenface was startled to see that he reached into the flames and picked up one of the steel skewers with his fingers. The thin gloves were evidently heat proof. The skewer was as long as his arm and was heavy with roasted, dripping vegetables. But vegetables didn't particularly interest Middenface, not when he had a suc-culent slab of beer-fed beef cooling on his own plate. He collected a knife and fork in a rolled napkin from a tray held out by a smiling gardener girl and set off to find a suitably quiet spot among the cacti to devour his personal feast. As he turned away he heard Asdoel Zo say, "You see, the barbecue is a purely western institution. In fact the word 'barbecue' is actually derived from 'bar-b-q' which was the brand a famous rancher put on his cattle. You get it? A bar, a letter 'b' and a letter 'q'."

"I get it, but who cares?" said HMK. "Spare us the lin-guistic insights and fill my plate, buster." Middenface winced as he sat down on a raised bank of plantings. He wished HMK wouldn't be so openly rude to their boss. It was embarrassing. He set his plate on his lap, impaled the big lump of steak with his fork and began to saw through it industriously with his serrated knife. Footsteps grated on the pebbled ground behind him and he looked up to see Johnny standing there, tall and grim in the night.

"Why so serious, pal?" said Middenface. "You should be down there by the coals getting a helping of steak."

"Suddenly I don't have much of an appetite," murmured Johnny.

"Why's that, partner?"

"I can't help feeling something's not quite right with this situation," said Johnny. Middenface sighed. But before he had a chance to begin lecturing Johnny about his perpetual paranoia and his inability to ever relax and take it easy, there was a scream from the barbecue pit.

Johnny spun around to see what was happening and Middenface followed, standing up so suddenly that his plate tumbled from his lap and his steak plopped in the dirt. There was more screaming now and both men ran towards the barbecue.

"All right!" boomed a deep, powerful voice. "Everybody freeze." Middenface stared in astonishment. At first he had thought the voice was coming from the direction of the barbecue pit. Now he realised it was coming from the pit itself. There, protruding among the glowing orange coals, was the helmet of what looked like a space suit. The black visor of the space suit jutted out of the coals, reflecting their hot light. Close to it, the barrel of a gun was poking out. As Johnny and Middenface watched, the helmet and gun continued to rise out of the barbecue pit, displacing and spilling coals. As the helmet cleared the surface, the shoulders, arms and torso of the suit were revealed. Middenface realised that it wasn't in fact a space suit after all but a kind of high temperature excursion suit like the ones used by furnace workers in nuclear power installations. The figure in the suit was rising out of the barbecue pit, holding a gun on them, shrugging and shedding a rattling shower of small glowing coals. The astonished party of revellers stood and stared at this bizarre apparition.

"How the hell..." said Middenface.

"Must have been buried in there, waiting for us," murmured Johnny out of the corner of his mouth.

The figure from the pit stood up, knocking over grills on either side, spilling meat and vegetables into the flames it had stirred up. "Who are you?" demanded Asdoel Zo. "How dare you ruin my barbecue? Do you have any idea how much those steaks cost?"

"Shut up," said the booming voice. The gun was pointing at Asdoel Zo now. "I've got no quarrel with you but if you get in my way I'll do you some damage, all right?"

Johnny moved fractionally closer to Middenface and spoke out of the corner of his mouth. "Do you have a gun with you?"

"No, I never thought–"

"Neither did I," muttered Johnny in disgust. "I guess they've got the drop on us."

"And as for your barbecue," said the figure in the furnace suit, "Why should I give a damn if I ruined it? Do you have any idea how uncomfortable it was lying in there for hours, peeking through my periscope, waiting for you to finish marinating your goddamned rack of lamb or whatever the hell you were doing?" A sudden kick from the figure sent one of the heavy grills rearing into the air amid sparks and fragments of coal. Vegetable-laden skewers flew through the air, shedding their load of impaled titbits, one narrowly missing Middenface and another landing at Johnny's feet.

There was silence for a moment after the grotesque figure's petulant outburst. Then Hari Mata Karma spoke up. "You said you've got no quarrel with Mr Zo."

The gun moved to cover HMK. "That's right, girlie."

"Very well. Then who *do* you have a quarrel with?"

"Her!" said the figure with a venomous hiss. The gun moved and pointed to Stella Dysh.

"Her?" said HMK, with what sounded suspiciously like delighted amusement in her voice. "And what exactly does your quarrel with Ms Dysh entail?"

Middenface was trying to keep up with what was going on. The revelation that the gunman in the coals was only after one of their party had at first provoked a profound wave of relief in him, followed by shame at the cowardice of his own reaction and a determination to do something about it. But what? Just then, he noticed that Johnny was moving, with stealth and caution...

"It entails taking her out of here and popping her back in that undersea prison where she was rightfully incarcerated in the first damned place."

"You want to put her back in prison?" said Asdoel Zo.

The gun swung back to cover the billionaire. "What are you sonny, some kind of parrot?"

"No," said HMK nonchalantly. "But if you want a parrot, we have several up at the house."

"You be quiet now, sarcastic girlie," said the gunman. "Like I said, I ain't got no bone to pick with none of you others."

"Bone to pick. What a delicious turn of phrase," said HMK. "And so appropriate to the occasion. Barbecue. Bone. You see what I'm driving at?"

"I see what you're driving at, all right. You're trying to distract me or rile me, or make me careless, girlie."

"And I love 'girlie'. It's so complimentary to a woman of my modest but inexorably advancing years."

"But you ain't going to distract me or rile me. And if necessary I'm going to plug you one, right in the guts. If you're lucky I'll use a non-lethal round, but even one of them means you're taking your meals through a tube for the foreseeable future. So just shut up."

Surprisingly enough, HMK did indeed shut up. The figure turned the gun back to Stella Dysh. "None of you interfere and none of you'll get hurt. But I aim to take this one back with me."

"Sorry," said Johnny Alpha, "but I can't let you do that." As the figure swung the gun in his direction, Johnny suddenly kicked the steel skewer that was lying at his feet. He kicked it upwards so it bounced into the air at shoulder height where he grabbed it, turned it and threw it with great force and accuracy. The figure in the heat suit was still trying to point the gun at Johnny when the sharp end of the skewer went right through its forearm.

There was a snarling scream, amplified by the suit's helmet, and the gun dropped among the coals as the figure clutched its impaled arm and, all at once, seven Strontium Dogs pounced.

Stella Dysh grabbed the fallen gun from among the coals, cursing as she burned herself. But she ignored the burns and turned to the other Strontium Dogs who were busy dragging the figure out of the barbecue pit by its heels, Ray and Bel each holding onto one leg. The figure in the suit was kicking and punching, but its attempts at resistance were hampered by the steel skewer protruding from its right forearm.

"Nice shot, Johnny," said HMK.

"Went right through the suit," said Middenface.

"Those suits are designed to resist heat, not mechanical force," said Johnny. "Now let's get a look at our gate-crasher."

"Yeah, let's get a look," echoed Slim Drago. His big fingers fumbled at the helmet release for an instant before he snatched them back. "Ow! It's hot!"

"Well it would be, Slim," said HMK sardonically. "It's been buried in a pit of burning coals for several hours."

"Here, let me," said Johnny. He snapped a pair of heat-resistant gloves out of the box Asdoel Zo had used earlier, pulled them on over his hands and reached for the release catches on the helmet.

The helmet came off with a rush of refrigerated air, scented with cheap shampoo and liniment, revealing the wizened face of a scrawny old woman. Her sparse, silver hair was drawn into a tight bun over the strange ridges and bumps that rose on the back of her skull and ran down her spine, marking her as a mutant. Her bloodshot, brown eyes gazed up at them in fury. She opened her cracked, thin lips and revealed uneven, yellow teeth.

"Well, what the hell are you staring at?" Without the amplification of the suit's speakers, her voice was high and frail and querulous.

"It's Granny Haxer," said Hari Mata Karma.

"Who?" said Middenface. He couldn't believe it.

"Granny Haxer."

"She's a little old lady."

"Hence the Granny."

"But she had seven of the toughest bounty hunters in the spiral arm at gunpoint."

"That's right, sonny," cackled Granny Haxer, a long thread of saliva spanning her mouth. "And don't you forget it."

"That's because she too is one of the toughest bounty hunters in the spiral arm," said HMK.

"Why thank you, girlie," said Granny Haxer. "Now if you don't mind, I've got a great big whazzing steel skewer sticking through my arm and I'm bleeding right copiously in this expensive rented suit."

"Yeah," said Slim Drago. "The poor little old lady's bleeding in her suit. We gotta get her some medical attention."

"A bit less of this old lady stuff," snapped Granny Haxer. "I'm a paid professional like the rest of you."

"Medical attention?" said Stella Dysh. "She was going to drag me back to that hell hole of an underwater prison planet. I say we forget about her wounded arm. I say we just roll her back into the barbecue pit but this time without her suit. Let her fry in there."

Granny Haxer chuckled. "You're a girl after my own heart, Ms Dysh. Fry old Granny, huh? I reckon you wouldn't get much eating meat off a tough old bird like me."

"It would serve you right for ruining my party, though," said Asdoel Zo, who was holding a cannabis cigar between trembling fingers, puffing on it to calm himself in the aftermath of the unexpected violence of the last few minutes.

"Sorry about that, mister," said Granny Haxer with patent insincerity. "I sure enjoyed your little speech about the history of the barbecue, though. I had a heat resistant surveillance device down there as well as my periscope." But Asdoel Zo wasn't listening. He moved away, puffing on his stogey, walking back to a cluster of cacti where his gardening girls were waiting to make a fuss of him.

Meanwhile, Hari Mata Karma, who a moment earlier had been glaring furiously at the old woman, turned to glare at Stella Dysh. "What's all this about a hell hole of a prison planet? Ever since Johnny rescued you from there you've been bitching about it and saying you wanted to go back."

"If she wants to go back, I'm the old gal to take her," rasped Granny Haxer.

"Don't be stupid," said Stella. "I never want to see that dump again."

"You've certainly changed your tune," said HMK.

"A woman has a right to change her mind," sniffed Stella.

"That's right," said Slim Drago, smiling worshipfully at Stella. "A woman has a right to change her mind."

"Oh, shut up, you oaf," said HMK.

"I hate to interrupt," said Granny Haxer, "but I'm still bleeding here with this meat skewer through my arm."

Johnny Alpha leaned over the old woman, studying her with his eerie eyes. "Sorry about that, Granny."

"Hell, don't be sorry, son. It was a great throw. I should never have knocked those skewers where you could reach them. It was my own damned fault. Bad temper is my abiding sin, it's true. I got a mite tetchy waiting for all those hours in that pit full of hot coals."

"Why did you do that?" said Middenface. "Why hide in a ridiculous place like that when you could just have come up to the house to get us?"

"Would I have caught you with your pants down like that if I'd just moseyed up to the house?" cackled Granny Haxer.

"No, I suppose not."

"I'm still bleeding here, children."

"We'll see that you get full medical attention in just a minute," said Johnny. "First, I've got a question."

"Fire away, son." The little woman stared up at him with amusement gleaming in her eyes. "I'm just lying here pumping out my life blood through that gaping hole you tore in me. No need to hurry or nothing."

Johnny smiled. "You said you were a paid professional like the rest of us."

"Did I?" The merriment faded from Granny Haxer's eyes.

"Yes you did."

"I don't recall."

"My question is, who paid you?"

Granny Haxer rolled her head and stared at Stella Dysh. "The same party who paid me to put her away in that watery prison in the first place. As soon as they heard she'd been sprung they hired me to catch her and take her back."

"And who is 'they'?" said Johnny.

Granny turned her head back to look at Johnny. Her eyes were guileless and sincere, her smile sweet and affable. "No idea at all, son. Anonymous client approached me through a computer communication. Paid me the same way."

"And you never thought to ask who they were?"

"Never asked, never wondered. Now either carry me up to that big house and patch me up, or take me out onto the lone prairie and leave me alone so I can die in peace."

"It's a ridiculous idea," said Hari Mata Karma.

"I don't see why," said Asdoel Zo. "And Johnny's with me on this, aren't you, Johnny?" He looked across the room at Johnny Alpha, who nodded but remained silent.

"Oh, for God's sake," said HMK, looking at Middenface for support.

Johnny, Middenface, HMK and Asdoel Zo were sitting on the leather chairs and sofa in Zo's study. The other Strontium Dogs had turned in for the night and Granny Haxer was lying in a sedated sleep in one of the numerous guest bedrooms with med robots tending to her. Asdoel Zo cleared his throat and rose from his chair. "Anyone care for a night-cap?" He walked across the room to the old, roll-topped desk and opened it. Inside was a well equipped mini bar. Middenface was startled. The last time he'd seen the desk opened it had contained a communications con-sole. He reminded himself that Asdoel Zo could afford the most ingenious and baffling gadgets that money could buy. It might not even be the same desk as last time.

Zo reached into the bar and selected a bottle. "Bourbon, anyone?"

"Stop trying to change the subject," said HMK.

"I'm not." Zo put the bottle on a lacquered wooden tray and added glasses and a small ice bucket. "I'm just trying to promote a rational and civilised discussion."

HMK snorted. "If this discussion was rational we wouldn't even be considering the possibility of hiring this insane old bitch as part of our team. And if it was *civilised* we'd be discussing ways of shipping her back to whatever retirement home she was snoozing her senile snooze in before she turned up here to spoil the barbecue. Your barbecue, I might add."

"Bourbon?" said Asdoel Zo, lifting the bottle. It looked like a very old and very expensive bottle. Middenface felt his mouth water. "I'll have a wee dram," he said.

"Excellent. Johnny?"

"No thanks," said Johnny Alpha.

"Got to stay sharp, eh?"

Zo turned back to the bar in the roll-top desk. He winked at Johnny. "Worried that someone might spring on you if you let your guard down and have a little intoxicating drink? Worried you won't be at your best?"

Johnny smiled a thin, tolerant smile. "Always pays to be sharp. You never know when someone might be popping out of a pit full of coals brandishing a gun at you."

Asdoel Zo laughed appreciatively as he delved among the glinting bottles. He poured two drinks and gave one to Middenface.

"Right," said HMK, "now that everybody who wants a vile drink has got a vile drink, what's all this nonsense about allowing that old crone to join our posse?"

Johnny looked at HMK. "When we were out by the barbecue, you seemed to have quite a bit of respect for the 'insane old crone'."

"Respect? What do you mean?"

"Didn't you say something about her being one of the top bounty hunting professionals?"

"So what if I did. She is, isn't she? Of course I've heard of her. Haven't you heard of her?"

"Sure," said Johnny. "I've heard of her. Never seen her before, though."

HMK scowled. "I am merely pointing out that this woman had us all at gunpoint a little while ago. And Johnny threw a meat skewer at her wrist. Now suddenly, with her drugged to the eyeballs upstairs, you're holding a conference about making her a member of the team."

Asdoel Zo shrugged. "I think she'd be a valuable addition to the posse."

"I see," snapped HMK. "And what arrangement would you make with her? Join us as soon as she's finished dragging Stella Dysh, a fellow valuable posse member, back to jail?" Middenface noticed that Stella, who earlier that evening had been thoroughly reviled by HMK, had suddenly been promoted to the status of valuable posse member.

"Johnny and I have already discussed that," said Asdoel Zo equably.

HMK turned and stared at Johnny. "You have, have you?" she said in a reproachful tone.

"Mr Zo can just buy out her contract," said Johnny. "If Granny Haxer's amenable, she can simply notify her previous employer that she's no longer working for them."

"She could be a useful member of the posse," said Middenface.

"She did get the drop on seven other Strontium Dogs," said Johnny laconically.

"Seven. That's another thing," said HMK. "If she joins us there won't be seven of us in the posse any more."

Asdoel Zo suddenly laughed. "Is that what's bothering you? That there will be eight of you instead of seven."

HMK shrugged diffidently. "Seven is a good number for a western adventure, you should be the first to appreciate that."

Asdoel Zo laughed again and shook his head. "By God, that's all that's bothering her. She isn't worried about Granny Haxer being potentially treacherous or dangerous or a spy planted among us. She's just upset that there won't be seven of you any more."

Johnny got up from his chair. "By the way," he said, "Ray/Bel only counts as one."

"As one what?" said Asdoel Zo.

"One member of the posse, stupid," said HMK. She had a thoughtful frown on her face. She looked up and smiled at Johnny. She had a dazzling smile. "You're right, Johnny. Ray/Bel or Bel/Ray, or whatever we call him/her basically constitutes a single, mutually dependent organism. Therefore there are only seven of us." She chuckled. "All right. Excellent." Astonishingly, she seemed mollified.

Granny Haxer proved amenable to the new arrangement and, thanks to the ministrations of Asdoel Zo's medical 'bots, she was on her feet and able to join the rest of the posse on their visit to the Weapon Shops of Usher (formerly Isher) Ltd.

The weapon shops were located in a low, orbital mall that was spinning around Wexler VII. The mall was a space station devoted to shopping, with the usual mix of stores and restaurants, though the weapons shops had become so successful that they now occupied nearly half of the entire mall area. But there was a hierarchy among the weapons shops, starting with low-rent gun dealers on the outermost hub of the vast rotating space station, where a redneck might go to pick up his Saturday night special, and progressing through increasingly posh establishments as the shoppers made their way inwards through the spiral access tunnels of the mall until the central cluster of retail premises was reached. Here, at the hub of the space station, the big yachts and cruisers docked. This was where the rich space travellers disembarked and this was where the most high-end weapons shops plied their trade.

Asdoel Zo took his posse to the most elite weapons shop of all, Quinn Moseby Arms, and had the entire place closed down to normal customers so it could tend to Johnny and his companions. Mr Moseby himself served them, getting them kitted out for their mission. The Moseby shop boasted the finest examples of weaponry in the known universe. The hard-bitten bounty hunters were like kids in a candy store – or a lethal toy shop. "Look at this!" whooped Granny Haxer, lifting a Velvett vibrosaw – a device no larger than a cigarette lighter but which, when activated, extruded a long, flat blade of vibrating energy which could cut through almost anything – or anyone. She clutched the vibrosaw in her right hand, which was still swathed with a flesh-coloured dressing, the last vestige of her wounded forearm, which had been so artfully repaired. "You could do a lot of damage with this little beauty. Just the thing for a lady's purse."

Hari Mata Karma and Stella Dysh seemed to agree. All three women selected vibrosaws – in different colours and styles, of course, and Asdoel Zo was there to pay for them without complaint. When the other Strontium Dogs realised that all this fine weaponry was on the house, they got caught up in a frenzied orgy of spending. Slim Drago insisted on getting into the spirit of their old west style adventure and selected a brace of retro-looking blasters with silver plating, carved ivory handles and twin holsters, on a leather belt embossed with turquoise beads. Ray and Bel raced through the shop, picking weapons up and putting them down. "Now that I know I can have anything..." said Ray, the brother.

His sister, Bel, completed his thought, "I can't think of what I want..."

"Why don't you just buy everything?" said Asdoel Zo. So they did.

Johnny Alpha, however, remained unmoved, sticking with his own austere collection of tried and tested weaponry, including the Westinghouse variable cartridge blaster he favoured, contenting himself with replenishing his supply of ammunition and choosing some sophisticated explosive devices. Middenface was swept up in the excitement at first, but soon lost interest. Once he acquired enough weaponry to fit in a small pack, he stopped, reasoning that there was no point in having more equipment than he could carry. Who knew what hardships they would face in their pursuit of Preacher Tarkettle? He didn't want to lumber himself with any unnecessary burdens.

Middenface left the others happily browsing in the weapons shop, with Johnny supervising and occasionally vetoing their more fanciful choices and Asdoel Zo uncomplainingly paying for everything. Walking on his own through the mall, Middenface felt a strange sense of excitement and freedom. The weapons shop had been all right in its own way, but this was what he really wanted to be doing. Strolling, on his own, with no particular destination, savouring the excitement and anticipation and fear that always came on the eve of a long and dangerous hunt.

Asdoel Zo had promised a final briefing, on the starship after everyone had finished in the shops. So Middenface made sure his wanderings took him steadily in the direction of the docking bay and the starship. He had no intention of missing a vital briefing. But there should be a little time yet. For sightseeing. And at the moment the sight Middenface was seeing was the rhythmic tightening and sway of a magnificent backside. The backside was clad in tight, red rubber and belonged to a tall voluptuous woman who was swaying along a walkway just ahead of Middenface, where she had been for some time. She was wearing a black hat like a sombrero.

The sombrero woman had been ahead of him for some time because Middenface was deliberately following her, enjoying the view. Having savoured her hindquarters fully, he then intended to saunter past her and glance back casually, steal a look at her face and cleavage, and to determine whether they lived up to the promise of those firm, swaying buttocks and shapely legs. After all, a face could so often disappoint. Take his own, for example.

But before Middenface could execute this manoeuvre, the woman suddenly cut off to the right and entered a palatially posh jewellers. Ah well, thought Middenface, in the interests of scientific enquiry... He followed her into the shop.

The shop was a bewildering matrix of velvety shadow and isolated shafts of light, illuminating small high tables on which choice examples of the jewel makers' craft were displayed. Here and there, just to confuse matters, were clusters of mirrors, which reflected the isolated spotlights and the velvet blackness, multiplying it into confusion.

Middenface spotted the sombrero woman, bending over an illuminated display of rubies on a white velvet cushion. He wasn't yet at an angle where he could see her face, which was bent attentively to the gleaming gemstones, but he could at least glimpse her hair, which up to now had been concealed under the broad hat she was wearing. And her hair was striking – boldly striped in black and white, like a zebra.

At just that moment, the woman glanced up at Middenface, as if she sensed she was being watched. Their eyes locked for an instant, and as he stared at her, Middenface had the odd feeling that he knew the woman from somewhere. Then the woman looked abruptly away, spun on her heel, and walked swiftly off. She seemed annoyed at Middenface's attention. All he could see of her was the broad sombrero swaying above those memorable buttocks, and her right elbow jutting out, as if she was speaking on a phone. Another moment and she had vanished into shadows at the rear of the large store.

Middenface was left standing alone and feeling a little foolish. It was embarrassing being spotted watching the woman, as though he was some kind of stalker. He shrugged and started off in the direction of the entrance. Never mind. He just wished he could remember where he had seen her before...

He was just nearing the exit when he heard a soft foot-fall behind him, a swish of motion in the air at the back of his head and an oddly intimate cracking sound. The next thing he knew, his knees were folding under him, pain was flooding through his skull and the black ceiling of the store seemed to be descending to engulf him.

When he came back to consciousness, Asdoel Zo was standing over him. "What the hell happened to you? I didn't pay you to get into a fight in a jewellery store."

CHAPTER SEVEN
LANDFALL

Charlie Yuletide marched across the desert, his saddle across one shoulder and his banjo across the other. His boots crackled on the dry ground and then began to make a tapping sound as each footfall touched rock. The nature of the terrain was changing. The desert rose into foothills, then narrowed into the shadowed throat of a rocky canyon. Charlie Yuletide marched into the opening. It was a narrow, meandering cleft between two high shoulders of rock. At the far end was a third wall of rock, turning the canyon into a dead end.

There was an opening, perhaps once a natural cave mouth, but extended and elaborated by man. Into the dark opening ran the twin rusty steel rods of a small gauge railway. Beside the railway were the tumbled hulks of the ore cars, which had once rolled along the rails into the mouth of the mine. Besides the rusting rail and ore cars, the canyon was filled with dumped rock, the odd dead tree and a large metal trough full of water, fed from an underground spring.

Standing drinking noisily from the verdigrised trough was a beautiful palomino pony. Charlie Yuletide stood and stared at the horse. "Hey, hey, hey. What do you know about that?" he said in cracked voice parched by the long miles he'd walked through the desert. He set the saddle down on the ground and his banjo carefully beside it. From one of his saddle bags he drew a large coil of rope.

Charlie Yuletide hefted the rope and looked at the horse. The horse finished drinking, lifted its large, dripping muzzle from the trough and looked back at him with big, intelligent eyes. Charlie Yuletide considered those eyes for a moment, then set the coil of rope down on the horn of his saddle.

He approached the horse with his hands empty, held out in front of him. The horse watched the man as he walked towards it, closer and closer. The horse's tail flicked nervously and water dripped from its mouth, but other than that the palomino was utterly motionless. Charlie Yuletide closed in on the horse. He was close enough now to smell its hot, sweet breath and, for its part, the horse sniffed at him with its big nostrils. Charlie Yuletide rolled up the sleeves on his torn shirt and held his wrist up to the horse.

The horse promptly reached down and began to lick the man's wrist. "You like the salt, don't you boy?" said Charlie, patting the horse. After a few minutes stroking the horse, he returned to his saddle and took a bridle out of the saddle bags. The horse didn't resist as he slipped the bridle on. "Looks like I got myself a new steed," said Charlie, smiling.

He tethered the horse to one of the dead trees, then sat down in the shade nearby with his banjo in his lap. The horse stirred and snorted as Charlie Yuletide began to sing.

"Preacher Tarkettle has gone into hiding. But Johnny and the posse are coming a-riding..."

Asdoel Zo and the posse were aboard his U-class starship, the *Charles Neider*. The billionaire stared at the Strontium Dogs who were assembled before him. Zo was standing in the white space of the launch chamber, with a variety of lifeboats, drop ships and shuttles racked in their dimly lit docking bays behind him. His expression was serious.

"Friends," he said, "I'm sure you're sick to death of hearing about how dangerous I believe your prey,

Preacher Tarkettle, to be. But believe me, ladies and gentlemen, I cannot overstress this simple fact. Tarkettle is a diabolical fiend of the utmost ruthlessness and resource. It would be far better if you didn't even think of him as your prey. Such a term is too suggestive of an innate advantage on your part."

Middenface heard Bel suppressing a contrived yawn behind him, and her brother Ray snickered appreciatively. HMK also emitted a low chuckle. "When is this chump ever going to stop talking?" she murmured.

"If you think of yourselves as the hunters and Tarkettle as prey then you run the risk of overconfidence," said Zo. "You might slip into the trap of believing that your victory is inevitable, that your advantage is supreme. This is not the case. Tarkettle is a formidable foe, the most adroit of adversaries. Please, my friends, think of him in that light and no other. If you underestimate him, that will be your undoing."

In the front rank of Strontium Dogs, Johnny Alpha spoke up. "I reckon we didn't get this far in our careers by underestimating our opponents."

Zo smiled grimly. "Perhaps not, Johnny, but I don't think that even in your eventful career you've ever come up against anyone quite like Tarkettle. The man is a demon in human form. He took my loved ones away from me..." Zo's voice faltered.

"I hope he's not going to start snivelling about his dead family again," whispered Hari Mata Karma and Middenface felt himself flush with anger. How could the wee woman be so callous? The poor bastard had lost everyone he loved.

Asdoel Zo took a deep, tremulous breath and continued speaking, his voice harsh and low but under control. "He killed my beloved children, Lorna and Jodi..."

"Oh no, here we go," sighed HMK. Middenface shot her a furious glance and took a step sideways, distancing himself from her. He couldn't believe how cold and heartless the woman was.

"And my dearest wife Kathleen," continued Asdoel Zo. Middenface heard HMK snort derisively. What was her problem? But under his irritation he felt something else, an odd sense of urgency. This disquieting feeling was accompanied by a stirring of half-formed memories. It was as if there was something that he had to remember, that it was vitally important for him to remember, but he couldn't quite capture it in his mind.

Middenface put a hand to his lumpy skull and felt the medical patch which he was still wearing after the attack on him in the jewellery store two days earlier. Middenface tried to think clearly. Something Asdoel Zo had said was significant. It triggered a chain of memory that remained tantalisingly inconclusive. Middenface massaged his skull. His recent head injury didn't help.

Asdoel Zo was still talking. "Although you may be seven (or eight, depending on how you count the twins) of the deadliest bounty hunters who ever existed, you may still prove be no match for Preacher Tarkettle. I say this, not to sow the seeds of fear, or to undermine your confidence. Quite the opposite. I merely wish to prevent any dangerous overconfidence that might lead you to your doom."

Hari Mata Karma moved close beside Middenface again. She leaned over to him and whispered, "This is a cheery little pep talk, isn't it?" Middenface ignored her.

"Friends," said Asdoel Zo. "We are now in orbit around Santo Segrelle, the desert world where Preacher Tarkettle lurks." He took his wafer-thin, gold phone out of his pocket and pressed a button on it. A spherical hologram appeared in the air behind him, a shimmering image of Santo Segrelle. The planet was a rust coloured sphere, streaked with bands of deeper red and pale blue. "This is a desert planet, and indeed a deserted one. There is no indigenous population of intelligent life forms. Tarkettle is alone on this world, a situation which suits him just fine. He regards this planet as his personal fortress and he has tailored it to suit to his purposes."

"So now he's dug in like a tick," said Johnny Alpha.

"Correct."

"But I thought you said Tarkettle hated all kinds of modern technology."

"Correct."

"Then why do you think he's such a danger to us, dug in or not?"

Asdoel Zo shook his head in exasperation. "It's true, Tarkettle is a Luddite. But this doesn't mean he doesn't possess killing power. He owns an extensive collection of vintage firearms. And even with no weapon deadlier than a Winchester and no explosive more powerful than dynamite, he is the most dangerous of adversaries. Now, if there are no further questions, I wish you all good luck and pray that you return from your mission swiftly and safely."

"At last," sighed Hari Mata Karma, in a voice that was far too audible for Middenface's liking.

"You will be landing on Santo Segrelle in two separate drop ships," said Asdoel Zo. "One for the posse members and one for your weapons."

"Why?" said Johnny.

"Because it's too dangerous to have you travel with all that lethal equipment in the same ship. If there's a malfunction or a hard landing or, God forbid, Tarkettle manages to attack you in some fashion, it could kill you all. Now, if there really are no other questions, I suggest you get ready, ladies and gentlemen." Asdoel Zo pressed a button on his phone and the hologram of the planet rippled and vanished. He turned and left the docking bay, exiting through a whispering fan of doors. The cluster of

Strontium Dogs broke up, talking and laughing, simmering with energy and repressed excitement. Only Middenface remained standing where he was, staring at the point in mid-air where the image of the planet had hovered a moment earlier. There was something about the way the hologram had flickered as it disappeared... The sight had triggered the same frustratingly incomplete cascade of memories that had bothered him earlier.

Middenface had the uneasy feeling that there was something he must remember. He tried to concentrate as, all around him, the others chattered.

"I wonder how long it will take us to find Tarkettle?" said Slim Drago. "Do you think we'll have enough food?"

"I say we'll get him within twelve hours," said Ray.

"Six hours," said Bel.

"Want to make a wager?"

"Yes." The brother and sister shook hands.

"When I get hold of this Tarkettle fella, I'm going to hang him up by a very personal piece of his anatomy over a slow fire," said Granny Haxer.

"I really like your simile," said HMK, going up to Johnny Alpha.

"My what?" said Johnny.

"'Dug in like a tick'," said HMK, smiling. "It was just delightful. You're really getting into the spirit of things with your western, folksy phraseology."

Johnny Alpha just looked at her and shook his head. "Don't you take anything seriously?" he said.

The smile faded from HMK's face. "As a matter of fact I do, partner. Would you like to know what I take seriously?"

"Sure," said Johnny, regarding her coolly.

"What I take seriously is Middenface getting clobbered by some unknown assailant," she said.

"I take it quite seriously myself," said Middenface, rubbing the medical pad on his head.

"Who did it?" said HMK. "And why?"

Johnny nodded. "I've been wondering that myself. It wasn't a robbery, because they didn't take anything."

"Right. There's something fishy about it," said HMK. "And here's another fishy thing. Asdoel Zo telling us−"

"Not to take our weapons in the drop ship," said Johnny.

"Right!" exclaimed HMK. "What the hell is all that about?"

"But Mr Zo explained," said Middenface. "It's too dangerous."

"I've never heard of any safety rules like that before," said HMK. "If you ask me, what's really dangerous is landing on that planet without a gun between us."

"But the drop ship with our supplies will be landing at the same time we do," said Middenface.

Johnny Alpha shook his head. "I agree with HMK. I think the three of us should each take one small, easily concealed weapon on board our drop ship. Just in case."

"A man after my own heart," said Hari Mata Karma.

Middenface felt an odd sense of guilt as he went through his equipment and selected a suitable sidearm to conceal on his person. It was as if he was betraying the confidence of Mr Zo by breaking his rules. Nonetheless, he was willing to trust Johnny's instinct − and HMK's. Finally, Middenface settled on a T-rifle, a high velocity projectile weapon that consisted of a telescoping barrel, which contained its own supply of three rounds of ammunition in a cylinder no larger than a pen. The cylinder could be extended to half a metre in length and was then attached to a wooden stock, which allowed it to be aimed and fired with precision. But there was a secondary trigger mechanism on the barrel itself, so Middenface left the cumbersome stock with the rest of his luggage and slipped the pen-sized object into his boot. Once on the planet, he could always improvise a crude stock out of local wood and attach the barrel to it. Or even, in a pinch, use the telescoping barrel without a stock at all. There would be a consequent reduction in accuracy and ease of use, but the T-rifle would still be a formidable weapon.

Middenface met Johnny and HMK in the *Charles Neider*'s lounge bar by prior arrangement, an hour before landfall. The spacious, mahogany-lined bar was deserted except for the three of them. Chrome and bottles gleamed behind the black marble bar and the orange globe of Santo Segrelle hung in a field of stars on a wide viewing screen above the low, dove-grey couches and armchairs that filled the room. "So what did you chose?" said HMK. Her face was flushed with excitement and Middenface didn't know if this was the result of the mission they were about to embark on, or the conspiracy they had just entered into.

Middenface showed her the T-rifle and she squealed with delight. "Excellent," she said. Johnny just nodded with approval. Middenface slipped the weapon back into his boot.

"What about you two?" he said. Johnny showed them a compact handgun which, he had dismantled and placed inside the canteen that he wore on his belt. The component parts of the gun nestled snugly in the canteen, with some soft wadding added to prevent a telltale rattle.

"Ingenious. You just have to remember not to fill it with water," said HMK.

"I reckon so," said Johnny. Middenface smiled. His friend would never make a foolish blunder of that nature, although Middenface had occasionally been known to do something like that.

"And as for myself," said HMK, producing a polished ebony cigarette lighter. She grinned expectantly at Johnny and Middenface.

"It's a cigarette lighter," said Middenface. Although he already suspected what the little woman had done, he had no intention of spoiling her fun.

"So you might think," said HMK triumphantly. She thumbed the lid of the lighter and, instead of a tiny flame, a large, wavering tongue of optically distorted air shimmered above the lighter. "It's a Velvett vibrosaw. I got the idea from the weapons shop. They kept going on about it being no bigger than a cigarette lighter so I thought, why not conceal it inside a cigarette lighter?" She snapped the weapon off and smiled at them.

"Do you smoke?" said Johnny.

"Do I what?"

"Do you smoke cigarettes?"

"No. Why?"

"Because it might seem strange for you to be carrying a cigarette lighter if you don't smoke," said Johnny.

"Details," said HMK, shrugging dismissively.

From the lounge bar, Johnny, Middenface and HMK went directly to the launch chamber to board the drop ship. they didn't need to worry about their equipment because a team of the starship's crew was busy collecting it from their cabins and loading it onto the second drop ship. The crew was dressed in striped blue and white jumpers, navy blue leggings and plimsolls. They were all attractive young women. Middenface believed he recognised several of the gardeners from Zo's mansion among them. "The man certainly likes a pretty girl," he said to Hari Mata Karma.

"Yes he does, doesn't he? The disgusting, pathetic old pervert."

"He's not so old," said Middenface and they both chuckled as they followed Johnny onto the drop ship designated for personnel. The others were already on board: Slim

Drago, Stella Dysh, the twins and Granny Haxer. They were all sitting upright in the contour couches that were set in twin bays of vertical alcoves facing each other at the rear of the drop ship. The whole front section of the ship was sealed off on the far side of a steel bulkhead. "Where's the crew?" said Middenface.

"No crew," said Johnny. "It's robot controlled." He sat down in a contour couch facing Granny Haxer. "About time you showed up, sonny," she said. "I was beginning to think we'd have to go without you."

"How could I miss going on a trip with a beautiful young lady like you?" said Johnny and Granny Haxer erupted in ribald, phlegmy laughter.

"Your friend's such a charmer," said HMK to Middenface as they settled in their contour couches and buckled in. They had Johnny to their left and Slim Drago to their right. Opposite them sat Bel and Ray, flanked by Granny Haxer and Stella Dysh. The eight Strontium Dogs looked at each other and fell silent for a moment.

"Let's get this show on the road," said Johnny. He touched the communications patch on his shoulder and said, "Ready for launch."

The drop ship was a wedge-shaped dart painted in the yellows and browns of desert camouflage. It dropped from the silver belly of the *Charles Neider*. Flame flared briefly in the tail of the drop ship and its nose dipped towards the great reddish arc of the planet below them. As it descended towards the outer atmosphere of Santo Segrelle, the second drop ship – an identical vehicle – emerged from the *Charles Neider*, flared its manoeuvring rockets and followed its sister in a controlled descent.

Inside the first ship there was a brief, stomach-heaving interval of weightlessness before they hit the atmosphere of the planet below. "I hope I don't lose my dinner," said

Granny Haxer. "Those were some mighty fine pork chops we had for our farewell meal. It would be a real shame to waste them."

"I hope I don't lose *our* dinner," said Ray, looking at his sister and stressing the plural.

"Yes," said Bel. "It would be a shame before I got a chance to do my half of the digestion."

"Stop it you two," said HMK, "or I'm liable to lose *my* dinner."

"Screen on," said Johnny, as their descent steepened, the drop ship accelerated and the G-forces began to build. An oval of air about a metre high shimmered in the space between the Strontium Dogs, flickering to life in a holographic image of the planet below. At first it was impossible to make out any details, just smears of orange, white and pale green. But in a moment these vast, abstract streaks began to resolve into desert, cloud and ocean. The white mass of cloud grew steadily until it filled the holo screen.

"Entering atmosphere," said Johnny. "Brace yourselves for turbulence."

The drop ship entered the thin upper air of Santo Segrelle, falling nose first and gathering speed as the planet's gravity drew it down to the great deserts below. The tan nose of the drop ship began to flare and flash as the friction of air warmed it and within a few seconds it was glowing a fierce bright red.

Inside the well-insulated ship, the Strontium Dogs felt no change of heat, but they did feel the impact of the high velocity winds that shrieked and whooped outside, haunting the upper atmosphere of the planet in a wild banshee chase. As Johnny had predicted, there was considerable turbulence. The drop ship was buffeted violently as it plunged towards the orange world.

The Strontium Dogs were thrown around in their seats, but the contour couches held them firm in their protective, jelly-like grip. The high impact cushion systems moulded themselves to their bodies and compensated for any external motion, but the couches couldn't compensate for the motion of the ship as a whole and when it hit a pocket of spectacular turbulence there were involuntary cries from Slim Drago and Stella Dysh.

"We'll level out in a minute," said Johnny. "Everyone just hold tight."

"Hold tight, hell. I'm enjoying the ride," said Granny Haxer. "It's a regular bucking bronco."

"Bucking bronco?" said HMK. "Has that damned Asdoel Zo got to you as well, with his insane wild west fixation?"

"Mr Zo was gentleman enough to show me around his library," said Granny Haxer.

"Some library," sniffed HMK. "Three hundred different editions of Zane Grey. Not exactly the greatest literary achievements of man."

"Oh hell," said Granny Haxer. "I liked his cowboy books well enough, but they didn't set me off. I've always been a cowgirl at heart."

The drop ship bucked wildly again, lifting up in the atmosphere then dropping again. Granny Haxer whooped with glee and HMK began to look distinctly bilious again.

For some time the holo screen hovering before them had shown an unrelieved expanse of fluffy white. Suddenly the cloud cover broke and they got their first real look at the planet. "God, look at that," said Stella Dysh in awe.

The landscape below was an endless stretch of coral pink with deeper red-brown streaks. It was a vista of desert and mountain, with spiked peaks of rust coloured rock rearing up into the atmosphere like jagged fangs hundreds of kilometres high. Squeezed between the clusters of mountain peaks was a long, thin crack of valley, like a scar stretching and twisting across the pale pink flesh of the desert. Deep in the valley, which must have been several thousand kilometres in length, there was the threadlike green glint of a river.

"Yes, it's just a picture postcard," said HMK, swallowing hard. "Let's hope we get to send some snapshots home."

"Change vantage point," said Johnny to his control patch. "Present view above ship."

"Why do we want to see above the ship?" said Slim Drago. Then he said, "Oh, I see," as the image changed to a view of white clouds. The brown-green dart of the second drop ship was bright against them and growing in size.

"Just checking that we haven't lost the other ship with all our luggage," said Johnny. "Resume forward viewpoint." The holo screen snapped back to its original image of the planet's surface growing below them. The sharp spires of mountain were growing from stalagmites to giant towers as the drop ship descended towards them. The largest of the peaks was in the centre of the screen and the drop ship seemed to be heading directly for it. The red stone scarp of the mountain grew in their view with unnerving speed.

"Uh, this ship does know how to land itself, doesn't it?" said Middenface.

"I guess we're about to find out," said Johnny.

The mountain peak filled the screen and Middenface could see that the upper slopes of the giant fang were streaked with irregular chevrons of white. Ice. The walls of the mountain, which had seemed like a smooth and uniform pink, began to reveal networks of black cracks and fissures. Deep in the black cracks there was the intermittent silver glint of running water as the melt from the ice descended the steep mountain slopes in endlessly falling streams. The drop ship seemed to be targeted on one of these winding, stream-filled fissures at the extreme left of the screen. The fissure moved inexorably to the centre of the screen, swiftly filling it. The thread of water also grew and Middenface realised that it wasn't merely a stream, but an enormous tumbling river. The silver glint of it fragmented into white splashes of wild foam and roiling green surfaces of moving water as the river grew in their vision. Middenface could see trees and thick mats of vegetation clinging to the steep banks the river had carved in the red mountain slope.

The river quickly filled the screen. "At least if we're going to crash it'll be in water," said HMK.

"Don't talk about crashing, please," said Stella Dysh. "It's tempting fate."

"I agree," said Bel. Her brother, for once, remained silent.

"A person makes their own fate, is what I reckon," said Granny Haxer.

"It's what I reckon too, Granny," said HMK. She winked at Middenface, who reflected that with the drop ship plummeting towards an uncertain, problematical and possibly even fatal landing it was the women who were busy chatting and wisecracking while the men remained tensely silent. He tried to think of some devil-may-care thing to say, but it just wouldn't come. His eyes were fixed on the holo screen and the wild-twisting surface of the river which was rushing towards them, foam and floating logs visible on the shifting water. Middenface closed his eyes and braced himself for a violent splash-down. Even as he did so, he felt the drop ship level out. He opened his eyes and saw that they were flying over the surface of the river, following its course, with the steep banks of mountain rock flitting past on either side.

"We're following the river," he said.

"I guess this must be the best way of getting to wherever we're going," said Johnny, tersely.

The drop ship sped along in the semi-darkness of the narrow river canyon, twisting and turning in smooth high-speed manoeuvres along the apparently endless river until, finally, Middenface glimpsed daylight ahead of them. The drop ship rose above the rushing green water and burst out of the shadowed river canyon into bright daylight.

"Well, would you look at that," said Granny Haxer in awe.

They had emerged at the base of the mountain, where the river spilled over a wide shelf of rock and fell dozens of kilometres to the ground below, spray rising in hectares of boiling mist. "It's a waterfall," said Slim happily. "A pretty waterfall."

It was more than a pretty waterfall. Middenface esti-mated the speed of their flight against the length of time it took them to cross the width of the falls and performed a quick calculation. "It's about ten times the size of Nia-gara," he said.

"Just the place for a honeymoon, then," said Granny Haxer.

"Or ten honeymoons," giggled HMK.

"You ever been married?" said Johnny. HMK glanced at him, giving him the strangest look for a moment. Then it passed and she looked away, gazing at the holo screen.

"What's that?" she said.

"I don't see anything," said Middenface, still wondering what that strange look meant.

"I see it," said Johnny. "Down there on the left, in that range of cliffs."

"What is it?" said Stella Dysh.

"Some kind of structure," said Johnny, peering at the screen with intense concentration, as though his strange eyes could discern hidden details. Middenface squinted at the screen, too. At first he couldn't see anything except a tumble of gargantuan rocks, each one bigger than a space station, that littered the skirts of the mountain's lower slopes. Below the jumble of rocks the mountain slope levelled out and then ended abruptly in a steep shelf, similar to the one that had created the giant waterfall.

This shelf descended to the desert below in a broad flat cliff face, riven and pocked in places by earthquakes, landslides and glacial erosion. It was in one of these depressions in the cliff face that Middenface spotted it: a group of buildings apparently carved from the native stone.

The drop ship was descending swiftly towards the hole in the cliff face and the sandy coloured stone buildings clustered inside it. At first Middenface thought they were heading directly towards it, but then the attitude of the craft changed and he realised that they were merely going to fly by it, passing it on their left. By now Middenface could get a proper look at the structure and he realised that rather than a group of buildings it was one large building with several towers jutting from it. "A man-made structure," said Johnny.

A narrow passage in the cliff face wound up towards the building at a steep angle, providing access along a kind of primitive road, which ended at the foot of it. The walls of the building rose up from this point, ending in what Middenface remembered was called a crenellated pattern, a series of openings and screens like gaps in teeth.

"A man-made structure?" said Slim.

Middenface realised that the place was a fort.

"But there aren't supposed to be..." said Bel.

"Any men here..." said Ray.

"Except for Preacher Tarkettle," said HMK.

Middenface suddenly remembered why forts had that crenelated pattern on their battlements. They allowed defenders to look out on any approaching force and fire on them...

At that exact instant, Middenface belatedly noticed the ranks of cannon poking their muzzles out through the crennelations. Muzzles that flickered with sudden flame.

"Hang on!" shouted Johnny, just as the first cannon balls struck the craft with a sound like a giant hammer striking a giant anvil.

CHAPTER EIGHT
THE FIEND TARKETTLE

Charlie Yuletide leaned against a cactus in the blazing sun of the desert. His horse stood patiently waiting, tethered to the cactus, as he plucked chords on his banjo and began to sing.

"Johnny and the others were in a heap of trouble. Their ship was going to turn into a heap of rubble."

There was a sudden banshee shriek of feedback and the horse reared back in alarm as Charlie Yuletide gave a scream of pain and tore something from his ear, flinging it to the ground. It was tiny, gleaming disc of metal. The kind used for audio communications.

Charlie Yuletide rubbed his ear, wincing. "You idiots," he said, his western accent strangely gone. "You nearly deafened me. I'm activating the injury clause in my contract."

For a moment after the iron tremor of impact, Middenface thought that nothing had happened to the drop ship. His mind was racing, weighing and selecting facts. Fact: it was a fort. Fact: there were cannons on the battlements. Fact: the cannons were aimed at them, firing at them, and had hit them.

But there were other facts, equally salient and equally important. Asdoel Zo had told them that Tarkettle was the only person on the planet, so he must be firing the cannons. Zo had also said that Tarkettle had an aversion to any kind of modern weaponry. So the cannons must be of an old fashioned variety. The kind that would have been used in the American west in and around the nineteenth century.

Surely such antiquated weapons couldn't do any harm to a sleek, super-fast, modern craft like the drop ship?

These thoughts raced through Middenface's mind in a kind of instantaneous collage of cognition, interacting and overlapping to form an impression, a result and a conclusion. They were safe. Everything was going to be all right. Middenface just had time to realise this, and to begin to smile with relief, when the port wing fell off the drop ship, neatly sheared away by a cannon ball.

"Hang on!" roared Johnny. His voice was lost in the screaming turmoil of the craft as it began to tumble from the sky. The remaining starboard wing created a fatal imbalance for the drop ship, both in terms of stability and aerodynamics. What, seconds earlier, had been an airworthy shape suddenly turned into an ungainly crippled chunk of metal weighing several hundred tonnes.

What was left of the drop ship was essentially a central tube with one wing jutting from it. This surviving wing caused it to spin as it fell like a deformed sycamore seed, whirling chaotically. Inside the ship, the Strontium Dogs were held tight in the gelatinous embrace of their contour couches, spinning wildly with the blood rushing in and out of their brains, alternately starving their senses and gorging them with a blinding wave of red darkness. Beside Middenface, HMK began to vomit violently, an acid spray of half-digested food that whipped around the sealed compartment in a yellowish cloud. Stella Dysh was screaming with undisguised terror, Slim Drago was chattering a childish prayer in a ululating voice, Ray and Bel were silent and Granny Haxer and Johnny Alpha were vying to see who could utter the most vicious curse.

Middenface was busy trying to stay alive.

He was coated with a thin layer of vomit that clung wetly to his face and the front of his shirt. The violent whipping G-forces of the tumbling ship clouded his brain and threatened to black him out. He had been in tight situations before, but on those occasions it had always seemed that there was something he could do. Now he couldn't lift a finger if he wanted to. Between the embrace of the contour couch and the demonic acceleration of the cartwheeling drop ship, he was pinned in place. Even if he could move, there was still nothing he could do. If he released himself from the couch he would start to tumble around in the ship like a mouse in a spin dryer, and probably with about as much chance of survival.

Middenface stared at the holo screen, hoping to get some clue as to their fate, but the screen just offered a sickening, high speed spin of images. Ground, mountain, sky, distant desert, ground, mountain, sky.

It seemed that Johnny had got the same idea, and that he had a better plan for implementing it. "Compensate for spin," he yelled, and the screen responded. Clearly the control systems of the craft were still intact. Its onboard computers obediently compensated for the wheeling motion of the drop ship and the screen suddenly offered a constant view – of the rocky desert terrain rushing up to meet them, like a great red fist of rock.

Middenface braced himself for a cataclysmic terminal impact. The view on the screen was misleading. It offered an artificially stable view, as though they were sliding down a smooth slope towards the ground below, whereas of course they were still rotating on their remaining wing with maniacal speed.

It was the wing which hit first, snapping off as cleanly as its counterpart, and sending the surviving midsection of the drop ship catapulting towards the distant desert floor. Middenface watched with detached fascination as the screen showed their shadow growing on the ground as they fell towards it. The loss of the wing arrested their spin and the remains of the ship began a slowing roll as it descended.

It had almost stabilised by the time they hit.

The drop ship was state of the art. It might have lost a wing to an iron ball from an ancient cannon, but it knew how to deal with a crash landing. It had been built to survive just such a scenario. The onboard computers had begun to order litres of crash foam pumped up from the deep wells of the ship even before the second wing had broken off. With the final wing gone and the ultimate impact point of the craft becoming evident at last, the cushioning foam was forced into the jet nozzles distributed over the hull and was blasted out.

The foam hardened into a gelid mass as soon as it hit the air and, although it couldn't entirely negate the massive velocity the ship had picked up in the wild course of its terminal, plunging fall, it did manage to reduce it enough to keep the outer hull largely intact. Inside the ship, more foam was being sprayed, to seal any cracks and to cushion any spaces inside that might otherwise be vulnerable to collapse.

The passenger compartment, luckily, was not sprayed full of foam because its occupants might well have suffocated. Instead, the contour couches clung to them with a grip like a giant hand as the ship came to a standstill. Even when it stopped, Middenface's couch continued exerting such pressure on him that he found it hard to breathe and he felt like his ribs were going to start popping.

There was eerie silence in the passenger compartment, and complete darkness. At first, Middenface thought that the lights had failed, but then the bunched pressure in the muscles of his cheeks alerted him that his eyes were shut, squeezed tight shut since the moment of impact. He opened them and saw Ray and Bel, sitting opposite him, slowly emerging from their contour couches, twisting and rising and leaning forward at an odd angle.

"How did you manage that?" said Middenface. Ray and Bel stared up at him, puzzled. "Get out of your couches," he said. "How did you do it?"

"Just say 'release'," said Bel.

Her next words were drowned out by a thunderous noise from outside the drop ship. It sounded to Middenface like a building collapsing nearby, but there were no buildings nearby. The sound was followed by a shockwave that shook the earth and caused the ruined drop ship to tremble all around them. "Oh, Christ," said HMK. "What's happening now?"

"Shit," said Johnny Alpha, who had a pretty fair idea.

The posse emerged from the wreckage of their vessel one at a time, blinking in the bright daylight of Santo Segrelle. The drop ship had crashed tail first, collapsing and telescoping the rear of the hull, with the vessel's nose pointing upright towards the Sol-type sun glowing in the clear sky above. The ship's attitude meant that the access hatch was suspended about five metres above the ground and each of the survivors had to cling to the edge of the opening, lower themselves as much as they could in this fashion, and then let themselves drop the rest of the way to the ground. Only Stella Dysh had come to any harm, apparently twisting her ankle as a result of a clumsy landing.

As soon as it was clear that their party was complete and safe, Johnny went around the wreck of the drop ship and stood on the far side. Middenface and HMK followed him. He was staring off into the distance where about three kilometres of smoke was rising into the clear desert sky.

"What's that?" said HMK.

"That's what made the sound you heard a little while ago," said Johnny. "The sound of a spacecraft crashing."

HMK blanched. "You mean it's the other drop ship? The one with all our equipment on it?" Johnny said nothing. He just nodded.

HMK shook her head and gave an odd little animal snarl. "Well, isn't that just dandy?" she said. "It looks like we're just shit out of luck today, doesn't it?"

Middenface looked at Johnny. "Do you think any of our gear survived the crash?"

"There's one way to find out," said Johnny.

Johnny, Middenface and Hari Mata Karma left the others at the wreck of their drop ship and set off to investigate the other crash site. As they left, Stella Dysh was sitting in the shade of the wreckage, nursing an injured ankle, while Granny Haxer was industriously gathering fragments of wood from the surrounding area with a view to making a fire. "It may be hot now, but there's a definite tendency for it to get cold in the desert at night," she said. Slim Drago was giving her a hand with the larger pieces of wood, including entire tree trunks which he obediently dragged back to their improvised encampment. Meanwhile Bel and Ray had scrambled back into the ship through the open hatch, as nimble as monkeys, to see if there was anything that could be salvaged from the wreck.

It turned out that the other drop ship was farther away than it looked and it took Johnny and his party the best part of an hour to walk to the crash site. "If the damned thing was going to smash itself to pieces, why couldn't it at least do it more conveniently nearby?" said HMK.

"Just be glad it didn't land right on top of us," said Johnny.

"Good point," said HMK. "Looked at that way, I suppose one could regard it as luck."

"That's something we could do with a wee bit more of," said Middenface. "Good luck."

"Well here's another piece for you," said HMK. "Our weapons."

Middenface squinted at the smoking wreckage in the distance. "What about them?" he said. "They're probably all melted or crushed, or burned by now."

"She means the ones we concealed before takeoff," said Johnny.

"Oh those! I'd forgotten all about them." Middenface paused for a moment, crouching to feel inside his boot. The familiar cool shape of the T-rifle was still there. He smiled at the others. "Now, isn't that a comforting thought."

"If we hadn't brought those with us, we would be down here on a barren planet facing a well equipped hostile, totally unarmed," said HMK.

"It was a good idea bringing them," said Johnny, tapping the canteen strapped to his belt. The canteen made a muffled sound that indicated that it contained gun parts instead of water. Middenface squinted upwards for a moment at the unyielding glare of the sun in the sky, and wondered if there would come a time when they'd wish that Johnny had water in his canteen, instead of a handgun.

They reached the wreck of the second drop ship about ten minutes later, and it was even worse than they feared. The smoke, which had been pouring into the sky in an oily black column, was just about spent by the time they arrived. But it had only ceased because there was nothing left to burn.

The remains of the ship lay in a scorched and blackened crater in the sand. It was a twisted, carbonised mess that looked like an esoteric example of abstract sculpture. The heat from the fire that had consumed it was still so intense that they couldn't get very close. But they didn't need to. It was clear that the vessel was a complete write-off. "The fuel tanks must have blown," said Johnny.

"Makes you think how lucky we were," said Middenface. "Do you suppose there was any crew on board?"

Johnny shook his head. "Nope. Just the robot pilot."

"And all of our lovely equipment and supplies," said HMK.

They spent the next hour making a thorough search of the area, just in case anything useful had been thrown clear of the explosion. All they found was some smouldering seat padding and the mangled remains of what had once been a self-inflating pup tent. "That's a shame," said HMK, examining the half-melted mess. "I could do with a nice, self-inflating pup tent just about now." She spoke for all of them. They were feeling footsore and weary and by the time they got back to the first drop ship, with the swift desert night falling around them, Middenface was tired, dry-mouthed and hungry.

"Welcome back, intrepid travellers," said Granny Haxer. "We were waiting for your return before we did the honours."

"What honours?" said Middenface grumpily.

"Come and see," said Granny, grinning. She led them around the side of the ship, which provided the most shelter from the prevailing wind and there they saw a large mound of dried branches and dead wood. "Instant camp fire," said Granny. "We were just waiting until you got back before we lit it. I don't suppose any of you have got a light?"

The three shook their heads. Granny peered at them, bright-eyed. "That's funny," she said. "I could have sworn you had a lighter, HMK. Well never mind. A good, old fashioned kitchen match will do. Slim! Fetch the matches, there's a good boy." As Slim brought the matches, the other members of the posse drifted towards the pile of wood. They all looked as exhausted and bedraggled as Johnny's trio. Stella Dysh was still ostentatiously limping on her injured foot. Middenface wondered how badly damaged it really was, and resolved to keep an eye on her. If he caught her forgetting herself and favouring the wrong ankle, he'd give her a boot up the arse.

Granny Haxer took the waterproof aluminium box of matches that Slim brought her, extracted one and struck it on the abraded strip on the side of the box. The tiny flame flared in the gathering dusk and Granny cupped her hands around it to protect it, as if it was something precious. Middenface supposed that it was. She bent over the pile of wood, inserting the match at its base and silence fell over the small group. It was as though the Strontium Dogs had gathered together for a solemn ceremony, here in the desert night of this alien world. A moment later there was a crackling sound and big yellow flames began to lick upwards from the mound. The posse gathered around the expanding core of heat.

"Now if we just had something to cook on it," said Middenface.

"We do," cackled Granny.

"But I thought all our supplies were on the other ship."

"They were," said Granny. "But this boy here smuggled a bit of food on board our vessel with him." She slapped Slim Drago on his broad back. "Seems he's fond of his food, all right."

"Is that right, Slim?" said Middenface. "You brought some food with you?"

"Uh, yeah," said Slim. His big, bland face was flushed. "I guess I did smuggle some stuff on board. I'm sorry."

"Don't be sorry," said HMK. "We're delighted. What have you got? Some protein bars or something?"

"Uh, five steaks, some pork chops, some lamb chops, a dozen sausages, two hamburgers and two and a half roast chickens."

"What?" HMK whooped with delight. "Slim, you're a gem. Where did you hide all that?"

"I, uh, removed one of the cushions on my contour couch before take-off when nobody was looking and replaced it with a chiller chest. It was really cold to sit on."

Everybody burst into laughter. "Just two hamburgers?" said Middenface.

"I'm trying to give up the junk food," said Slim.

Slim Drago's cashe of smuggled food proved sufficient to feed the entire party – except perhaps Slim himself – to their wolfish satisfaction. "Seems like crashing in a spaceship gives a person a healthy appetite," said Granny Haxer, licking the grease from a pork chop off her fingers.

The flames of the campfire gradually subsided to a blue flicker above a bed of orange embers. The posse drew in close and disposed themselves on the ground around the fire, using spare clothes and seat covers from the drop ship as makeshift blankets. Johnny arranged a system of sentries, nominating various members of the posse to keep watch through the night while the others slept. Johnny took the first watch, Middenface the second. Hari Mata Karma relieved Middenface a few hours before dawn and he crawled gratefully under the covers of his improvised bedding and fell deeply asleep.

He awoke to Johnny roughly shaking his shoulder. The light of the desert dawn was creeping over the mountains in the distance, and the air was cold, clean and fragrant with the last lingering woodsmoke from the dying campfire. "What is it, Johnny?" said Middenface, blinking up at his friend.

"Trouble," said Johnny. HMK hurried over to join them. She had a worried expression on her face. Middenface found that he was suddenly fully awake.

"What's the matter?" he said.

"Someone took our weapons," whispered HMK.

"What?"

"My canteen's gone," said Johnny. "And somebody got her vibrosaw lighter. They took them while we were asleep."

"Well, I've still got my telescoping rifle," said Middenface, fumbling for the boots that he had carefully stashed under his covers while he slept. He pulled out one boot, then the other, shaking them, then peering inside them with increasing desperation. He looked up at HMK and Johnny. He didn't need to say anything.

"We don't have any weapons," said Johnny tersely.

"It's worse than that," said HMK. "We've got a traitor in our midst."

CHAPTER NINE
FLINT KNIVES

Charlie Yuletide stood beside the cactus where his horse was tethered. He was saddling up. He tied his banjo onto his bedroll then made some final checks to make sure that his saddle was tied on tight. He kneed the horse in the belly and the animal snorted and stirred. "Sorry boy," said Charlie. "But I know you horses have a trick of bloating out your bellies and then sucking them in after a saddle's been tied on. It makes it more comfortable for you, but it means a fella is likely to slip off his mount. Which is kinda embarrassing as well as painful."

He stroked the animal comfortingly on its side, then rolled up his sleeve and presented his bare wrist to the horse. "Go on boy, lick some salt off me."

The horse bent its big head down diffidently, and suddenly snapped its teeth down on the man's wrist. Charlie Yuletide shrieked and snatched his hand back. "That damn horse!" he yelled. "It *bit* me."

"A traitor," said Middenface. "Are you sure?"

He was speaking in a low voice, so none of the others could hear. Slim Drago had dragged in enough wood to renew the campfire and a cheerful efficient blaze was already flaring over the old ashes. Granny Haxer was busy frying up the sausages and the rest of the leftovers from the previous night's feast, using a reflector panel from the hull of the drop ship as an improvised frying pan. Ray, Bel and Stella Dysh sat on the ground nearby, watching alertly, like baby birds waiting to be fed.

Johnny, Middenface and HMK stood some distance away, in the lee of the wrecked drop ship, watching the breakfast preparations. "There isn't any other explanation," said HMK.

"She's right," said Johnny. "Somebody took our weapons last night, and it has to be one of us."

"Why couldn't it be Preacher Tarkettle?" said Middenface.

"What?" said HMK. "You mean he just slipped past the guard on duty and snuck into our camp like a stealthy, silent wraith and absconded with them while we slept?"

"Yes," said Middenface.

"Oh come on."

"You're the one who was saying we keep on underestimating the man," said Middenface. "Maybe we're still underestimating him."

HMK stared at him, then looked away and shrugged. "I still don't buy it."

"Neither do I," said Johnny. "If he could slip into our camp like that, why not just slit our throats while we slept?"

"Ughh," said HMK. She shook her head. "But even assuming you're right, which I don't concede for a moment, how did he know where our weapons were hidden?"

"They were all high-tech ordnance," said Johnny. "Even Middenface's rifle had a computer-assisted sighting mechanism."

"So what?" said HMK. "Oh, I see what you mean. Anybody with an energy emissions detector could have found the weapons, no matter how carefully we hid them."

"Right," said Johnny. "I'm beginning to wish we'd brought along something more low-tech. Like mechanical handguns. Or even knives."

"Or sharp rocks," said HMK sardonically.

"Plenty of those around," said Johnny, scanning the desolate desert landscape with his glittering eyes. He frowned. "You know, maybe that's not such a crazy idea after all."

"Is this the right kind of rock, Mr Alpha, sir?" said Slim Drago. His big fists were full of samples gathered off the desert floor near the wreck of the drop ship. Johnny paused in his labours and sorted through the pile of stones. Three he selected, the rest he discarded.

"What we're looking for are flints," said Johnny, patiently. He kept two of the stones he had selected and handed the third back to Slim. "Look for more like this one."

"Like that one. Sure. Thank you, Mr Alpha." The big man lumbered off.

"He's not quick, but he gets there in the end," said Middenface. He moved closer to Johnny to see what progress he'd made. "How's it going there?"

"Slow but sure," said Johnny.

"Slow but sure?" said a third voice. They turned to see HMK standing beside them. "I'd say *fast*, but sure. My God, I hardly turn my back for five minutes and I come back and find you've turned into an assembly line."

"Not quite," said Johnny. "But we're not doing badly." On the ground in front of him was a pile of thin stone fragments, each no larger than a thumbnail. These were the discarded fragments from his work. In his lap were the fruits of his labours: three flat grey pieces of stone, leaf-shaped, thick at the centre and thin at the tip and each about the size of a man's hand.

"May I?" HMK picked up one of the pieces of stone and tested its edge with her thumb. "Ye gods, that is sharp. You managed that just by knocking pieces off it with another stone?"

"It's how our ancestors made their weapons," said Johnny.

"God bless human ingenuity," said HMK. "How many have you made altogether?"

"Three so far, plus the pair Middenface is working on."

Middenface reddened and looked at the misshapen chunks of stone that sat heavily in his own lap. "Actually, Johnny, I'm not sure I've got the hang of it. Maybe you should take over before I ruin them."

"Here, let me have a go," said HMK, sinking to the ground beside them. She took the pieces of flint from Middenface and, under Johnny's supervision, began to chip away at them with a chunk of harder rock, gradually flaking off pieces until the flint began to take shape as a deadly weapon. She was soon working swiftly and expertly. "You know, this is quite good fun," she said.

"Just wait till the blisters start," said Middenface, inspecting his own red ruin of a hand.

"You'll never guess what I saw out there in the scrub vegetation a moment ago," said HMK. "I went out there to attend to, ahem, a call of nature. And you'll never guess what I saw. Ray and Bel. Also attending to a call of nature. But they were going *together*."

"Must be another consequence of that shared digestive system."

"I have only one thing to say about that," said HMK, "and once again that's *ughh*."

Two hours later, the desert sun was high and remorseless above them, blazing steadily down, and the entire posse had shifted into the shadow of the wrecked drop ship. The work on the flint weaponry was going surprisingly well.

Johnny was using one of the flint blades he'd fashioned earlier to smooth and thin some lengths of wood gathered by Middenface. When he was finished, they resembled rods. Once he finished each one, he passed it to Granny Haxer, who carefully split the end, inserted one of the flint blades and bound it in place with strips of leather cut from the furnishings of the drop ship. "What we really need is animal tendons," she said as she tightened the leather strips on one spear. "Kill an animal, pull the tendons out, and use them to tie the head to the spear."

"How are you going to kill an animal?" said Stella Dysh, recumbent in the shade of the drop ship.

"Why with this little beauty here," said Granny, hefting the spear and admiring it. It was an impressive piece of handiwork. "It'll do until we can improve on it."

"And what are we going to do once we have all our spears and our little flint knives?" said Stella. There was a note of sarcasm in her voice that set Middenface's teeth on edge. If the damned woman couldn't help, why didn't she at least shut up?

Johnny took the spear from Granny Haxer and added it to the two they'd fashioned earlier. They lay on the ground beside half a dozen finished hand blades. Johnny inspected the pile of weaponry with a faint smile. "What are we going to do?" he said. "Well, I've got a plan. It's not perfect, but it's a plan. We're going to do exactly what we came here for. To go after Preacher Tarkettle and bring him down."

"How are we supposed to find Tarkettle?" said Middenface.

"We go to that fort," said Johnny.

"You mean the fort we saw in the mountains? The one with the cannons?"

"Do you know any other fort?" said HMK.

"Anyhow, that's my plan," said Johnny.

"But that's going to be a couple of days' march," said Middenface. "Maybe three."

"That's what I reckon too," said Johnny.

"And even if we can salvage some water from the drop ship, we've only got enough for another day, or maybe two," said Middenface.

"That's what I meant about it not being perfect," said Johnny.

"Maybe we'll find water on the way," said HMK. "I mean, there was that humongous waterfall with a giant river attached to it."

"The river and the falls are on the far side of the mountain," said Middenface. "They'll take even longer to reach."

"But we might find some other source of water along the way," persisted HMK.

"We might," said Johnny. "Now, I suggest we don't spend any more time talking about things we can't predict. Everybody who doesn't have guard duty should turn in for the night."

Middenface bedded down on the ground between the camp fire and the drop ship. He deliberately chose a spot near where Hari Mata Karma was sleeping. Although he didn't actually admit it to himself, he liked the woman and he felt that if she was in close proximity during the long desert night, something might happen. Something that would result in the two of them slowly and innocently snuggling together for warmth, and then, innocently and drowsily shedding their clothing and...

A moist tongue crept over Middenface's chin and cheek with a silky motion. His confused mind surfaced from sleep, an astonished delight mingling with anxiety at the fact that dawn was already breaking over the desert – he could see the glow of daylight through his closed eyelids. It was wonderful that his dream was coming true, but HMK had left it rather late. It would soon be full daylight and Middenface didn't fancy pursuing their dalliance with others awake and able to see them. "Couldn't you have slipped over a bit sooner, darling?" he murmured.

"I would have," said Johnny Alpha, "but our friend here just arrived."

Middenface's eyes snapped open. He found himself staring into two enormous, dark brown eyes staring down at him along either side of a black and tan muzzle. A wide, pink tongue lolled out between large teeth and licked his face again. Middenface rolled back, suppressing a shriek. It took an instant for his mind to identify the monster that was licking him.

"A horse!" he said.

"And he seems to like you a lot," said Johnny, staring down at his friend with amusement. He had one hand on the horse's flank, stroking it as the animal whipped its tail gently back and forth, apparently utterly content with its new friends.

Middenface scrambled to his feet. "Where the hell did it come from?"

"The same place as the others, I guess," said Johnny, patting the horse.

"Others?" said Middenface. He stared around the encampment and saw that there was a group of horses clustered over by the rear of the wrecked drop ship, where Granny Haxer was feeding them something from the survival kits by hand. There was a mist covering the area up to about knee height and some of the horses were of a greyish colour that made them look like phantoms, as though they were fashioned of the mist itself.

"A total of eight altogether," said Johnny.

"Without riders?"

"Without riders or saddles, though they seem tame enough. They came wandering into camp in the middle of my watch. I guess they smelled the food or something."

Middenface heard hooves pounding across the earth and turned to see HMK galloping towards them from the misty distance of the desert, riding bareback on a magnificent, black animal. He backed hastily away as she steered the horse towards them, but HMK brought it to a halt, reining it in with a professional flourish. She grinned down at Middenface. "Not bad, eh?" she said.

"HMK has already been taking them for a test drive," said Johnny dryly.

"Where did you get that bridle?" said Middenface. He felt he had to say something.

"Granny Haxer improvised it from some strips of leather leftover from the spear-making," said HMK. She slid down off the horse, patting its sweaty, trembling flank. "Good boy," she murmured.

"Uh well, that Granny is certainly handy with her... hands," said Middenface, lamely. He was still having trouble adjusting to this situation, and it didn't help that he'd been thinking he had HMK nuzzling him when in fact it turned out to be a great, hairy beast.

"Give her a couple of hours and she'll have made bridles for the rest of them," said HMK happily.

"The rest of them?"

"Naturally. We can get by without saddles, providing we use blankets or something to cushion the ride for some of the candy-asses in the posse." HMK stared around the camp with a critical eye. Granny was still feeding the horses, but now Ray and Bel were helping her. Slim Drago was clumsily trying to stroke and pet the animals, who seemed to be suffering his attention with forbearance, but little enjoyment. Stella Dysh was sitting by the embers of the campfire eating breakfast, and completely ignoring the horses. "But we're all going to need bridles of some kind if we're going to ride them."

"Ride them where, exactly?" asked Middenface.

"To Tarkettle's fort," said Johnny.

"You're not proposing..."

"That's exactly what I'm proposing." Johnny nodded at the horse. "We'll be able to make good time riding these new friends of ours. A lot better than on foot. We might even be able to reach the fort fast enough so we don't have to worry about running out of water."

"Running out of water? Look, Johnny," said Middenface, "What do you think these beasts run on? They'll need water themselves, and quite a fair amount of it."

"I know it," said Johnny Alpha. "But they look pretty well watered now, and if we share our rations with them we ought to be able to make it."

"You're not serious about this?"

"Do you have a better plan?" said Johnny.

Middenface looked at HMK, hoping she might offer him some support against this hare-brained new scheme. But she merely slapped the black horse affectionately on the side and clambered back onto him. "Mount on up, cowboy," she said to Middenface, "and get those doggies rolling. In this case, Strontium Doggies." She giggled and coaxed the horse away in an accelerating canter, dust rising from its hooves as it left Middenface and Johnny standing.

Middenface turned helplessly to Johnny. "But these horses..."

"I know," said Johnny.

"They're well looked after and well watered – you said so yourself–"

"I know."

"And there's exactly eight of them. And exactly eight of us."

"Right."

"Don't you find that just a bit convenient, Johnny? Don't you find it a wee bit suspicious?"

Johnny looked at him. "I've thought all the same things myself and I've come to one conclusion..."

"Don't look a gift horse in the mouth?"

Johnny grinned. "I wouldn't put it quite like that."

"How would you put it, then?"

Johnny slapped Middenface on the shoulder. "Partner, we just don't have any choice." He turned towards the campfire, where Granny Haxer was now stirring the embers and adding kindling. Middenface hurried after him.

"But they could be booby-trapped, Johnny. They could have bombs inside them! Imagine that. Eight horses with bombs inside."

"That would make a hell of a mess all right," agreed Johnny. "What's for breakfast, Granny? We've got a long ride ahead of us."

The ride towards the mountain took the best part of the day. The posse made amazingly good time, considering that several of them had no previous experience on horseback. Both Johnny and Middenface were competent enough, HMK, of course, had demonstrated that she was something of an expert and Granny Haxer had done cavalry training in her days with the Colonial Marines. "Once you've learned to ride a horse you never forget," she said. "It's like riding a bicycle or making love."

"Two closely related pastimes," said HMK, bobbing along on horseback beside her.

Stella Dysh, too, proved to a surprisingly competent rider. "At last she's good for something," murmured Middenface, watching her trot along at the front of the group.

"Maybe the horses like the smell of her," said HMK. "All males seem to."

But Slim Drago was spectacularly incompetent on horseback, and both Ray and Bel were startlingly inept.

The root of the problem seemed to be their fear of the animals. It was a totally unjustified fear, since all eight of the horses were gentle, patient and co-operative with their clumsy novice riders.

"They're obviously accustomed to humans," said HMK.

"They're more than that," said Johnny. "They're telepathic."

"Telepathic? Really?" HMK chuckled. "Will they be able to tell me what playing card I'm thinking of?"

"I doubt it, since playing cards don't really exist in their frame of reference. But they will be able to understand the mindset of a novice or unfamiliar rider and compensate for their lack of knowledge." Johnny patted the mane of his own horse, a beautiful grey and white dappled mare.

Middenface's animal was equally handsome, with bold black and white markings, which somehow seemed naggingly familiar. He had the feeling, every time he looked down at his mount, that there was something he should be remembering, something of vital importance. But the memory always remained just out of reach of his conscious mind. It was certainly an unusual colour combination for a horse. It made the animal look almost like a zebra...

"Telepathic horses," said HMK. "You're making this up."

"Nope," said Johnny.

"Are they mutations?" said Middenface.

"Like us," laughed HMK.

"Maybe they started out like that. But now they're the results of deliberate breeding and they have been for generations. They're very interesting animals. They've been bred to exist symbiotically with humans. Unlike your ordinary horse, they actually want to be ridden and they seek out human beings."

"They certainly sought us out," said Middenface.

"How sweet," said HMK. She caressed the broad power-ful neck of her horse, stroking its gleaming black coat.

"They develop a kind of psychic rapport with their rid-ers," said Johnny. "Which is why even Slim Drago is managing to make some headway."

"You mean the horse is in charge, rather than the rider?" said Middenface.

"Something like that," said Johnny. "If the human can just manage to stay sitting on it the horse can sense the destination they have in mind and do the rest."

There was a cry of despair, followed by a loud dull thudding noise and a shriek of pain. Johnny and the others looked back to see Slim Drago lying on the ground, covered by a thin coating of dust, with his horse standing patiently beside him, nudging for him to get up.

"*If* the human can manage to stay sitting on it..." said HMK.

They arrived at the upward gradient that marked the beginning of the mountain slopes an hour before sun-set. The horses slowed down, picking their careful way among spills of fallen rocks and finding trails that would have been invisible to the humans even in full daylight.

By nightfall they reached the fort.

The stone face of the structure gleamed in the cold light of a rising moon. Johnny ordered the posse to dis-mount while they were still a kilometre and a half away. "We go the rest of the way on foot," he said.

"Why?" hissed Stella Dysh in a piercing whisper that was louder than most people's normal voice. "So we can have sore feet when Tarkettle kills us?"

"So he won't hear us coming," said Middenface. He didn't bother to try and disguise the impatience or hos-tility in his voice.

"What makes you think he won't have hypersensitive audio tracking, motion sensors and spy cams?"

"Because he hates modern technology, you great fool," said Middenface. He turned his back on her and went over to join Johnny, who was busy distributing flint knives and spears.

Middenface expected the doors of the fort to present difficulties. They were large, each one about two metres wide and six metres tall and had been fashioned from thick planks of some kind of tropical hardwood. Each one was equipped with a black lock and handle made from wrought iron.

But the doors opened at the first tentative push and, in a way, that was much worse than if they'd been sealed and bolted. "Somebody *wants* us to come in here, Johnny," said Middenface in a tense, low whisper.

"Everybody have your weapons handy," said Johnny, "and be ready for anything."

"That's useful advice," said Hari Mata Karma tartly. The little woman was obviously feeling the tension, thought Middenface. But who wasn't? He braced himself and shoved on the tall door. It swung fully open, but emitted a blood-chilling, grinding shriek as it gave way.

"Someone needs to oil them hinges," said Granny Haxer. Johnny was the first one through the doors, moving nimbly, spear held high and at the ready, with Middenface at his side. Behind them came Hari Mata Karma and Slim Drago, followed by Granny Haxer and Stella Dysh. Ray and Bel brought up the rear. They flitted silently into the courtyard beyond the tall doors, jagged shadows in the moonlight with ancient weapons at the ready.

The courtyard was about twenty metres square with a set of steps straight ahead, leading up to an arched doorway on the second floor. There were stone troughs on the left and the right of the courtyard, full of water that glinted in the moonlight. The high shadows of the fortress rose all around them, silent and menacing. Their feet struck on the cobbled square of the courtyard, the echoes rattling off the stone walls all around them.

"Middenface, HMK, come with me," said Johnny, moving towards the steps in the far wall. "Ray and Bel, check out the door to the right. Granny, Slim, take the one to the left. Stella, stay here. If anyone sees or hears anything, shout long and loud."

Stella took up a position in the middle of the courtyard square. The others melted silently into the shadows. Watching them disappear, Middenface was reminded forcefully that these were some of the finest bounty hunters in the galaxy. But would they be any match for Preacher Tarkettle if they found him? There was no time for doubts, though. Johnny was already jogging up the steps to the arched doorway, HMK close behind him. Middenface had no intention of being the last man through the door. He set off at a run.

The moon was setting the mountain range that flanked the fortress by the time they finished searching the place. Middenface and HMK stood behind the battlements at the top of the fort, among the antique cannons that had proved so lethally effective against their ships a few days earlier. There were seven cannons in all, with pyramids of steel cannon balls and barrels of gunpowder stacked between them.

But there was no sign of their prey anywhere. Preacher Tarkettle simply was not at home. As this finally became clear, Middenface had said to Johnny, "I guess he thought we were dead."

"Or he's out hunting for us."

Tarkettle may have been absent, but his fortress was fully equipped. The posse took advantage of this fabulous stroke of good luck to feed themselves on his fine foodstuffs – pork and beans and chilli con carne cooked by Granny Haxer on the cast iron stove in the damp basement kitchen – drink sourmash whiskey from his liquor cabinet and ransack his collection of vintage guns. The guns had been in a small underground armoury that was to the left of the courtyard, part of a cellar complex that had been built into what looked like a series of natural caves. The caves themselves had been adapted into an extensive powder magazine, equipped with enough dynamite and barrels of gunpowder to start a small war.

On the other side of the courtyard, a separate cellar complex contained the kitchen and a library, in which Johnny discovered a collection of maps, which charted the arid wastes of this desert world.

Now, well fed and fully armed, albeit still in a low-tech fashion, the posse was ready to confront the fiend who ruled this world. Hari Mata Karma and Middenface stood on the battlements, keeping watch.

"Maybe he knew we were coming and just took off," said HMK.

"Instead of staying and blowing us to pieces with his artillery?" Middenface sat down on the cold barrel of one of the cannons.

"There's no guarantee he would have succeeded," said HMK. "Maybe he realised that. We're a pretty mean team, you know. When he didn't manage to blast us out of existence on that first day, maybe he decided that discretion was the better part of valour and high-tailed it for the hills."

"Maybe," said Middenface. "Anyway, Johnny's getting ready for him in case he's only gone temporarily."

"That's right," said HMK with satisfaction. "If he comes back he'll have quite a surprise waiting for him." She lifted her rifle so it gleamed in the dying moonlight. The rifle was a vintage Remington No. 1 rolling-block, and it was just one of many vintage weapons they had found in an arsenal on the third floor of the main building of the fort. HMK had chosen the Remington and a bandolier of spare ammunition, which she now wore diagonally across her chest, draped from shoulder to waist, making her look like a diminutive, but dangerous brigand. For his part, Middenface had chosen a pair of chromed Colt six-guns, which provided a comforting symmetrical weight in the holsters on his hips. He had also chosen a large and vicious bowie knife that he wore in a sheath on his belt, for fighting at close quarters.

He had felt strangely sad, though, to set aside the flint daggers and spears they had so painstakingly constructed. It seemed a shame to discard them, never having used them.

"Yeah, we'll give Tarkettle a warm welcome all right," said HMK, working the action on her Remington with a well oiled click.

Middenface smiled and nodded, but said nothing. He moved away from the cannons and the battlements, back to the inner wall that overlooked the courtyard. He stared down at the horses in the moonlight. Once the fort had proved empty, Johnny had ordered them brought in for the night – or what was left of it. Granny Haxer and Slim had returned back down the path and found all eight animals placidly waiting. Now they were happily tethered by the troughs in the courtyard, thirstily drinking the cool, moonlit water.

As Middenface stared down at the horses in the moonlight, he felt oddly light-headed. He told himself it was just fatigue after the long day's ride and the thwarted anticipation of violent action. But he had never felt like this before. He gazed at his own horse amongst the others, busily drinking. In the fading moonlight it was utterly monochrome, a black and white beast, zebra striped.

Zebra striped.

Middenface felt something giving way in his mind. He closed his eyes and rocked back unsteadily on his feet. "Middenface. What's wrong?" said HMK, a note of fear in her voice. He tried to answer, but couldn't. His legs seemed to be made of springs instead of muscle and bone, and feeble, over-stretched springs at that. They gave way under him and suddenly he was tumbling to the cold stone pavement between the cannons. The world spun dizzily for a moment.

Middenface awoke to find someone wiping his face with a damp cloth. He looked up to see HMK and Johnny bending over him with identical expressions of puzzled concern on their faces. Johnny was wearing a pair of binoculars he had found in the room with the maps. They dangled on a strap around his neck. HMK was wielding a damp cloth, wiping it across his forehead. "I don't know what happened. He just went down," she said.

"Looks like he's back now," said Johnny.

Middenface stared up at his friends and, seeing them, he remembered everything. He remembered the black and white horse, and all the memories it had triggered. "It's a trap," he said, his voice hoarse and clumsy.

"What's a trap?" said Johnny.

"This place."

"The fort?" said HMK. "Of course it's a trap. And if Preacher Tarkettle returns we'll spring it on him."

"No," said Middenface. "It's a trap for us, and we've walked right into it."

CHAPTER TEN
AMBUSH

Charlie Yuletide walked alone through the desert night. His horse was nowhere in sight in the desolate, moonlit landscape.

On his wrist, where the horse had bitten him, Charlie wore a clean bandage. He was carrying his banjo and as he walked he played it, strumming awkwardly with his injured hand. His voice, though, was clear and steady as he sang.

"Watch out, Johnny, Tarkettle's coming. Somewhere in the night, hooves are drumming. The hammer of a gun, someone is thumbing. Watch out, Johnny, Tarkettle's coming."

The moon was slipping behind the distant range of jagged mountains. In the shadows of the fort's battlements, Middenface lay on the cold flagstones between the long iron bodies of the cannons. Johnny and HMK stared down at him. Johnny said, "You think this fort is a trap for us?"

"It's not just the fort," said Middenface, struggling to sit upright. As he did so, the blood rushed to his head. "It's this whole shite-heap of a planet."

Johnny and HMK exchanged a silent glance. Middenface felt anger flare in him. "I'm not mad or paranoid, or having a funny turn. Just listen to me."

"We're listening, partner," said Johnny, calmly.

"It's been bothering me ever since we visited the weapons shop," rasped Middenface. His voice was hoarse, his throat dry, but he didn't want to waste time asking for a drink of water. He felt a terrible urgency. He had to tell what he knew before it was too late.

"Since you got bashed on the noggin at the jewellery shop," said HMK.

"Yes," said Middenface. "I knew there was something I had to remember. I knew it was important, but I couldn't remember it no matter how hard I tried. Then suddenly just now, it all came back to me, and it was too much. I blacked out."

"Sounds like a psych truncheon," said HMK thoughtfully.

Johnny nodded. "She's right. If somebody hit you with one of those, it would set up a mental block in your brain that would prevent you remembering any of the events immediately preceding the attack. They'd be sealed away in your mind for weeks, or months."

HMK smiled at Middenface. "You've done well recovering so quickly, champ."

"It was the horse," said Middenface. "My horse. It's black and white, almost like a zebra."

"It's a genetically modified thoroughbred," said Johnny.

"But the thing is, it reminded me of what I saw just before I was coshed in the jewellers. I saw this woman. She had hair like that. Black and white. Zebra striped."

Johnny and HMK exchanged another silent, sceptical glance. "I'm not going nuts!" said Middenface. "Let me explain it. I saw this woman with the weird hair and she reminded me of someone, so I followed her into the jewellers, so I could get a good look at her. And I did. Just for a moment. Then somebody knocked me out, because they didn't want me to tell you what I'm telling you now."

"And what are you telling us?" said HMK gently.

"I'd seen that woman before. The woman with the striped hair. I'm sure of it. Exactly the same woman."

"Where did you see her?" said Johnny.

"In Asdoel Zo's mansion, that first day he invited us there for our job interview."

"So what?" said Johnny. "There were lots of women there. Asdoel Zo likes his women."

"No," said Middenface. "She wasn't one of the gardening girls. She was the woman in the hologram."

"In what hologram?"

"His wife," hissed Middenface. "It was Asdoel Zo's wife. The one who's supposed to be dead."

Johnny and HMK stared down at him in silence. The blood red light of the desert dawn began to spread across the cloud streaked sky. "Are the implications beginning to seep in?" said Middenface. "Do you see what this means?"

"And you're sure you're not mistaken?" said Johnny.

"I'm damned sure."

"But you only got a quick look at the hologram, and that was some time ago now."

"Johnny–"

"And it was a very odd hairstyle," said HMK gently. "Two quite different women with the same weird hair-do would tend to look alike. You'd notice the bizarre hair colouring rather than anything else about them, like their faces."

"It was the same woman," said Middenface stubbornly. "I know what I saw."

"And you said yourself you only got a glimpse of this woman in the jewellery shop before you were knocked unconscious."

"I'm sure about this!"

There was silence on the battlements again, except for the distant calling of a bird. A small winged shape swooped across the dawn sky and disappeared into the shadows of the desert below.

"Johnny," said HMK, "I think he's right."

Both Johnny and Middenface looked at her in surprise. "You said it yourself," she went on. "Middenface only got a glimpse of the woman before someone knocked him out. Maybe he got a look at something he wasn't meant to. Why else would anyone go to the trouble of hitting him with a psych truncheon and scrambling his memory?"

"If that's what happened," said Johnny.

"It is what happened!" snarled Middenface. He staggered to his feet, clinging to the iron mass of a cannon to maintain his balance, ignoring the attempts of the others to help him. He stared at Johnny. "You do see what this means?"

"If you're right..."

"Let's assume for a second I am right."

"I think he *is* right," said HMK.

"You do see what this means, don't you Johnny?"

"If Asdoel Zo's wife is still alive, then he was lying to us about Tarkettle murdering her."

"That's right."

"So, how much else was he lying to us about?" Johnny's eye blazed with disquieting anger.

"That's also right."

"It doesn't make any sense, though," said HMK. "Why would he go to all the trouble of hiring us and convincing us that his family had been killed?"

"One thing at a time," said Johnny.

"It all begins to fall into place," said Middenface. "All the strange events and coincidences. Like those eight horses just happening to turn up exactly when we needed them."

"And our drop ships taking us on a convenient course, right past these guns, so we could get blown out of the air."

"That's right," said Middenface. "Asdoel Zo is playing some kind of game with us. He can't be trusted. Maybe he's in league with Preacher Tarkettle. We must tell the others."

"I don't know," said HMK.

"A minute ago you said you believed me."

"I know, I know. But it all just seems like a lot to assume, based on one woman having the same hair colouring as another woman."

Middenface could feel his teeth clenching with frustration. "But you said yourself, they used the psych truncheon on me. Why else would they do that?"

"I don't know," said HMK, biting her lip. "It's one thing for us to discuss the notion up here, just the three of us. It's something else to go the others with it as if it's definitely the truth."

"We can't tell the others," said Johnny.

"Why the hell not?"

"Have you forgotten what happened to our weapons on that first night?"

Middenface stared at his friend. Johnny continued in a patient, measured voice. "There's a traitor among us, old friend."

"That's right," said HMK.

"If you're correct in everything you're assuming," said Johnny, "then Asdoel Zo is manipulating us for unknown reasons. And if there's a traitor in the posse, maybe they're working for Zo."

"You're right," said Middenface wearily. He leaned his weight on the cold iron of the cannon barrel. He still felt dizzy and disorientated.

"And if Zo's planted a stooge among us, we can't tell the others what we've discovered, because one of them *is* that stooge. And the only advantage we have at the moment is that they don't know how much we know."

"All right," muttered Middenface. "So we'll keep our mouths shut. But what are we going to do about it?"

Johnny opened his mouth to reply, but he was cut off by a cry from above them and to their left. At either end of the battlement chunky towers rose, square in section with observation posts on their roofs, equipped with antique telescopes. Johnny had posted Bel and Ray in one of these towers – he had tried to split them up and assign one to each tower, but the twins had refused to separate – and now they were calling out in excited voices, their words overlapping and blending.

"Look, Johnny!"

"Out there!"

Johnny and the others turned to the battlements and saw what Ray and Bel had spotted. A speck, approaching in the distance. Johnny took hold of the binoculars dangling around his neck and pressed them to his eyes. "What is it?" said Middenface and HMK simultaneously. Johnny didn't reply. He lowered the binoculars, then slipped them off his neck, passing them to Middenface.

It took a moment for Middenface's eyes to adjust to the primitive, twin lenses. At first, two images danced independently before his eyes, then they merged to reveal a surprisingly sharp view of a figure, about four kilometres away, heading in their direction.

It was a man, riding on a burro, small clouds of dust rising under the animal's feet as it picked its slow way up the mountain trail towards the fortress. "For God's sake, let me see," said HMK. Middenface passed the binoculars to her. He looked at Johnny as HMK peered eagerly through the glasses.

"Tarkettle?" said Middenface.

"Looks like it," said Johnny. "Let's see if we can arrange a little welcome home party for him."

Middenface whistled from the battlements when Tarkettle and his burro disappeared into the old river hollow, a few kilometres from the fort. Johnny sent the twins and HMK out the doors of the fort and followed them, checking out their positions among the rocks. "Where's Granny?" said HMK, setting her bandolier of ammunition on the sloping, inner face of the boulder where she crouched, in easy reach for reloading.

"Still stabling those precious horses of hers," grunted Johnny. He left her there and inspected the cluster of rocks Ray and Bel had chosen for their lair. It offered a field of fire, which covered the path and the entrance to the fort without compromising HMK's position. He tersely nodded his approval and left them there, checking their guns. HMK waved cheerfully to him as he headed back towards the doors of the fort and Johnny gestured savagely for her to get back into hiding behind the boulder.

He trotted back into the courtyard, his boots echoing urgently on the rough flagstones in the pregnant stillness. Slim and Stella watched him from either side of the doorway, stationed behind barrels of grain, which they had found in the kitchen and which Slim had laboriously hauled up the stairs. The troughs had proved to be too far from the doors to offer both protective cover and a clear shot at Tarkettle the instant he stepped inside. But the barrels were perfect.

There were swift tripping footsteps from the doorway to his right and Granny Haxer emerged from the shadowed corridor that led to the stables. Her face was gleaming with sweat. She hurried to join Johnny. "Sorry I'm late, boss man. Those damned horses just wouldn't co-operate."

"Forget it. Take up your position outside. Make sure you leave a clean field of fire for the twins and HMK." Johnny hesitated. "On second thoughts, I'd better go with you. They're so well hidden, you probably won't be able to see them. And I've given them orders to keep their heads down until Tarkettle's safely past."

Granny Haxer paused to scoop up her weapon – an impressive silver-filigreed, double-barrelled shotgun that was almost as long as she was tall – and a hat full of shot-gun shells, which she had left beside one of the troughs. Then she trotted towards the tall doors of the fort with Johnny at her side. "I know you're pissed off at me about stabling the horses, son. But I just couldn't bear the thought of them poor innocent beasts taking a stray round."

"Don't worry about it. It's a good idea having them out of the way. They might have made a noise, or Tarkettle's burro might have smelled them. Or they could have got in the way when the shooting started. It was a smart move putting them in the stables."

Granny Haxer grinned as she trotted along at Johnny's side, heading for the doors of the fort. "You're just being kind to an old lady. But I appreciate it. I'm just sorry those damned, fleabitten nags took longer to get bedded down than I expected and–"

There was a low, urgent whistle from the battlements above. Johnny immediately stopped and stood still. "What was that?" said Granny.

"Middenface. Tarkettle's coming out of the dry river basin now. He'll be able to see us in a few seconds." As he spoke, Johnny hurried to the big doors and swung them shut. He looked at Granny Haxer. "It's too late for you to take up your position. You'll have to stay inside."

"Shitfire!" said Granny Haxer, a savage grimace of disappointment on her wizened face. "Those damned horses."

"You stick with me now. We'll wait on the steps overlooking the courtyard."

"But I've got this double-barrelled fowling piece," said Granny. "It's no good at that kind of distance. It just doesn't have the reach."

"You'll have to forget about it, then."

"Let me go back to the arsenal. That fella's got all kinds of guns in there."

"Too late, Granny. Here, take this." Johnny gave her the six gun that he was wearing in a holster strapped to his hip, a Colt Army .45. That left him with the rolling block Remington sporting rifle he had slung over his shoulder, a double for the one HMK had chosen. She had opted for a ladylike .22 calibre model, whereas Johnny had gone for the .58 calibre, the most massive configuration the weapon came in.

"Are you sure?" said Granny Haxer, taking the Colt revolver and studying it.

"Just don't shoot me with it." Johnny turned and loped back across the courtyard, to the far wall and the steps leading up it. Granny jogged behind him, hurrying to catch up.

Middenface had turned to the wall overlooking the courtyard when he had whistled the second signal, so he had seen the business with Johnny and Granny Haxer. He cursed the old woman for being so slow and spoiling Johnny's plan, which had called for her to be with the ambush party outside. Who knew what complications would ensue from being short-handed in the rocks outside the fort? And he had cursed her doubly when he saw Johnny hand the old crone his sidearm. So what if the stupid old biddy had chosen a useless weapon of her own? It had been her choice. Let her live with it. But, no, that wasn't Johnny's way.

So now they were launching the ambush with an inadequate complement of men outside the fort and with Johnny short of a gun inside. Plans had gone bloodily wrong as the result of smaller changes than that. Middenface kept cursing as he turned back to the outer wall of the battlements and lifted his binoculars again, careful to shadow both lenses with the palms of his hands as Johnny had suggested, to prevent Tarkettle seeing the tell tale gleam of reflection.

The man on the burro leapt into view again, startlingly close now. For the first time, Middenface could get a really good look at him.

Preacher Tarkettle was a small man wearing a black frock coat, buttoned tight against the cold of the desert morning, with black and white checked trousers and pointy black shoes with big, silver buckles on them. Middenface couldn't see a gun on him, but there might well be one, or more, under that frock coat. On the back of the burro, behind his saddle, there was a cylindrical bundle with a tartan green and blue blanket on the outside, secured with knotted lengths of yellow rope. There could well be a rifle in that bundle.

If there was, it wouldn't be easy to get it out and ready in a hurry, any more than it would be to draw a handgun from under that tightly buttoned black coat. But Middenface had no intention of letting himself be drawn into a false sense of security. They'd already seen how deadly effective this man could be. Even if he rode into the fort stark naked with a flower between his teeth, Middenface intended to keep a gun on him every step of the way.

The burro made its slow way up the rubble-strewn path towards the fort, seeming to chose each step with deliberation. Sitting, rocking on its back in a relaxed posture, Tarkettle seemed to be in no particular hurry. Middenface could clearly make out the man's features now. He remembered the first time he'd seen him, on the screen in Asdoel Zo's study.

Middenface felt a cold flutter of disquiet. Preacher Tarkettle's sharp-featured face was like that of an oily rodent, chinless with a long pointed nose. The thick, sensual red lips that Middenface remembered were parted and pursed as if the man was whistling as he rode along on his burro in the desert morning. His tousled, greasy hair fluttered in the breeze, stirring in disarray over his tiny ears. He was

wearing the same misshapen black felt stovepipe hat that
Middenface remembered. And it might well have been the
same frayed and stained white shirt with a pearl pin
across the collar, and the same narrow, black tie.

The narrow eyes flicked upwards and for a moment
seemed to be staring right into Middenface's eyes, boring
inexorably into his skull, his brain, his soul, reading all his
secrets. Middenface backed away from the almost physical impact of that gaze. Was it possible that Tarkettle had
seen him, crouched here over the battlements, binoculars
in his hands? Middenface forced himself to remain calm
and stay motionless. The only way that Tarkettle was
likely to see him was if he was foolish enough to make a
sudden move, and allow the sun to flicker across the
lenses of his binoculars.

Tarkettle glanced down again, and Middenface sighed
with relief at no longer having that dark gaze drilling into
his own. The black felt of the man's hat filled the binoculars and Middenface lowered them to get an estimate of
how close he actually was. He was startled to see that the
burro was already wending its way up the last curve of the
primitive path that led up to the fort. Tarkettle seemed
cheerfully unaware of the fact that he was riding into a
trap. Middenface saw a faint stir of motion in the rocks to
Tarkettle's right and he held his breath. HMK was rising
up behind a boulder, Remington in her hands. Middenface cursed and tried to focus his willpower on the little
woman, as if he could command her to remain still and
out of sight.

But HMK was still sheltered by the bulk of the boulder,
and Tarkettle showed no inclination to look in her
direction anyway. He just sat, casually rocking on the
back of the burro, loosely clutching its reins as the beast
ambled up the rocky path. He was approaching the mass
of rocks on his left where the twins Ray and Bel were

waiting. Middenface murmured another blend of curses and prayers, hoping that the symbiotic siblings would stay put. From his vantage point on the battlements, he could see them kneeling in a hollow amongst the big rocks, eyes fixed on the man on the burro. But they didn't stir from their hiding place. "Good kids," whispered Middenface.

Now Tarkettle was almost at the wall of the fort itself. He rode up the path into the shadow of the building and disappeared from sight below. The only way Middenface would be able to see him was by leaning out from the battlements at a dangerously visible angle. So instead he drew back out of sight, listening carefully. He heard the burro's hooves on the rocky path, slowing to a halt. Then he heard the man twisting on the saddle, freeing himself from it and jumping to the ground, landing with a little gasp of exhalation. His footsteps rattled on the path as he approached the doors of the fort. There was a moment's silence, during which Middenface held his breath. Had Tarkettle spotted something? Had he sensed that he was being watched?

Then Middenface heard the unearthly metallic shriek of the rusty hinges as the big doors were pushed open, and he knew everything was all right. He turned and scuttled back across the battlements, keeping low, heading for the inner wall. He peered over into the courtyard, no longer worrying about being seen. Tarkettle was riding into the jaws of their trap now. There was another pause that seemed to last for an instalment of eternity as Tarkettle apparently climbed back onto his burro to ride it into the fort. Why was the man riding it in? He'd already got off the bloody beast. Why didn't he just lead it in on foot? Middenface cursed. Who knew what the fiend had in mind? Maybe he knew an ambush was waiting for him and being saddled on his animal was part of a master plan for defeating the Strontium Dogs.

A cold shiver of apprehension tickled Middenface under his breast bone. He leaned out over the courtyard and felt sweat gathering on his chin. Tarkettle rode into the fort, his burro's hooves clipping the flagstones. Middenface could see the top of Tarkettle's black hat passing below, nodding gently with the swaying motion of the rider as he entered the courtyard. Middenface saw Stella Dysh and Slim Drago crouching behind their barrels in the shadows on either side of the open doors. He glanced at the far end of the courtyard and saw Johnny Alpha step out of the arched doorway at the top of the stone steps, Remington rifle held in his hands, Granny Haxer following him with the revolver pointed.

Middenface didn't wait to see any more. He turned and ran to the steps leading down to the courtyard. Despite what Johnny had said about his staying up here, he had no intention of missing the fun. He hit the steps at a dead run and was down them in a few bone-jolting leaps. He followed the stone spiral to the right, raced through the doorway and out into the sudden sunlight of the court-yard just as Johnny yelled, "Hold it! Put your hands up!"

Middenface saw the expression of astonishment on Tar-kettle's face as he looked up and saw Johnny Alpha and Granny Haxer facing him at the far end of the courtyard. "Get down off that animal!" barked Johnny. Tarkettle hes-itated and Johnny yelled "Now!" with such force that the man automatically obeyed. He swung down from his burro, which was stirring restlessly, spooked by the sud-den appearance of strangers. Johnny trotted down the stairs, Remington held high, pointed dead at Tarkettle's chest. Granny Haxer scampered after him. Tarkettle stared at them. Then Stella Dysh and Slim rose up from behind their barrels, and Middenface ran out into the courtyard.

Preacher Tarkettle looked wildly around at the three newcomers, all with guns pointing at him, and he gave a little wordless moan. The crotch of his black and white checked trousers darkened and a puddle of urine began to gather at his feet.

The kitchen of the fort was a cool, underground room with the a smell of damp earth. Preacher Tarkettle sat on a chair in the middle of the stone floor with his hands tied behind his back and his feet tied to the two front legs of the chair, his legs spread open and the shaming stain on his crotch was plainly revealed. Middenface cringed a little every time he looked at it.

Slim Drago had been left on guard outside, although with Tarkettle captive it was a moot point who was left to be on guard against. Nonetheless, Johnny had insisted on the arrangement. The other seven members of the posse were in the kitchen. Six of them were arrayed around the room, some standing and some sitting, but every one pointing a weapon at the little man in the chair. Only Granny Haxer had her back to him. She was busy at the old black iron stove, preparing a pot of coffee. "No reason we can't be comfortable and have some nice hot Java during the interrogation," she opined.

"Interrogation," quavered the little man in the chair. "Why do you want to interrogate me?"

"We'll ask the questions," snapped Stella Dysh.

Johnny corrected her. "I'll ask the questions." He took a chair, reversed it, and sat facing Tarkettle, his powerful arms folded across the wooden back of the chair, his face expressionless.

"You don't need to interrogate me," said Tarkettle desperately. "I've already told you everything. I am indeed Tarkettle. Hieronymous John Tarkettle, called Preacher by some because of my academic lecturing style. But I had nothing to do with the destruction of your ships."

"It was the cannons on this fort that shot them down," said Middenface. "We saw them."

"Perhaps so, sir. I mean no doubt, if you say so, sir. But when was this?"

"About four days ago," said Middenface.

"Then I couldn't have had anything to do with that tragic occurrence. I've been away from this fort for the best part of a week."

"Doing what?" said Johnny.

"Surveying. You may have seen the maps of this planet in my library."

"We saw some maps."

"Then you'll know what I was doing. It's my job. Or rather my hobby, while I'm doing my official job."

"And what exactly is your official job?"

"Caretaker of this planet."

"I don't believe you," said Johnny.

"Well, no, not just a caretaker. That's not entirely correct. I'm sort of a combination caretaker, librarian, custodian and planner."

"Planner?"

"Yes, my employer wants me to study this world and plan how it could be used to enact a series of scenarios."

"Scenarios?"

"Scenarios evoking the old west, sir."

"You mean scenarios like blowing us up and shooting us one by one."

"No! Nothing like that. Educational vignettes that will capture the vibrant, lusty charm of the frontier days of the American west. Offering painless and colourful history lessons set in the grandeur of the desert wilderness of this world."

"A likely story," cackled Granny Haxer. She spat on the hot surface of the stove and listened to the spittle hiss. Nodding with satisfaction, she set the coffee pot onto the searing metal. "Be ready soon. Do you want me to pour a cup for the prisoner, Johnny?"

"Please," said Tarkettle. "Why am I your prisoner? I don't understand it. I don't understand any of this. You say that you're a posse..."

"What do we look like, sonny?" said Granny Haxer, fetching a rattling assortment of tin cups from one of the cupboards fixed to the white-washed stone walls. "We're the most dreaded, cold-blooded, sharp-shooting bounty hunters in this part of the spiral arm."

"Yes, yes, you certainly look the part. I just don't understand why anyone would want to send such a distinguished delegation after me."

"Because you murdered his family," said Johnny, glancing over at Middenface as he spoke. "You murdered a man's children and his wife."

"That's preposterous. I'm an academic. I've published numerous papers and several highly regarded books."

"That's why you've got such a well equipped arsenal," said Johnny, lifting the Remington from his lap and pressing the barrel gently against Tarkettle's forehead. The man squeezed his eyes shut and began to weep.

"Not to mention fully functional cannons up there on your battlements, with plenty of powder and shot," said Middenface.

"And a healthy stash of dynamite, too," added Hari Mata Karma. "In fact, there's an entire cave system under this place that's just packed with gunpowder and explosives."

"That's the replica powder magazine," said Tarkettle desperately. "It's just for show."

"Sounds pretty damn lethal just for show," said Johnny. But he lowered the gun from the man's forehead and returned it to his lap.

"My employer insisted on installing it," said Tarkettle, his voice trembling and frail. "That is the raison d'être of this world. A well-stocked, authentic recreation of the old west. Like a living museum."

"Well, there's going to be one fewer living exhibit in this museum if we don't believe your answers," said Johnny, casually studying his Remington.

"Please. What can I do to make you believe me?"

"You can look me in the eyes," said Johnny. And he raised his eerie pale gaze towards Tarkettle. The little man blinked nervously, but gradually lifted his own moist eyes to look into the mutant's.

"Tell me the name of your employer," said Johnny.

"He's called Asdoel Zo. He's a wealthy man with an educated interest in the old west. An interest that I share. You might say he is a patron of the arts, or rather a patron of the study of history."

"And you killed his wife and children," said Johnny, his gaze relentlessly fixed on the other man's eyes.

"No! I've never met his family. I've never even met him. All our communications have been via computer. He advertised for an academic with an interest in this period of American history, and I applied for the job and I was accepted. My salary is paid directly into my bank account. I've never met the man. Please believe me."

Johnny stared silently at the man for a moment longer. Then he rose abruptly from his chair, turning away from Tarkettle. "I do believe you," he said.

"You can't be serious," snarled HMK.

"He's obviously lying!" said Stella Dysh.

"Johnny's generally right about these things," said Middenface, mildly. "He can look into a man and see the truth."

"Mystical bullshit," said Stella Dysh.

"For once I'm inclined to agree with our smelly friend," said HMK.

Granny Haxer bustled over to the stove with a stack of tin cups and started pouring coffee from the bubbling pot. "I reckon you should listen to Johnny," she said. "After all, he's the man in charge here."

"In charge of getting us killed by the sound of it. This murderous Tarkettle spouts some lies to us and Johnny Alpha just rolls over and believes him." HMK looked around at the others for support. Stella Dysh nodded vigorously, but Ray and Bel refused to meet her gaze. HMK turned to Middenface.

"I'm with Johnny," he said.

"If Johnny is so damned good at looking into the souls of men," sneered HMK, "why didn't he see that Asdoel Zo was lying to us all along, since that's what he's claiming?"

"All I got from Zo when I checked him out was a deep sense of pain and loss," said Johnny. "Just like you'd find in a man who really had lost his wife and kids. The emotion was so intense that it blotted everything else out."

"Highly convenient. So what are you suggesting? That Mr Zo had these emotions hypnotically implanted specifically to baffle your ability to read people?"

"I'm not suggesting anything," said Johnny harshly. "For all we know, Asdoel Zo may have nothing to do with any conspiracy against us."

"But you heard what this Tarkettle said! He didn't harm a hair on the head of any member of Zo's family. And you believe him."

"He also said he'd never met the man," said Johnny. "And I believed him when he said that, too."

Granny Haxer moved around the room, offering cups of steaming coffee. She held one out to HMK, who shook her head impatiently and turned away, to look at Johnny. "So what are you saying? That there are two Asdoel Zos? The real one and an impostor?"

"Maybe," said Johnny, accepting a cup of coffee. "Thanks, Granny."

"Mind, it's hot. And those tin cups do radiate the heat. Don't scald yourself, son. Should I pour one for our prisoner here?"

"You'd better untie him first," said Johnny. He looked at Ray and Bel. "Keep your guns on him, just in case. If he looks like he's going to throw that coffee at someone instead of drinking it, drill him without hesitation."

"I don't mind if I don't have any coffee," said Tarkettle. "Just please don't drill me."

Middenface drew the large, glinting bowie knife from the sheath in his belt and walked over towards Tarkettle. The little man gave a squeak of pure terror. "Oh, for heaven's sake man, isn't it obvious I'm going to cut your bonds with this thing? Really." Middenface muttered in disgust as he sliced the ropes that held the man's hands and feet fastened to the chair. "Anyway, it's your own bloody knife. From your own bloody collection." The ropes dropped away from Tarkettle and Middenface stepped back, half expecting him to spring into action in a desperate attempt to slay his captors.

But the little man just sat there, trembling and looking more like a rodent than ever. Granny Haxer handed him a cup of coffee. "Here, this will put lead in your pencil," she said. Tarkettle accepted the cup with shaking hands. He sipped at it gratefully, but the tremor in his hands was so bad that he spilled as much as he drank.

"And when he's finished that, let him change his pants," said Middenface. "The poor bugger's as wet as a baby."

Johnny shrugged. "All right. So long as the twins follow him everywhere he goes. And if he picks up a gun instead of some clean trousers..."

"We know," said Ray.

"Drill him," said Bel.

"Please don't drill me," said Tarkettle. "I don't mind staying in wet pants."

"Well I mind," said Middenface. "Just the thought of it is making me uncomfortable."

Suddenly there was the sound of footsteps on the staircase leading down into the kitchen, heavy, frantic, lumbering footsteps. Slim Drago burst into the room, his face pale. "Johnny," he gasped. "There's a big spaceship. And it's landing outside."

CHAPTER ELEVEN
MOONLIGHT MEETING

Morning sunlight fell on the desert. Charlie Yuletide was standing in the foothills of a majestic mountain range with a huge waterfall tumbling into a curtain of gleaming mist in the background. Charlie's hand was still bandaged, but now the horse was back with him, tied to a scrubby tree nearby. Charlie was also holding his banjo, but he wasn't playing the instrument and his face had a set, stubborn expression on it.

"I'm not doing it," he said. "I'm not working with that horse again. The damned thing bit me. The next time it might take my whole, damned hand off."

He appeared to be talking to himself. Suddenly there was a shimmer in the air and holograms of two teenage girls appeared – a pair of sun-tanned, lithe redheads.

"Daddy says you have to," said the older girl.

Charlie Yuletide shook his head. "I refuse."

"Daddy says you have to appear with the horse or you won't get paid."

"This is outrageous," said Charlie Yuletide.

"The horse is a deal breaker," said the older girl. The hologram flickered and she disappeared. The younger girl remained for a moment longer.

"The horse won't bite you again," she said. "So long as you don't do anything stupid, like sticking your hand in his mouth."

"Stupid?" Charlie Yuletide's voice went up an octave. "Horses love to lick the salt off your wrist. It was a genuine piece of authentic western lore!"

"Just don't stick your hand in his mouth any more and you'll be fine," said the girl. "I have to go now. Daddy wants to take us to visit some stupid fort."

Then she, too, disappeared, and Charlie Yuletide was left alone with the horse.

Slim Drago was right. There was a spaceship, it was big, and it was landing outside the fort. The Strontium Dogs gathered on the battlements of the fort, interspersed between the cannons, watching the craft descend. Preacher Tarkettle, wearing a fresh pair of trousers and a rope around his wrists stood with them. Granny Haxer held a gun at his back. A powerful hot wind blew in their faces, blasting from the underside of the ship onto the rocky desert slope below the fort. It carried a smell of hot metal and ozone with it. The ship was a pale blue vessel consisting of a heart-shaped central section, with sweeping twin fins at the rear.

"It looks kind of familiar," said Slim Drago, who seemed to be taking a proprietary pride in the space ship, having been the first to spot it.

"That's because it's the shuttle from the *Charles Neider*, you great oaf," said HMK.

The ship settled over the dry river basin a few hundred metres down the hill from the fort. The basin provided a patch of level ground just large enough for the shuttle to use as a landing site. As soon as the ship had eased to the ground, its pointed nose split open and a small hover platform came shooting out, heading straight for the fort at high speed. The Strontium Dogs jerked their guns hastily up and took aim – except for HMK and Johnny.

"Don't waste your ammunition," said Johnny. "The dome over that platform is bullet-proof." Standing under the transparent dome on the hover platform were three people: Asdoel Zo and his two gold-skinned, copper-haired daughters.

"They're not dead, then," said Middenface. "I wonder where his wife is?"

The platform flickered swiftly over the steep broken ground at a height of about twenty metres, banked swiftly and rose up to hover on the same level as the battlements, just on the far side of the wall. Middenface reflected that Asdoel Zo was close enough to hit with a rock if he wanted to throw one at the billionaire. Not that there was much point in trying that. As Johnny had noted, a shatterproof dome enclosed the man and his daughters.

"Good morning," called Asdoel Zo affably, his voice amplified by a speaker on the platform. "How are you all enjoying the desert air?"

"There's a burro down there in the courtyard," replied Granny Haxer. "Why don't you go and have sex with it?"

Asdoel Zo chuckled. "Now really, Granny, is that any way to talk to a man in front of his children?"

"I said 'have sex' didn't I?" said Granny. "I coulda been a lot blunter in my vocabulary."

Asdoel Zo smiled and shrugged. "In any case, I take it from your suggestion, and from the fact that you've got our friend Tarkettle with you, that you've worked out the true nature of my little game."

"I wouldn't say that," said Johnny, his voice dangerously calm. "We know that you lied to us and that you brought us here under false pretences. We also know that you blew our drop ship out of the sky and left us to die in the desert."

"Come now, Johnny. You're being far too melodramatic. I didn't blow you out of the sky personally. I sent down a specialist crew of technicians from the *Charles Neider* to do that. I flew them back up afterwards and, incidentally, gave them a slap-up dinner in return for a job well done. As for leaving you to die in the desert, I knew that you'd survive the crash. Those drop ships are sturdy and well built."

"That's good to know," said Johnny.

"And who do you think sent those horses for you?"

"We worked that out. We just haven't worked out why."

Asdoel Zo leaned forward on the rail of the hover platform. He looked tanned and relaxed, like a man on a
pleasure cruise. "Tell you what, Johnny, why don't you
and I have a little chat in private? I'll take this platform
down into the courtyard." Without waiting for a reply, he
adjusted some controls and sent the platform sailing up
over the battlements, dropping steeply to descend into the
courtyard of the fort.

Johnny turned to the others. "You aren't going to nego-
tiate with that bastard are you, Johnny?" said Middenface.

"That's one of the things I'm going to do," said Johnny.
"But there's something else I want to do, too." And he
issued a terse series of instructions to the other Strontium
Dogs before he turned and strode down the stairs to the
courtyard.

Asdoel Zo looked up as Johnny approached. He remained
standing on the platform, which was now sitting in the
middle of the stone courtyard between the two troughs.
The two teenage girls beside him looked bored, but Zo
seemed to be having the time of his life. "I expect you
want me to tell you what this is all about?" he said.

"I don't care what it's all about," said Johnny. "I already
know enough to know that I don't want any part of it."

"Johnny, how can you say that?"

"We've been playing your game since the day you hired
us, but that's all over now."

"Listen, friend. I'm paying your fee and you'll do as
you're told."

"I'm not your friend," said Johnny in a dangerous voice.
"And I dropped off your payroll as soon as I learned that
you'd been lying to us. And so did every other Dog in the
posse."

"You really think you speak for all of your colleagues, Johnny?"

"I know that I do. You're not pulling our strings any more."

Asdoel Zo smiled. "Are you sure about that? You do realise that the weapons system on my shuttle is targeted on this fort right now?"

"I'm not that easily intimidated, Mr Zo," said Johnny.

"I should hope not, considering the money I've been paying you."

Johnny's eyes flashed and a note of impatience entered his voice. "I suggest you go back on that shuttle right now and take your daughters with you, before things get nasty."

"Very well. We wouldn't want things to get nasty. Hold on Lorna, hold on Jodi." Asdoel Zo pressed some buttons and the platform shot straight up vertically then streaked away over the battlements, back towards the shuttle. Johnny turned and ran back towards the steps. Just as he reached them, Granny Haxer, Preacher Tarkettle, Stella Dysh and the twins came hurrying down.

"It's all set," said Granny Haxer. "Just like you said, Johnny."

"Good. You'd better take cover in one of the underground rooms. I'd advise the kitchen. You want to be as far from the powder magazine as possible. Just in case things go bad."

Granny nodded and led the others away, while Johnny set off up the stairs at a run. When he reached the battlements he found Middenface, Slim Drago and Hari Mata Karma waiting for him. "Are you ready?" he asked.

"We only managed to get four cannons loaded," said HMK. "Then we saw that platform flying back and we knew we'd run out of time."

"Four should be enough," said Johnny. "Are you sure you aimed them properly?"

"HMK was in charge," said Middenface. "She seemed to know what she was doing."

"Let's find out." Johnny took out a pack of matches and handed them around to the others. "Right. Let's give our former employer something to think about. We'll blast the engines off that vessel, so it won't be going anywhere without some major repairs."

He stepped up to the front wall of the battlements. Four of the seven cannons had been loaded with powder and shot, and trained on the shuttle sitting on the slope below. Johnny struck his match on the rough iron of the gun and watched it flare into flame. Standing beside him, Slim, HMK and Middenface did the same. Johnny put the burning match to the fuse that jutted from the rear of the cannon. The other three followed suit. Four short fuses began to fizzle.

Johnny just had time to say "Cover your ears," and to notice a flicker of movement at the edge of his vision before the fuses sizzled down into the cannons and hit the charges inside. Then there was a split second pause, followed by an explosion that tore the world apart.

Johnny emerged from a red-hot haze. He blinked his eyes, trying to see. There was something all over his face, a thick, sticky liquid. He tried to reach his hands up and feel what it was, but his hands wouldn't move. Instead he licked his lips, and tasted the salty flavour of his own blood.

"The cannons blew up," said a voice to his left. It was a familiar voice, but for a moment Johnny's dazed mind failed to identify it. He looked over and saw that it was Middenface. Middenface was kneeling on the flagstones of the courtyard, with his arms behind him. He looked in a bad way. There was a gash in his misshapen skull and he had blood all over his face. Johnny imagined that he looked much the same himself. More worrying was the fact that Middenface had chains on his arms and legs. As Johnny tried to move again he discovered that there was a set of chains on him, too.

"I hope HMK is all right," said a voice to his left. Johnny glanced over in that direction and saw that Slim Drago was kneeling there, also in chains. "I can't see her anywhere."

"The reason that you can't see her is that she wasn't blown up and taken prisoner," said Middenface in a sour voice. "She scarpered just before the cannons exploded in our faces." His words brought a fragment of memory back to Johnny. A glimpse of HMK running from the battlements just as the fuses burned down to the critical point...

"You mean she managed to escape?" said Slim happily. "That's good."

"No, it's not good, you great lummox," snapped Middenface. "The reason she managed to escape is because she knew the cannons were going to blow up in our faces. And the reason she knew that was because she sabotaged them. She did it right in front of me. I was a damned fool." Middenface looked over at Johnny. "She said she was adding an extra charge to the cannons and because she seemed to know about the things, I believed her. What a damned fool. What she was really doing was sabotaging them, so they'd blow up on us."

"I don't understand," said Slim.

"There was a traitor among us," said Johnny. "And HMK was the traitor."

"That's such a nasty word," said a woman's voice. The three men twisted around to see Hari Mata Karma approaching from the steps that led up into the fort. She had changed her clothes, bathed and looked fresh, well groomed and elegant. There was something else about her that had changed, but Johnny couldn't immediately identify what it was. "Hello boys," she said.

"You wee bitch," snarled Middenface.

"Now, that's not nice, is it?"

"Do you like it better than traitor?" said Johnny.

"Don't try and be witty, Johnny Alpha. That's my job."

"No, your job is sticking a knife in the back of your fellow Strontium Dogs."

HMK sighed. She strolled up behind Johnny and patted him lightly on the head. It was only the gentlest of touches, but it caused a gruesome surge of agony in his wounds. Johnny winced. HMK took her hand away and walked a little further down the courtyard before turning and looking at the kneeling, chained trio of men. "That's not strictly true," she said. "Because I was never a Strontium Dog myself."

Johnny suddenly realised what was different about the woman. Instead of having one brown eye and one blue eye, they were both a cool amused blue.

"You're not a mutant," he said.

"No. All that was just a story we cooked up to get you to accept me."

"Who are you, then?" said Johnny.

"Oh, I'm Hari Mata Karma all right. But that's my maiden name. My full name now is Hari Mata Karma Zo."

"Zo?" whispered Middenface incredulously.

"Just call me HMKZ."

"You're his wife?" said Johnny.

"But that can't be," murmured Middenface. "The woman I saw in the jewellery shop..."

"And the hologram in Asdoel Zo's study..." said Johnny.

"That zebra-striped harlot was an associate of my husband's. A rather too close associate, and I'm going to have words with him about that. She was what you might call my stand-in, for the deeply emotional hologram we showed you of the dead family. She was supposed to be me. After all, I couldn't appear as myself, because I was also going to be a member of our posse."

"But what was she doing in the jewellers?" said Johnny.

"Good question. She wasn't supposed to be there. She wasn't even supposed to be in that solar system. But as I said, she had formed a rather disgustingly close association with my husband. He kept her around instead of just paying her off and sending her on her way. And the empty-headed little slut let you spot her." She smiled at Middenface. "So unfortunately you had to be clubbed with a psych truncheon to stop you putting two and two together."

Middenface shook his bloody head wearily. "So all along, when you were pretending to be such great pals with us, you were planning this."

"No, not exactly *this*. We were improvising to a large extent. Making it up as we went along. We didn't know exactly what was going to happen. We just knew it was going to be fun."

"Fun," said Middenface, disgustedly.

"And I wasn't pretending to be pals with you. I really was your pal."

"Sure you were," said Middenface.

"What was the point of it all?" said Johnny. "What did you want from us?"

"Something that money couldn't buy," said Asdoel Zo. The three chained men glanced back to see Zo approaching them from the same direction his wife had come from. He was dressed in khaki shorts, sandals and a dark blue, short-sleeved shirt, puffing contentedly on a cigar. "An experience like no other."

"Take these chains off me," said Johnny, "and I'll give you an experience like no other."

Asdoel Zo chuckled, emitting a mouthful of sweet herbal smoke. "A tempting offer, but no thanks."

"I don't get it," said Slim. His voice was mournful and pained, the cry of a confused beast in a snare. "Why did you bring us all here?"

"I was just getting to that," said Asdoel Zo. He strolled over and stood beside his wife, reaching out to put his arm around her shoulders. She shrugged off his embrace and moved a small distance away from him. Zo puffed on his cigar, not visibly upset by her rebuff. "You may feel that I've lied to you fellows..."

"Lied?" spat Middenface. "Is there one thing you've told us that was true?"

"Plenty," said Zo affably. "It's absolutely true that I'm an old west enthusiast and that I'm a passionate man who'll spare no expense pursuing my passions."

"Good for you," said Middenface.

"Don't sound so bitter, my friend."

"He's no friend of yours," said Johnny Alpha grimly.

"You're right there, Johnny," said Middenface.

"Frankly I don't understand all this hostility," said Asdoel Zo. He glanced at his wife. "Do you, dear?"

"No, I can't say that I do. But you know what they say."

"No, what do they say, dear?"

Hari Mata Karma Zo smiled a bright smile. "The rich are different."

Middenface stared up at her through bloodstained eyes in a ravaged face. "You can say that again, you wee back-stabbing whore."

"Watch the mouth, McNulty," said Asdoel Zo, striding forward and standing directly in front of Middenface. He drew one leg back, shifting his balance, and Middenface braced himself to receive a brutal kick in the face. But the kick never came.

"Don't do that, Asdoel," said HMKZ, who was restraining her husband. "Don't hurt the poor fellow. I quite like the salty dialogue. It sort of adds to the sense of occasion, don't you think? Lends a certain piquant authenticity."

"Whatever you say, dear," said Asdoel Zo. He abandoned his kicking stance and instead, inhaled deeply on his cigar and blew a mouthful of blue smoke at Middenface. Middenface coughed and shook his head helplessly. "You should thank me for that," said Zo. "These are very expensive cigars. You're privileged to share them."

"Besides," said HMKZ, "where do you get off, suddenly pretending that you care about my feelings?"

Asdoel Zo looked at her in surprise. "What do you mean, darling?"

"We'll talk about it later. After you've finished filling the boys in."

Asdoel Zo shrugged and turned back to the three kneeling men. "There's not much to tell, really. Tarkettle was never the real threat. He never harmed my family. He was merely a decoy."

"A hunting decoy," said Johnny.

Asdoel Zo smiled around his cigar. "Why, that's right, Johnny. It seems I still enjoy a good, old fashioned bloodhunt... So I assembled the galaxy's top bounty hunters for an entertaining little extravaganza, in which they are played off against each other."

"Sorry to spoil your fun," said Middenface, "but it won't work."

"Don't be so sceptical, McNulty. You haven't heard the whole plan."

Slim Drago stared at him in confusion. "What plan?"

"We don't need to hear it," said Middenface.

"He's right," said Johnny. "You're not going to get us to fight each other for your amusement."

"Not just for my amusement," said Asdoel Zo. "There's an exciting bonus prize." He glanced over at his wife. "Isn't that right, dear? Tell the boys."

HMKZ sighed and said, "The lucky survivor will be given their freedom plus their fee, plus the fees of all those who have died."

"Everybody else's fee?" said Slim Drago.

Asdoel Zo gave an encouraging smile. "That's right. And it will add up to quite a handsome jackpot."

"What do we have to do?" said Slim. He suddenly sounded interested. Middenface and Johnny exchanged a glance.

Asdoel Zo took a last puff on his cigar, then dropped the smouldering stub to the flagstones and ground it out in a shower of sparks under his sandal. "It's quite straightforward. The whole deadly game will be played out using old west-style weaponry. We set you down out there," he gestured towards the vast desert beyond the fort. "You'll be armed to the teeth and provided with enough food and water to last you a week, which should be plenty of time. All you have to do is hunt down your erstwhile colleagues and dispatch them." He leaned close to Slim Drago and smiled at him. "Sound good, big fella?"

To Middenface's horror, Slim smiled back and slowly nodded his head. Asdoel Zo turned to Middenface and Johnny and beamed at them. "You see? It doesn't matter if you two don't want to play. Enough of the others have agreed to set the ball well and truly rolling."

"I don't believe it," said Middenface.

"It's true," said HMKZ in a wistful voice. "Sorry about that, Middenface. I guess it makes you rather disappointed in human nature."

"Who's agreed to this murderous bloody scheme?" demanded Middenface.

"Hmm." Asdoel Zo frowned and counted on his fingers. Then the frown disappeared and he smiled brightly. "It's easier to tell you who *hasn't* agreed to it. Because it was only one person."

"Granny Haxer," said Johnny.

Asdoel Zo grinned at him. "That's right! Granny Haxer was as outraged as you and McNulty here. But apart from the old girl, everyone else in the posse has agreed to the arrangement. In fact the idea actually sounds pretty good to them, especially the bit about the survivor collecting everybody's fees."

"Except that there won't be a survivor," said Johnny.

"My, what a cynical thing to say." Asdoel Zo took another cigar from one pocket of his shirt and his golden, wafer-thin phone from the other. He used the phone to slice off one end of the cigar and ignite the other. He puffed on it meditatively. "Why would you think a thing like that?"

Johnny stared up at him, his unearthly eyes full of cold hatred. "Because whatever Strontium Dog manages to kill all the others will simply be used as prey in a safari by you and your family." Asdoel Zo glanced at his wife. She looked steadily back at him. Neither said anything, but some kind of brief, silent communication went on between the two of them. After a moment, Asdoel Zo looked back at Johnny.

"Whatever gave you an idea like that?"

"You're a hunter," said Johnny. "You like to hunt, not just watch." Middenface, who had been horrified by his friend's blunt accusation, remembered the trophy room in Asdoel Zo's mansion, full of the heads of beasts slaughtered on safari. He realised that Johnny was probably right.

"Don't try to psychoanalyse me, Johnny," said Asdoel Zo. His wife was studying the diamond-encrusted watch on her wrist. She looked at Zo and he caught the look. "My better half is reminding me of the time, so we'd better wrap this up."

"Wrap it up any way you want," said Johnny. "We're not playing your game."

"I'm afraid you don't have any choice, my friend. You see, after your little contretemps with the cannons, I had my medical team check you over. They made sure there was no serious damage. But they also put some depot meds in you."

"What's that?" said Slim anxiously.

"Nothing to worry about, my ox-like friend. Merely some implanted drugs timed to go off at specific intervals. That's why you all woke up at the same time. And it's why you're all about to go back to sleep."

"Back to sleep?" said Slim. His voice was beginning to slur and his head lolled forward as Middenface watched. Middenface tried to turn his head and see what was happening to Johnny, but it was too late. A welling flow of blackness rose up within him, swamping his vision and floating him away towards a dark, vast ocean.

Middenface awoke feeling bright, alert and free of pain. He sat up, pleased to discover that he was no longer in chains. He put a hand to his face and found that it had been cleaned of blood and that his wounds had been expertly tended to. Only then did he look around at his surroundings.

He was no longer in the courtyard. As a matter of fact, he was nowhere near the fort and didn't recognise the terrain at all. He seemed to be in a small box canyon filled with sunlight. It was a meandering cleft between two shoulders of rock. At the far end was an opening in a wall of rock, an opening into a man-made cave. The rusted rails that extended into the opening, the piles of rock and the old ore cars lying on their side suggested that it had once been some kind of mine.

Middenface had been lying in the open, in the middle of the canyon, on a thick blanket. A second blanket lay on the ground, rolled up in a bundle, with the stock and muzzle of what looked like a rifle jutting from either end. Middenface inspected this weapon first. It came with a set of instructions that explained it was a Hale percussion carbine with a tip-up breech which could be detached at the removal of a single screw, effectively turning the carbine into a pistol for close quarters fighting. The instructions were clear, informative, chatty and obviously written by a fanatical enthusiast – probably Asdoel Zo himself, Middenface decided with a scowl of disgust. He did practise converting the breech into a pistol, however, and found that it was surprisingly easy.

Then he unrolled the blanket and found that it also contained a hundred rounds of ammunition, matches, candles, a knife, a coil of rope and half a dozen bags of food. A quick inspection told him that the food was mostly dried fruit and beef jerky. Rationed judiciously it would last at least a week. There was also a large, metal canteen padded on the outside with grey and red striped felt. But the canteen was empty. What about water?

Then he noticed the large trough of water standing under a dead tree. He went to it and filled his canteen, holding it under the water until it was full. He sealed the canteen and slung it over his shoulder. The trough was fed by a pipe, which seemed to tap some kind of natural underground source.

There were all sorts of other dangers, though. Middenface quickly rolled up his supplies in the blanket again, added the second blanket to the unwieldy bundle, and carried it on his shoulder into the cool dark mouth of the mine.

Once he was inside he realised it wasn't a mine at all just a neat hole carved in the rock, an artificial cave that went back about fifteen metres in a slow curve. The rails only extended inside about three metres. Of course it wasn't real. It had only been built for appearance's sake, to provide one more authentic, western tableau for Asdoel Zo's amusement on this planet. Nonetheless, it made a good temporary refuge. Middenface moved along the curving tunnel until the daylight faded out of sight. Then he lit a candle and laid his new belongings out neatly in the flickering yellow light.

The floor of the cave was flat and smooth, obviously carved out by modern machinery. Maybe by lasers. The illusion of the old west on this planet was only superficial. Middenface wondered where Johnny was, and he hoped his friend had found himself as well situated and equipped as Middenface was.

There was no point speculating, or worrying, until he knew some more in the way of solid facts. Tomorrow he would set off in search of Johnny. But right now the sunlight outside was failing and the only thing that made sense was to rest and husband his strength. Middenface lay down on one blanket with the other rolled into an improvised pillow, and the Hale carbine in easy reach. Then he slept the sleep of exhaustion.

When he woke, the candle had long since burned out. His whole body seemed to be on fire with a terrible thirst. He rolled off his blankets and moved quickly along the tunnel. In his mind was the metal trough under the tree, with its sweet load of cold water. All he wanted to do was bury his face in that trough and drink and drink, until he was full. As he hurried through the tunnel, it occurred to him that he should be taking the carbine with him. But the need for water seemed to drive all such considerations from his mind. Middenface felt distinctly strange, feverish and light headed. He forced himself to stop. He was halfway along the tunnel. He should go back for the gun. It seemed such a weary, long distance to go. And the opening of the mine was just as near, and when he reached it he would be out in the night with the water...

Middenface found his feet moving again. Without conscious volition he was hurrying along the tunnel. There was a strange, nagging thought in his mind. He'd left something behind back there, with his gun and his supplies. Sweat ran down Middenface's brow. He tried to think clearly. What was he leaving behind, besides the protection of his weapon?

Then he remembered. The canteen. There was a canteen full of water lying within easy reach. He didn't need to go outside. But, oddly, the realisation didn't slow him down at all. He had rounded the curve in the tunnel and could see the moonlit mouth of the cave.

That was when he realised that it wasn't water, which he thirsted for, and it wasn't the trough that was drawing him outside.

He moved through the shadows of the tunnel, slowly but steadily, with the stride of a condemned man who was resigned to his fate. When he reached the mouth of the cave he stood for a moment looking out into the moonlight that filled the canyon. And he saw her, just as he knew he would.

She was standing under the skeleton shape of the old dead tree, beside the trough with its glassy water reflecting the pale shine of the moon. In her hands was a long rifle of some kind. On her head was a wide-brimmed cowboy hat. Her clothes were new, but he had no trouble recognising her, standing there in the shadows and the moonlight. He could have recognised her with his eyes shut.

Stella Dysh stood under the tree, patiently waiting. She wasn't looking towards him. She didn't need to. Whatever direction her prey came from, it would come willingly, and it would come to her and stand there patiently, not resisting, not complaining, as she did whatever she wanted. Middenface knew all this, but he knew it as an abstract, unimportant fact in a distant corner of his mind. The only thing that mattered was that he would step out of the cave and go to the woman who was singing the siren's song, and kneel before her in the moonlight and submit. It was the moment his whole life had been moving towards. It was the ending that would give meaning to everything that had gone before.

It was his destiny.

Middenface moved forward, to step through the mouth of the cave and out into the moonlight. And as he moved there was a sound from outside. A rattling shift of rocks, carelessly stirred by hurrying feet. Middenface watched as if in a dream, as a tall figure appeared at the far end of the canyon, silhouetted in the moonlight. The size of the figure left him no doubt in who it was.

Slim Drago came hastily into the canyon. He had a shotgun in his big hands, but it might as well have been a lute, clutched by a medieval swain rushing to serenade his true love. Slim obviously had no intention of firing the gun. He held it flat against his chest as he stumbled across the floor of the canyon to the tree where Stella Dysh was standing.

Stella had turned to face Slim, but apart from this small motion she hadn't stirred a muscle. She was neither surprised nor excited. Simply waiting patiently. As Slim approached her, she slowly lifted her rifle and pointed it at him. The rifle didn't discourage Slim. He didn't even seem to notice it. He gave a wide idiot grin as he approached Stella.

He reached the skeletal tree and stood under it, with her, in the moonlight. Stella said something that Middenface couldn't hear. Slim set his shotgun down, leaning it neatly against the trough.

Then he turned to Stella and she said something else. Slim smiled and obediently opened his mouth.

Stella put the barrel of her rifle in it. Slim did nothing to resist. He was still trying to smile, with the rifle barrel in his mouth, when she pulled the trigger.

The sound of the gunshot was muffled by Slim's skull but it was still a flat, hard sound that echoed around the canyon. Slim dropped to the ground, dragging the rifle, which was still in his mouth, with him. Stella cursed and slowly wrestled the rifle free of the corpse's jaws. Then she kneeled beside Slim's body and took out a knife. Middenface saw the knife blade gleam in the moonlight as Stella cut off a lock of Slim's hair, working fastidiously around the bloody ruin that was now the back of his head. When she was finished, she put the hair carefully in her pocket and turned and walked out of the canyon, the rifle slung jauntily over her shoulder.

When she was gone, Middenface slumped down in the mouth of the cave, sat on the rocks, and wept.

CHAPTER TWELVE
BLOOD HUNT

Charlie Yuletide was riding the horse that had bitten him, looking distinctly uncomfortable, with his banjo in his lap. He made his way along a familiar, dry river bed and up a slope into the box canyon with the old mine works in it. There, beside the dead tree, were Asdoel Zo and his wife Hari Mata Karma in matching safari outfits.

They were standing above a long, low mound of earth with a crude cross, fashioned from two sticks, stuck in at one end. They looked up from the mound as Charlie rode into the canyon. "Mr Zo!" cried Charlie with hearty insincerity. "What an unexpected treat. What brings you here?"

"I brought him here," said his wife. "I wanted to check on you."

"Check on me?"

HMKZ snorted. "I left this entire aspect of the operation up to my husband, so I thought I'd better do an inspection. Just to see what kind of a dog's breakfast he's making of it."

"Oh come on now," said Asdoel Zo. "That's uncalled-for."

"Is it? I'm only just discovering what you got up to with that zebra-striped Jezebel you hired to impersonate me."

Asdoel Zo shrugged and grinned. "One tiny slip..."

"One? What about those little gardening trollops of yours?"

"But dear. We had to maintain the fiction of your death. I was supposed to be a man alone, a widower. Nonetheless, a man with a man's needs. It would have looked strange if I..."

"A period of mourning *is* traditional, you know," said HMKZ in an icy voice.

Charlie Yuletide wasn't listening to either of them. He was staring down at the long, low mound with the crude cross stuck in it. It was a big grave, for a big man. He said, "There isn't really somebody buried in that, is there?"

Granny Haxer was in a fix. She had found herself what seemed like the ideal spot to hole up and get the drop on these varmints. Not Johnny or Middenface, of course. That spoiled little rich bastard, Asdoel Zo, had let slip that Johnny and Middenface had rejected the deal, just like her. They despised this situation as much as she did. Just like her they were unwilling participants.

The other varmints, the ones who were willing to kill their partners, people who'd been their friends just a day before, but were now willing to sell them down the river, or worse, just for the sake of money... Granny Haxer didn't have any trouble putting paid to low-lifes like that. And she had just the tool for the job. A fine buffalo rifle, a Sharps breech loader with an octagon barrel for long distance shooting. It was a weapon that could reach far and hit hard. She caressed the blue steel barrel of the rifle now, careful not to touch the sights, which she had so painstakingly zeroed-in the previous morning, using some rounds of her precious ammunition.

Yes, she had a fine firearm. And she'd found an equally fine place to hole up. After she'd got the Sharps sighted in properly with her test shots, she'd known she had to get moving in a hurry. Those shots were bound to draw the human jackals who were hunting her, hungry to shed her blood and pocket her fee for themselves.

The small hill, on which Granny had awoken, had been an advantageous spot. It had allowed her to check for pursuit in all directions. She set off, carrying the small rucksack she'd found beside her, full of dried food and spare ammo, and the canteen full of water. There was a lightweight sleeping bag tucked into the small rucksack and the rifle, too, was surprisingly light. Granny realised that the sleeping bag and the rifle were both anachronisms. Neither could have existed in the real days of the cowboys. The rifle might have looked like an antique buffalo gun, but it was obviously made of some kind of special low-mass alloy.

It seemed that the rich fool, Asdoel Zo, wasn't such a stickler for authenticity after all. He must have realised that, because Granny was smaller and less physically strong than the others, a proper old-fashioned weapon and roll of bedding would have weighed her down so much she would hardly have been able to move. And it seemed that Zo wanted a fair competition, by his own lights.

"Very well," Granny had said, setting off with her lightweight pack and her lightweight rifle, "if it's a fair competition he wants it's a fair one he'll get." She didn't feel one ounce of gratitude towards Asdoel Zo, though. Or towards his whore-bitch of a wife, that treacherous she-dog, Hari Mata Karma. If they'd seen fit to allow Granny these small advantages, then fine. She'd use them. Hopefully to blow both Mr and Mrs Zo back to whatever hell had spawned them.

So Granny Haxer had set off from the hilltop where she'd awoken, moving quickly in the hours just after dawn, before the desert day became unendurably hot. She'd been looking for a spot where she might be able to get a good shot at any fool unfortunate enough to pass under the sights of her buffalo rifle. And she'd got lucky. Within three hours of swift marching she'd come upon the wreck of an old stagecoach, lying on its side and studded with arrows from an Indian attack.

Granny knew that the stagecoach, like the arrows, was a complete fake. But that didn't bother her. All that mattered was that it was a *useful* fake. She reasoned that she could hole up inside where she'd be both out of sight and protected from bullets – at least badly aimed or hasty bullets – and have the opportunity to watch for any wayfarers and get the drop on them.

Unfortunately, they'd got the drop on her.

And what had initially seemed like an ideal refuge was beginning to smell like a death trap.

The stagecoach was built of wood on a steel frame. It lay on its side with one set of wooden wheels in the air and the only way in was through a set of doors, which were now on the top of the wreck. The other set of doors were pinned against the ground and therefore impossible to use. Granny had clambered up onto the stage and opened the doors on top, lowering herself into the dusty interior. The stagecoach seats were covered with velvet and smelled spicily of mould. Even though everything had been turned on its side, it was quite a comfortable place to take refuge.

She was sitting on what had been the doors on the left side of the stagecoach, and which were now effectively the floor. The actual floor of the coach, tilted up at right angles from the ground, now formed a wall to her left. The ceiling was a wall to her right. And the ceiling was the set of doors, which had been on the right of the stage. If she poked her head up through the window above her, or opened the door, she had a nice little spot for spying or shooting.

The stagecoach was situated on a slight rise in the ground and although the terrain was strewn with boulders and cut with ravines, it provided a reasonable field of fire over three hundred and sixty degrees. Granny reckoned she could take down any adversary, coming from any direction.

What she hadn't reckoned on were two adversaries, coming from two directions.

A bullet ploughed through the topsy turvy roof of the stagecoach, directly behind Granny Haxer, buzzed through the air past her ear, and lodged in the up-ended floor directly in front of her. Granny cursed and moved hastily to one side, although this wasn't necessarily a good idea. Since she didn't know which direction the next bullet was coming from she might be moving directly into its path. Still, it was human nature to dodge gunfire, and dodge she did. The next bullet, as it happened, came through the floor of the stagecoach. The floor was wooden, but fitted on the underside with steel plates, so the bullet entered at a crazy angle and ricocheted around the interior of the coach, most of its energy already spent. It landed in Granny's lap.

She quickly brushed it away, like an unpleasant insect that had landed on her, feeling the heat of the metal slug on her hand as she touched it.

"You're going to have do better than that, you dumb bastards!" she yelled. Since her opponents already knew where she was, she wouldn't give her position away by shouting, and she might do some good. She might rattle them, although admittedly they hadn't showed any signs of getting rattled so far.

"Don't worry," called Ray from outside.

"We will," called Bel.

Granny thought she had a pretty fair idea where both the twins were, based on the directions the shots had come from and the sound of their voices. She considered popping up through the window and taking a shot at one of them. But that was the problem. She could only shoot at one of them at a time, and while she was taking aim and pulling the trigger, the other one had a pretty good shot at *her*.

Holing up in this stagecoach hadn't been such a good idea after all. Granny was beginning to wish she'd stayed on that nice hilltop where she'd woken up. It would have given her a better command of the terrain, allowed her more freedom of movement, and wouldn't have required her to risk her life every time she took a look around her. "No point fretting over broken eggs," murmured Granny, and she checked her Sharps. Outside the stagecoach, things were suspiciously quiet. She decided to take a chance on having a look outside. She stood up and cautiously thrust her head through the open window above her, twisting around to try and look in all directions. Immediately, two shots rang out and she dropped back into the coach, with a long scratch on the side of her neck for her troubles. She hadn't actually been hit, but one of the bullets had gouged long splinters of wood off the door and one of these cut her. The other bullet had damned near parted her hair.

But she'd managed to get a glimpse of what the twins were up to. The devils were almost upon her. Bel was lying flat on her stomach on the ground fifteen metres from the roof of the coach. Ray was about five metres further back, behind a rock that faced the underbelly of the coach.

There wasn't much Granny could do about Ray, what with him using that rock for cover. Plus the floor of the stagecoach being steel plated meant that Ray's bullets were unlikely to reach Granny, but also that her own bullets couldn't reach Ray. But the girl... Granny squirmed around on the velvet cushion where she was sitting until her back was to the floor of the coach and her rifle was pointing at the roof. She closed her eyes and tried to remember exactly where Bel had been laying. When she had a pretty clear picture in her mind, she gently squeezed the trigger...

The buffalo gun made an unholy noise in the confined space of the stagecoach, as she fired blindly through the wooden roof. Granny's ears rang with the aftermath of the blast. But she could still hear well enough to detect the gratifying cry of rage and pain from Bel, and the shocked, worried shout from her brother.

"I'm all right," called Bel, but her brother was already furiously pumping shots at the underside of the stagecoach. Granny could feel them hitting the steel plates at her back. She scooted around quickly, moving away from the floor of the coach, but none of the bullets were penetrating. The one that had got through earlier must have been a lucky fluke, slipping between the floor plates. "That's nice," yelled Granny. "It tickles a bit, but keep on shooting if you like, Ray. It gives me a nice back massage." In fact her back was still tingling from the vibration of the bullets on the steel plate behind her. Granny grinned with the fierce joy of being alive. A glint of bright sunlight caught her eye and she realised that her shot had blown a hole in the roof of the coach.

Granny slid across the dusty seat and examined it. The hole was about the size of her fist. Not big enough to render her visible, or vulnerable, to those jackals outside. But it was a useful size for spying on them. She squinted through it and saw that Bel had retreated a good twenty metres from her previous position and was now hiding in a dip in the ground. Excellent. Granny grinned. That would teach them. And with the hole to spy and shoot through, she'd be able to plug Bel if she so much as twitched a whisker.

The hole gave Granny an idea. She searched through her backpack and found the knife that had been provided for her. Then, she set about searching the floor of the stagecoach for the bullet hole that must be there. Finally she found it, a tiny speck of daylight that indicated where Ray's freak shot had come through. She'd been right. It had entered at a point between plates. To be more precise, at a point where the corners of four plates met. The steel plates weren't absolutely flush and the space between them was filled with wood. Using the point of her knife, Granny Haxer was able to enlarge the hole until it was big enough to get about three of her tiny fingers inside it. That was as big as she could possibly make the opening, because she was now up against steel plates on all sides. It was considerably smaller than the hole she'd blown in the ceiling, but it would suffice. She could peer out of it and, if necessary, poke the barrel of her gun into it and take a shot.

Making the hole had been a protracted, nerve-wracking business. She hadn't been able to work at it for more than a few seconds at a time. She constantly had to pause and squint through it to try and get a glimpse of Ray, and then dart back across the coach to look through the ceiling hole and keep watch on his sister. At one point she'd seen Bel trying to slink out of the hollow she was lying in and move to a more advantageous position. Granny had aimed her buffalo rifle and taken a shot that dropped Bel back into her hole right smartly. Granny cackled and reloaded the Sharps and then resumed her work. By the time she finished the hole in the floor, she had a satisfactory means of keeping an eye on both the twins.

The problem, of course, was that she couldn't keep an eye on both of them at once. And, with their eerie ability to anticipate each other's behaviour, the twins could co-ordinate their moves in a perfectly orchestrated attack.

That was what worried Granny. If they both made a move at the same time, she would be lucky to get even one of them. And the odds were that the surviving twin would get her. They were a sly pair, and she had a healthy respect for their abilities.

That was why, when she heard Bel shouting, she was sure it was a trap. "Come back!" shrieked Bel. "Ray! What are you doing?"

"I ain't stirring," murmured Granny. "You can't fool me. You're just trying to get me to poke my head out so you can blow it off." But Bel kept on screaming.

"Come back, Ray. Don't go to her!"

Her? Granny abruptly realised what was happening. The boy must have fallen under the sway of that Stella Dysh. Granny chuckled delightedly. "She's got him!" she shouted to Bel. "She's drawing him like a dumb hound to a bitch in heat!"

Bel's response was a wordless scream of rage, but Granny wasn't paying attention. She had her face pressed to the hole she'd fashioned in the floor boards. Sure enough, Ray had abandoned his position in the rocks and was walking away from the stagecoach, moving at moderate speed, but with an oddly somnolent stride. As if he wasn't in conscious control of his actions. "Which he ain't," chuckled Granny. "This is going to be like shooting turkeys in a tree." She scooped up her weapon, took one last look through the hole, then pressed the octagonal rifle barrel to it and braced herself.

It was difficult shooting through the tiny hole, because she couldn't look and fire at the same time. But she'd got a pretty good idea of Ray's position. She squeezed the trigger and once again the buffalo gun roared in the hot cramped space of the stagecoach. Granny quickly withdrew the rifle and peered through the hole. The bad news was that she'd missed. Ray was still marching mechanically off towards the distant blue hills.

The good news was that the boy hadn't reacted to the shot in any way at all. He wasn't taking cover, running or even changing direction. It looked like she was going to get plenty of chances to hit him.

There was a wordless cry of frenzied rage from Bel, who must have surmised what Granny was up to. Then there was a wild volley of shots from the girl. Granny ducked as half a dozen bullets tore through the ceiling of the coach behind her and ripped into the fat cushions of the seats, kicking up miniature clouds of dust. One bullet hit the stock of Granny's Sharps rifle and knocked it out of her hands. She cursed and groped for the weapon. The clouds of dust from the seat cushions danced in the golden shafts of sunlight that fell through the bullet holes in the roof.

"Leave him alone!" shrieked Bel from outside.

"Fat chance," murmured Granny in amusement. But she found she was having trouble picking up the rifle again. Her right arm felt numb, no doubt with the shock transmitted through the wooden stock of the rifle from the impact of the bullet.

She put her fingers on the rifle, but for some reason they wouldn't close on it. Then Granny felt something wet trickle down her wrist and she saw the blood. For a moment it puzzled her and then she realised what had happened. The bullet hadn't hit the rifle. It had hit her arm. That accounted for the numb feeling and the loss of strength in it. Granny cursed. What a time for this to happen. She tore a strip of fabric off her blouse, using her left hand and her knife and hastily tied it around her right arm just above the wound. "Won't do to lose any more blood," she murmured to herself as she worked. It was a difficult business tightening the makeshift bandage, but she managed by using her teeth.

When she completed the task, she took a quick look through the hole in the perpendicular floor boards and saw that Ray was still marching in the same direction as before, slowly but steadily receding into the distance. He still made a feasible target, though, if only she could lift her gun...

Then Granny realised that Bel had gone suspiciously silent. She quickly moved to the hole in the roof and peered out. Bel was nowhere in sight. "Shitfire," murmured Granny. The damned girl could be anywhere. "Where is she?"

Her question was answered a moment later, when the stagecoach gave a sudden ugly lurch, responding to the weight of someone climbing on top of it. Granny scrabbled frantically for her rifle, trying to grab it and lift it awkwardly with her left hand.

But it was too late. The door above her was flung open and Bel stood there, silhouetted in a square of blue sky. She had a Winchester rifle in her hands, aimed right at Granny's head.

Granny realised that it was all over. But she forced a smile onto her face. "Your brother's finished, dearie. That Stella Dysh has got her claws into him good and proper."

"I'll get to him and I'll save him," said Bel calmly, "as soon as I've put a bullet between your eyes and taken a cutting of your hair as proof of the kill. That is, if I can find any hair on that bald head of yours."

"Burn in hell, honey," said Granny Haxer cordially. She crossed herself and closed her eyes. The last thing she saw was the evil smile on Bel's face. Then the darkness behind Granny Haxer's eyelids was full of stillness and silence for a moment, followed by the sharp crack of a rifle firing. Granny didn't feel a thing. She wondered if this was what death was like. If so, it wasn't too bad. She was still breathing. She opened her eyes and saw Bel standing above her, wavering slightly as if she'd had too much to drink. There was something wrong with Bel's head. It was misshapen and there was a spreading stain over one eye.

As Granny watched, Bel toppled off the stagecoach and fell to the ground. The rifle dropped from her fingers as she went, falling into the stagecoach. Granny Haxer immediately grabbed it and shoved her head up through the open door to see what the hell was going on.

There on the ground beside the stagecoach, Johnny Alpha was standing over Bel's dead body. He had a revolver in his hand, a thread of smoke drifting up from its muzzle. Bel, who had seemed such a fearsome apparition only a few seconds earlier, now looked sad and frail, and abandoned in death. Johnny glanced up at Granny. "Where's the brother?" he said.

Granny pointed with her chin. "Over yonder, heading towards them hills. Seems he got a sniff of our Stella."

Johnny put his gun back in its holster. "Pack your things and get ready to clear out. We'll go after Ray. With a bit of luck we'll be able to nail him and Stella together."

Granny Haxer cackled appreciatively. "Now that's a nice thought. I ain't going to be much use to you, though, Johnny. I took one in my old wing." She lifted her bandaged arm, and winced at the pain that was only now beginning to make itself felt.

"That's all right," said Johnny. "I'll do the shooting. You can pass me the ammunition."

Middenface was making his way along a dry river bed that had been carved in the desert floor millennia ago. It was a couple of metres deep, with sloping sides, and he was walking along the bottom of it in the centre. It seemed a good way of making fast progress without being visible from a distance.

After last night's experience, Middenface had decided to abandon his nest in the mine. If Stella Dysh came back into the vicinity, he knew he was finished. So, at dawn he'd set off, moving quickly, without a backward glance at the box canyon that had been his sanctuary. Of course, there was no guarantee that he wouldn't run into Stella somewhere out here in the desert, but it simply felt safer to be on the move. He had buried Slim Drago in a makeshift grave mound marked with a wooden cross and then he'd set off. He was moving in the direction of the mountain with the fort at its base, which he could see as a massive ghost in the distance of the desert morning. He estimated that it would take him the best part of the day to get back to the fort. He had no idea what he'd do when he got there, but it seemed like the right course of action. It seemed like the sort of thing Johnny would do. When he'd found the dry river bed, which ran conveniently in the direction he was travelling, he had descended into it and followed it without hesitation.

The river bed twisted and turned, following some inscrutable rules of the land's topography, and each time Middenface came to a blind turning he slowed down, dropped to his knees, and peered around the bend. After a couple of hours, this strategy had begun to seem pointless and also a little craven, so now he was pressing along at full speed, taking each blind curve boldly, his rifle held high and ready.

He was moving like that, when he came around one bend and found himself face to face with Ray. Like Middenface, the boy had a rifle in his hands. He also had an odd, dream-like expression on his face, but Middenface didn't really register this until after he'd aimed, fired, and dropped Ray in his tracks.

Middenface darted forward and examined the boy. He was dead all right. The bullet had taken him squarely in the chest and killed him outright.

Middenface repressed a flicker of regret. Ray would no doubt have killed him with an equal lack of ceremony, if he'd had the chance. Middenface had just been lucky enough to shoot first. But something about the look of Ray bothered him. The odd, dreamy expression he'd had on his face, and the way he hadn't even attempted to use his gun. The fierce elation Middenface had felt on defeating his opponent began to fade, to be replaced by a profound sense of disquiet. He looked around the empty river bed. Something was wrong.

Where was Bel? He had never seen the twins separated before. He'd imagined that only death could keep them apart. Death, or...

Middenface remembered the odd expression on Ray's face, and the way he'd made no attempt to defend himself. It reminded Middenface of Slim Drago and how he'd gone obediently to his executioner in the moonlight. Despite the heat of the desert sun, Middenface found himself shivering. What if Ray had been under Stella Dysh's spell? What if he'd been on his way to her when Middenface had run into him?

Middenface left Ray's body where it fell and scrambled up the slanting wall of the river bed. He didn't know what was going on, but he was going to get the hell out of here. He struggled back onto ground level and found himself in a range of small hills, dotted with scrubby trees and dry bush. Some birds where wheeling high up in the cloudless blue sky. Their tiny black shapes made Middenface think uncomfortably of vultures. The bush around began to sway with the approach of a breeze and Middenface felt the slow, gliding rush of air cooling the sweat on his face.

The breeze brought more than coolness with it. It also carried an undetectable, but powerful, chemical scent and, although Middenface couldn't smell it consciously, he immediately felt its effect. He dropped his rifle and the rolled blanket he had been carrying. They no longer seemed important. He turned towards the foot hills that rose above him, slowly building in height, towards the blue mountains beyond. Middenface started up into the hills. He understood what was happening to him with total clarity. But that didn't seem important, either.

He found Stella Dysh sitting on the downwards slope on the far side of the hill. She had built a small fire and its tiny flames flickered invisibly in the daylight. Stella was eating something scorched and black, impaled on a sharp twig. "This beef jerky isn't so bad if you cook it up a bit," she said. She crunched a final mouthful of the seared jerky, then discarded the twig and stood up, dusting off the seat of her jeans. "I heard a shot," she said. "Was that you?"

"I shot Ray," said Middenface. It didn't occur to him to attack Stella, or to struggle, or attempt to flee. Anything like that was clearly impossible.

Stella smiled at him. "Good for you. That's one less for me to deal with and one more to add to the jackpot." She picked up her rifle from the ground. "Before I deal with you, you'd better show me where he is. I need a sample of his hair for proof of a kill."

"All right," said Middenface. He led Stella back down the far side of the hill. As they walked, he found himself noticing how beautiful the desert was, how vast and clear the sky. The mountains towering in the distance were grandly magnificent, exquisite in every detail. The world had never looked this beautiful to Middenface before. He supposed it was something to do with knowing he was going to die.

They reached the point where he'd dropped his rifle and bedroll. Stella Dysh paused. "I wonder if there's anything in your kit I could use? Oh well, I'll take a look at it on the way back." Middenface knew he wouldn't be with her on the way back. It wasn't a happy thought, but there was nothing he could do about it. "Which way now?" said Stella.

He led her down the sloping side into the dried river bed. When Stella looked like she might be about to stumble, he helped her. "Thanks," said Stella. "You're a real gent." Middenface led her through the winding river bed, along a blind curve, to the point where Ray's body was lying, just as he'd left it. "Good boy," said Stella to Middenface, giving him the sort of absent-minded pat on the head that you might offer to somebody else's dog.

She set her rifle down and kneeled by the corpse, taking out a knife which she used to cut a piece of Ray's hair. "I'm glad you didn't shoot him in the head," she said. "I made the mistake of doing that with old Slim last night and then, of course, I had to get a bit of his hair. Yuck! Talk about bad planning."

"I know," said Middenface. "I saw you."

"Did you now? In that box canyon? Sounds like I should have stuck around for a few minutes. I could have crossed you off the list, too. Never mind. I've got you now." She put the tuft of hair into the pocket of her jeans and stood up, picking up her rifle. "I'll shoot you in the chest, just like you got him. Sound all right to you?"

"No," said Middenface mournfully.

"No," agreed Stella with a chuckle, "but what are you going to do?" She raised the gun. "Say goodbye."

"Goodbye," said a voice from above them. A shot rang out and Stella Dysh dropped to the ground at Middenface's feet. He looked up to see Johnny standing at the top of the bank. Granny Haxer stood beside him. They came slowly down the sloping gradient towards Middenface, dust rising at their feet. Johnny helped

Granny, who had a bloody bandage tied on one arm. The old woman went to Stella's body and gave it a kick.

She looked up at Middenface and Johnny. "I don't know what you fellas saw in her," she said.

CHAPTER THIRTEEN
DUEL IN THE FORTRESS

Charlie Yuletide sat beside the old iron stove in the kitchen of the fort. He had his feet up and was strumming on his banjo and singing softly.

"They fought and they fought, to their last breath. Brave Strontium Dogs in a fight to the death."

"Oh, for God's sake, put a sock in it," said Hari Mata Karma Zo as she passed him, poured herself a cup of coffee, and wandered out again.

Hari Mata Karma Zo stood on the battlements of the old fort, sipping her coffee and staring out over the desert. The view was magnificent and the coffee wasn't bad, either, though oddly not as good as the vile-looking stuff Granny Haxer had brewed up. She felt a small twinge of regret about Granny and the others, especially Middenface and Johnny. They were out there in the desert right now, engaged in the tricky business of killing each other. HMKZ sighed and set her coffee cup down. On either side of her were the spaces for the four cannons, which she had sabotaged, and which had blown themselves to pieces. Her husband had ordered them to be removed for repairs by his team of experts. Within a few days they'd be back in place, fully restored and as good as new.

"Or as good as old," thought HMKZ, since they were already antiques. She smiled. The thought amused her. It was about the only thing that did amuse her at the moment. She turned away and moved to the inner wall of the fortress, looking down over the courtyard. The pale blue shape of the shuttle ship rested there in the heart of the fort, fitting neatly between the four walls. It was no surprise that it fitted so well, since the fort had been purpose built to accommodate the vessel. Asdoel Zo had moved it inside as soon as he dropped the drugged bounty hunters off in the desert to begin their game. "You never know what those desperados might get up to. They're really quite resourceful for a pack of primitive low-lifes," he'd said. "It'll be safer inside." But HMKZ knew that wasn't the real reason, and that if Asdoel had his way, the ship would be vastly less safe in its new berth.

"Penny for your thoughts."

She turned to see her husband standing there, smoking one of his cigars. She hadn't heard him approach. "Are you practising sneaking up on me?" she said. "You'd better, because that's the only way you're going to be able to exercise your conjugal rights from now on."

"Oh come now, honey," said Asdoel Zo. He was wearing his usual shorts and sandals and brightly coloured shirt – in this case one decorated with a motif of black horses' heads on a red background. "You aren't still mad about that stupid girl are you? She didn't mean anything to me." He took the cigar out of his mouth, blowing smoke. Blowing smoke is right, thought HMKZ. He's trying to blow smoke up my ass.

"Where is she?" said HMKZ.

"Where is who? Her? I got rid of *her* ages ago."

"That's what you said before."

"I left her back at the mall, I swear. The jewellery store was the last place I saw her. The last place I'll ever see her."

HMKZ sighed. "This all has a terribly familiar ring to it."

"It's the truth this time, my dove," said Asdoel Zo, bending to kiss her on the cheek. She dodged the kiss.

"You reek of that ganja," she said.

He grinned at her. "You used to say you liked the smell of it."

"I was just saying that."

"I know you're upset, darling," he cooed in his most annoying voice, the one of wheedling, unctuous sincerity. HMKZ had heard it many times before. Too many times. "But it will all be better when this is over. We'll be able to spend some time together and iron out any misunderstandings."

"There aren't any misunderstandings. I understand you all too well. That's the trouble."

"You'll feel better in a few days, dear. I know you're a bit upset because you bonded with those Strontium Dogs."

"Johnny and Middenface are both twice the man you are."

"I see. So on aggregate they're four times the man I am." Asdoel chuckled and sucked on his cigar, quite unruffled. He was so vastly arrogant, he was almost impossible to insult.

"Are you still determined to go through with this ridiculous stunt of yours?" demanded HMKZ.

"The grand finale you mean?" Asdoel exhaled smoke. "Of course I am."

"What if something goes wrong?"

"What could possibly go wrong?" Asdoel patted the stone wall of the battlements. "Except for this entire fort and the shuttle craft being blown to pieces, of course." He chuckled and winked at her.

"Where are the girls?" said HMKZ.

"Stop worrying. Lorna and Jodi are perfectly safe, back up in orbit on the *Charles Neider*." He peered at her. "Maybe you ought to be up there with them."

"No, I'll stay down here and see it through to the bitter end."

"That's my girl."

"But for God's sake, let's wrap it up quickly. I'm getting sick of the whole affair."

Asdoel consulted the clock on his watch. "It will be over sooner than you think. As a matter of fact, that's why I came up here to get you. They're already on their way to the powder magazine."

"They're here!" said HMKZ. "Middenface and Johnny?"

"And that old bat, Granny Haxer too. Remarkably enough she's one of the three survivors. She's a tough old bird all right."

"Tough, but stupid. She never worked out that you were the mystery client who hired her to get Stella Dysh, did she?"

Asdoel smiled. "Do you want to tell her?"

HMKZ ignored the question. She said, "What would you have done if Johnny and Middenface hadn't made it?"

"Oh, you know me," said Asdoel. "Mr Eventuality. I had scenarios prepared for any permutation of survivors. But this one just happened to be my favourite."

"I'm so glad it worked out for you," said HMKZ bitterly. "How did you lure them here?"

"I sent Tarkettle out into the desert to find them. He's led them back in through the secret entrance that leads to the powder magazine."

"Secret entrance?"

"You know, we had it dug last week. Designed to look like a clandestine escape route with an entrance near the waterfalls. Very nice piece of work. Anyway, Tarkettle met up with the Strontium Dogs and told them how he's appalled by my plan and the part he has been made to play in it, the cavalier treatment of humans as playthings, yadda yadda, being made to act out life and death games purely for my amusement, and blah, blah, blah. So he shows Johnny and Middenface, and old Granny, this concealed entrance to the fortress that takes them into the caves beneath it and through the gunpowder magazine. The idea is that they'll blow up the magazine, and the fortress and the shuttle craft – now handily docked in the courtyard – into the bargain and thereby eliminate the evil rich man."

"And his evil, rich wife," said HMKZ.

Asdoel laughed. "That's right!"

"And you seriously expect Johnny and the others to believe Tarkettle's story?"

"Why not? Tarkettle believes it. I had it implanted as a hypnotic suggestion while he was asleep last night. He woke up this morning with a desire for escape and revenge. He was all primed and ready and waiting for me to give him his cue, which I duly did. So he slipped out and went looking for Johnny and the other heroes. I gave him a little subliminal guidance, of course, based on their last known positions. He found them pretty quick and brought them back here."

"Like a Judas goat."

"Nice image. Of course Tarkettle knew all about the secret tunnel and the access to the powder magazine. By now he believes he thought up the plan himself."

HMKZ went back to the battlements and found her tin coffee cup. It was still half full. She took a sip, but it was cold and bitter. She set it aside again. "Well, if they're preparing to blow up the fort, don't you think you should be doing something about it?"

Her husband checked the time again. "In just a minute now, darling. Do you want to be there to see the big finish?"

HMKZ yawned. "I suppose so. Do you still plan that ridiculous, final confrontation we discussed?"

"Indeed I do. Thanks for reminding me." He dug in the pockets of his shorts and took out a silver box. He prised it's lid open with his thumbnail and took out a pale blue pill. "Better top myself up. I want to be at my best for the big showdown." He turned and walked towards the stairs that led down to the courtyard. But before he could go, HMKZ caught his arm. He turned to look at her. "What is it, honey?"

"Are you really sure you want to go through with this, Asdoel? You don't have to, you know."

"What else am I going to do?"

"Let Johnny and the others go. Pay them off and let them go. We've had our fun. Put an end to it now."

"Oh sure," said Asdoel Zo. "Like I'm going to do that." He laughed heartily and set off down the stairs, his sandals slapping as he went. HMKZ stared after him for a long moment, then followed.

First, her husband went into the underground kitchen, descending the steps on the right of the courtyard. "Where are you going?" said HMKZ. "The powder magazine is the other way."

"I know that, dear. I thought I'd collect our lackadaisical troubadour en route. He should witness the end of the drama. Maybe it will inspire him to compose a suitably poignant, final verse to sing on the video."

They went into the kitchen where they found Charlie Yuletide eating a large, messy bacon and egg sandwich and forced him to abandon it. Then they returned up into the courtyard and back down into the cellar on the opposite side, pausing in the armoury that adjoined the powder magazine. "What now?" said HMKZ impatiently.

"First we arm you, my darling." He inspected rows of rifles, gleaming dully in a glass cabinet and decisively opened it and chose one. "An original Volcanic repeating rifle, circa 1856. The perfect thing for the lady in my life."

"Do you mean me?" said HMKZ, sardonically lifting an eyebrow. After a moment, she accepted the rifle from her husband.

Asdoel Zo took a box of shells out of a drawer in the cabinet and handed it to her. HMKZ began loading the rifle with practised expertise while Asdoel turned to a wall covered with revolvers hanging on pegs. "And now I arm myself. After all, we can't have a final shootout without something to do the shooting with can we?" He looked at the rows of handguns and selected one. "Remington .44 calibre new army model, I think, designed for service in the Civil War."

"Just get on with it."

"Almost there, my dove." He opened a drawer in a tall wooden chest that ran from floor to ceiling, and selected a leather belt and holster. He strapped them to his hip, slipped the Remington into the belt and tried a few slow practice draws, watching himself in a mirror. The pistol cleared the holster cleanly every time.

"What's he doing?" whispered Charlie Yuletide.

"He's going to fight a duel with Johnny Alpha," said HMKZ in a voice of profound, flat neutrality.

"But, Mr Zo," said Charlie Yuletide. "That man's an experienced killer. You don't stand a chance against him."

Asdoel winked at Charlie. "That's what you think. But poor, old Johnny Alpha doesn't have the advantage that I have. A little blue pill I've been taking religiously for the last forty-eight hours. A pill that boosts my metabolism and turbocharges my reflexes. Alpha doesn't stand a chance against me. No ordinary human – or even mutant – can possibly beat me."

"My husband likes a fair fight," said HMKZ sarcastically.

Asdoel Zo just smiled and said, "Johnny Alpha is dead."

The powder magazine had been built in a natural cave system that ran under the fort. There were three cave chambers in all. Their walls were lined with a natural fungus that provided a constant illumination and which had the additional benefit of offering no risk of accidentally igniting the caves' contents.

The first two caves were small antechambers used to store small barrels of gunpowder. The third cave was the largest and contained several dozen more powder barrels and a few crates of ammunition, but its floor was mostly clear. Its rear wall was covered with tall stacks of wooden boxes, most of which were full of dynamite. Some of the boxes, however, were fakes and concealed the doorway that led to the secret tunnel. When the steel-lined door was opened, the fake boxes swung out with it. This door now stood ajar. Johnny and the others had entered through it some ten minutes earlier, led by Preacher Tarkettle.

Now they were busy preparing a surprise for Asdoel Zo. Granny Haxer and Tarkettle were occupied opening the dynamite boxes, taking out the slick, waxed, orange sticks and braiding their fuses together. Meanwhile, Middenface was moving carefully around the floor of the cave with a barrel of gunpowder, which had been punched open at one end with a knife. A steady flow of black granules spilled onto the floor. Middenface was engaged in creating a trail of gunpowder in an elaborate spiral pattern.

"Don't let the rings of the spiral get too close together," said Johnny. He was following Middenface, carrying bundles of dynamite with fuses that had been braided by Granny and Tarkettle. Johnny carefully trimmed the fuses to specific lengths and then laid the bundles of dynamite so that the fuses were buried in the trail of gunpowder.

"Ah, Johnny, you know how I enjoy home decorating," said Middenface. "Don't go intruding on my creativity."

"If you lay that gunpowder trail too close together the spark can jump the rings. Then the dynamite will go off prematurely. Which means before we have a chance to get clear back down the tunnel." Johnny displayed a crooked grin. "Then something will really intrude on your creativity."

"You're such a worrier, Johnny," said Middenface. "If you like, when I'm finished I'll go around the spiral with a piece of wood from one of the box lids and scrape it along the floor to guarantee an even spacing."

"Good thinking," said Johnny, accepting another bundle of dynamite from Granny Haxer.

"Johnny," said Granny. "Are you sure that Asdoel Zo's daughters won't be around when this little fireworks display goes up? I don't mind blowing up Zo and his henchmen, or even that viper of a wife of his. But I'd hate to put paid to a couple of kids."

"Trouble yourself not, my good woman," said Preacher Tarkettle, squinting with concentration as he twisted the fuses together on five sticks of dynamite. "Lorna and Jodi are safe in orbit on the *Charles Neider*. I had this information from none other than Mrs Zo herself, this very morning, so you may assume it's correct."

"And Middenface," said Johnny, "you'll be pleased to know that there aren't any of the gardening girls around either."

"No," agreed Tarkettle. "Mrs Zo has seen to that. Sent them packing. She is, to put it mildly, a jealous woman."

Johnny winked at Granny. "So no innocent women or children," he said. "We can enjoy this little explosion without guilt."

"It ain't going to be no *little* explosion," said Granny Haxer. "When the gunpowder ignites all this dynamite, half a mountain is going to drop on Asdoel Zo."

"Now, is that any way to repay the hospitality of your host?" said a voice from the doorway. Johnny and the others looked up to see Asdoel Zo standing there, holding a pistol on them. Beside him his wife stood with a rifle. Standing behind the Zos, and looking distinctly uncomfortable, was a man Middenface didn't recognise.

Asdoel Zo saw Middenface staring at the man and said, "Allow me to introduce Charlie Yuletide. I hired him as a kind of on-screen host for the video I've been making about this little adventure. He sings songs to link the segments. Oh, and by the way, everybody put your hands up."

Middenface set down his barrel of gunpowder and put his hands in the air. "You've been filming us? Without our consent? That's unethical."

HMKZ grinned. "Glad to see you've still got that dry sense of humour, Archibald."

"Only my friends call me that," said Middenface coldly.

"I suppose it *was* a little unethical," said Asdoel Zo. He stepped into the cave, keeping his pistol pointed unwaveringly at Johnny, whom he had clearly identified as the most dangerous person in the room. HMKZ followed him, keeping her rifle on the others. The man called Charlie Yuletide reluctantly followed her. He was apparently unarmed. "But nonetheless," said Asdoel Zo, "my lovely wife has been filming your adventures with a concealed camera from the start."

"That was one reason I was so pissed off that you wouldn't let me come along on the Queen Victoria undersea prison break," said HMKZ. "I missed out on some good footage."

"But hopefully we haven't missed any footage of your recent adventure in the desert. Some satellites orbiting over this planet have been recording it for me to watch when I get back."

"Let me get this straight," said Granny Haxer. "You rich ghouls have gone to all this trouble just so you can make some home movies of us?"

"I'd hardly call them home movies. And that wasn't our sole aim," said Asdoel Zo. "We also wanted to participate in your exploits with you. Especially my adventure-loving wife."

"And you're participating now, eh?" said Johnny. The cold glow of his eyes never moved from the barrel of Asdoel Zo's revolver.

"That's right," said Asdoel Zo. "I had to be here for this. It's the grand finale. That's why I asked Charlie Yuletide here to join us. I wanted him to witness it so he can write a song for the closing credits of the video. Something suitably heart-rending and home-on-the-range."

"I have to say I'm not comfortable with this, Mr Zo," said Charlie Yuletide. "I was employed as an actor and singer. No one said anything about being an accomplice to murder."

"Well, you're one now, so just shut up," said Hari Mata Karma Zo.

"You're not an accomplice, Charlie," said Asdoel Zo soothingly. "Just a witness."

"I still don't want any part of this," said Charlie Yuletide.

"Too bad," said Asdoel Zo, the soothing tone quite absent now. "Just stay put if you know what's good for you."

"So what happens now?" said Johnny. "You just gun us down?"

"That's entirely up to you, Johnny," said Asdoel Zo. "Things could go that way, sure. But I'd like to offer you one final chance of survival."

"Don't trust him, Johnny," said Granny Haxer.

"At least listen to my proposition," said Asdoel Zo. "I'm giving you the opportunity to go up against me, man to man, in personal combat."

"Me against you?" said Johnny contemptuously, looking at the soft body of the rich man, sleek with decades of good living.

"Sure, Johnny. Old west style. We walk ten paces, turn and draw. The fastest man shoots the other man down. And if you beat me, you and your friends go free; unharmed and handsomely rewarded." Asdoel Zo fished his phone out of his pocket and quickly stole a glance at the clock on it. His eyes flickered back to Johnny and his gun never wavered from Johnny's head.

"What do you know, it's high noon, local time. What do you say Johnny?"

"Let's do it," said Johnny Alpha.

Johnny and Asdoel Zo stood back to back in the courtyard. The shuttle had been flown back outside the fort to clear space for the duel. The high, hot sun blazed down on the two men and the onlookers. HMKZ held her rifle on Granny Haxer, Tarkettle and Middenface. Charlie Yuletide stood sullenly behind her.

Both Johnny and Asdoel Zo wore gunbelts, with a single holster strapped to their right hips. In Asdoel Zo's holster was the Remington .44. Johnny's holster contained the same Manhattan .36 that he'd been supplied with for the desert blood hunt. The two men stood waiting tensely for the command to begin.

It was HMKZ's job to issue the command. But she seemed to be characteristically milking the moment for all it was worth. "Asdoel," she said. "We don't have to do this, you know. We could all just go and have a drink and forget the whole thing."

"We couldn't possibly do that," said Asdoel Zo. "A man's got to do what a man's got to do, right, Johnny?" Johnny Alpha didn't reply.

HMKZ persisted. "Listen to me, Asdoel. It's not too late to shake hands and call it a day."

"I don't think Johnny wants to shake my hand," said Asdoel Zo. "Now, quit pissing around and give us the starting signal."

"All right, if that's the way you want it," said HMKZ. "Get ready and take your positions."

"We *are* ready," snapped Asdoel Zo, "we *have* taken our positions."

HMKZ opened her mouth to speak. Charlie Yuletide stepped forward. "Mr Alpha! Don't do it. He's taken some kind of pill to speed up his reflexes – *ooof*." This last sound was made by HMKZ stepping smartly towards Charlie and slamming him hard in the stomach with the butt of her Volcanic repeating rifle.

Charlie Yuletide fell to his knees, doubled over with pain. "Don't interrupt me when I'm about to give the starting signal," said HMKZ mildly. Then she pointed the rifle at Middenface and the others again. "And you lot can stay put too."

"Come on, let's get on with it," said Asdoel Zo impatiently. He was still standing back to back with Johnny Alpha.

Middenface looked desperately at his friend. "Johnny. You heard what that fella said. Don't go through with this."

"I don't reckon I have much choice," said Johnny.

"Now, that's the frontier spirit," declared Asdoel Zo. "Come on honey, let's get this show on the road."

HMKZ said, "One," and the men took a step away from each other across the stone courtyard. The sun was high in the alien sky, directly above them, so they cast no shadows. "Two," said Hari Mata Karma Zo. She slowly kept counting and the men slowly paced away from each other.

"Ten," she said finally, and the two men turned, drew and fired. Two guns went off, the sound of the shots strangely frail and trivial in the hot air of noon. Both men stood facing each other for a moment.

Then Asdoel Zo crumbled and fell backward on the flagstones. Johnny Alpha stood looking at him for a moment, then turned and aimed his gun at HMKZ. But

the woman had already dropped her rifle and was striding across the courtyard to her husband. She was moving
quickly and yet in a strangely controlled way. She didn't
run.

She knelt by Asdoel Zo and took his hand. There was a
spreading, red stain on his chest. His eyes were wide and
staring. "Get medics," he rasped.

"No dear," said his wife in a soft, comforting voice. "I'm
afraid it's too late for that."

"No... isn't."

"Yes, it really is, Asdoel. Listen to me, Asdoel. Those
blue pills you were taking were just sugar. Do you understand? I substituted sugar pills for the real pills."

He stared at her. "Why?"

"You should have left that big, zebra-striped slut
alone," said Hari Mata Karma, formerly Zo. "She was the
last straw."

Johnny and Middenface's ship, the one they had been
plying their trade in before Asdoel Zo had hired them,
had been transported in the hold of the *Charles Neider*
and was now sitting in the desert half a kilometre from
the fort. It was a battered but serviceable stellar clipper,
which had served them in good stead for years. "There's
plenty of room in it for an extra passenger," said Middenface.

"I'm obliged, boys," said Granny Haxer. "It's only a couple days back to my home on good old QS718. I won't be
underfoot during the journey. I'll cook for you." The old
woman stood with Johnny and Middenface outside their
ship as they waited for the horses to approach.

There were three horses, galloping towards them from the
fort in the mountains. Desert dust swirled around their
hooves. All three horses were black, and so were their riders.
As they emerged from the shimmering distortion of the heat

haze, the riders resolved into three women, or one woman and two girls. All were dressed in the black of mourning.

Hari Mata Karma and her daughters rode up to the space ship and reined in their horses. Middenface saw that the horses were sweating heavily and he saw why. In addition to their riders, the horses were also laden with black silk sacks, each the size of a large pillow. HMK swung out of her saddle and released the sacks onto the ground. They hit it with hard thuds. She had three sacks on her horse. Each of the girls had two.

Seven black sacks lying on the ground. "What's that?" said Middenface.

"Your payment," said HMK. "We were going to pay you with sacks of gold dust, western style. But that would have been a rather modest payment. So we opted for bags of platinum dust instead."

"Platinum?" said Middenface.

"Yes, and with the recent demand for the metal in implant technology I think you'll find that it is worth a considerable amount."

"Seven sacks," said Johnny.

"One for each member of the posse," said HMK. "Not counting me, since I was never really one of you. We're paying for all seven, and the survivors – which is you three – get to keep the dead member's spoils. That was Asdoel's little notion."

"We'll only take what's ours," said Johnny. "We'll leave the rest."

"Are you sure?" said Middenface hastily. "We could use the money for good causes, maybe donate some to charity and that sort of thing."

"We'll leave it," said Johnny. "It's got blood on it."

"What a romantic notion," said HMK. "Well, come on girls." She whirled her horse around and galloped off, followed closely by her daughters.

"Didn't even say goodbye," said Granny Haxer. Midden-face went to the sacks lying on the ground and picked up three of them. He carried them into the ship, sagging under the weight of them. Granny Haxer followed, but Johnny remained standing outside for a moment. He went to the remaining four sacks, took out a knife and sliced each one open. The slashed sacks spilled out pale metallic dust. The wind began to pick at the shiny dust and carry it off as Johnny walked back towards the ship. The hatch closed behind him with a heavy thud as he entered.

Then the engines of the ship screamed for a long moment, kicking up a wild swirl of sand. The mechanical blast also caught the platinum dust, swirling it out of the sacks.

The engines of the space ship began to empty the sacks and, as the ship moved upwards, disappearing into the endless blue sky, the desert wind took over, shaking the sacks and carrying away the precious powder, until the last of it was gone, scattered over the mountains and the plains, and the bones of the dead.

ABOUT THE AUTHOR

Andrew Cartmel started writing television scripts as a way of earning a living while concentrating on becoming a novelist, but things weren't quite that straightforward. His TV scripts led to him being head-hunted by the BBC to script-edit the legendary science fiction epic *Doctor Who*, then another hit show, the hospital drama *Casualty*, where he got to decide who would die each week. He tore himself away to become lead writer and script editor on the cult sword and sorcery classic *Dark Knight* for Five. Television work led to scripting comic strips (including *Judge Dredd*) and, finally, back to novels, including his eerie thriller *The Wise*. Cartmel's previous novel for Black Flame was *Judge Dredd: Swine Fever*.

NIKOLAI DANTE

The Strangelove Gambit
1-84416-139-0
£5.99 • $6.99

DURHAM RED

The Unquiet Grave
1-84416-159-5
£5.99 • $6.99

The Omega Solution
1-84416-175-7
£5.99 • $6.99

NEW LINE CINEMA

Blade: Trinity
1-84416-106-4
£6.99 • $7.99

The Butterfly Effect
1-84416-081-5
£6.99 • $7.99

Cellular
1-84416-104-8
£6.99 • $7.99

Freddy vs Jason
1-84416-059-9
£5.99 • $6.99

The Texas Chainsaw Massacre
1-84416-060-2
£6.99 • $7.99

FINAL DESTINATION

Dead Reckoning
1-84416-170-6
£6.99 • $7.99

Destination Zero
1-84416-171-4
£6.99 • $7.99

End of the Line
1-84416-176-5
£6.99 • $7.99

JASON X

Jason X
1-84416-168-4
£6.99 • $7.99

The Experiment
1-84416-169-2
£6.99 • $7.99

Planet of the Beast
1-84416-183-8
£6.99 • $7.99

FRIDAY THE 13TH

Hell Lake
1-84416-182-X
£6.99 • $7.99

Church of the Divine Psychopath
1-84416-181-1
£6.99 • $7.99

THE TWILIGHT ZONE

Memphis/The Pool Guy
1-84416-130-7
£6.99 • $7.99

Upgrade/Sensuous Cindy
1-84416-131-5
£6.99 • $7.99

Sunrise/Into the Light
1-84416-151-X
£6.99 • $7.99

Chosen/The Placebo Effect
1-84416-150-1
£6.99 • $7.99

Burned/One Night at Mercy
1-84416-179-X
£6.99 • $7.99